MOLLY

The Past will always catch up with you

Kerri and Stephen West

DEDICATION

We would like to dedicate this book to the people who gave us firsthand accounts of their experiences, knowledge, and professional opinions. Without you this book wouldn't make sense.

CONTENTS

ACKNOWLEDGMENTS

We would like to acknowledge "Amazon Kindle Direct" for their work on making this dream come true by getting this book published.

1 RAVEN

Raven Debardot is just getting ready for school. She threw on a hoodie, tied her boots, and slipped black jeans over the top of her boots. She let her long, jet-black hair flow over her shoulders. She picked up a bagel, grabbed her nap sack, and headed out the door keys in hand to lock the door on the way out. Her folks had already left for work and walked down to the bus stop. There was a crowd of other kids hanging around. It's lightly raining. The bus comes and everyone standing around lines up to get on the it. Raven sits at the back of the bus and looks out the window. She takes a bite of her bagel. The bus makes one more stop before heading to the school. It was early fall in 1976. Raven had just started her last year of school at Manistee High. It was just after the first nine weeks. Her folks were addicted to prescriptions pills. They kept their jobs but didn't really pay much attention to her. She was promiscuous and slept around with the jocks at school even though she spent more time with rockers and goths. Everyone saw her as loose and easy. She didn't seem to care as she felt it was the one thing that she got pleasure from. It was something she felt she had the most control over. The bus stopped at the side of the school, and everyone got off. Raven headed to her locker to swap out her books from the previous day's homework so she could get the first three books she needed for the morning courses and headed to her first period class, which was science. She sat down in her assigned seat. Jackie, one of her closer friends, approached her. "Hay Raven! Did you hear about the party going on tonight?" said Jackie.

"Hell, yeah, I did! It's supposed to be a get together at a rave, right?"

"Yeah, Jonas will pick us up after school and head down there"

After school Raven met with Jackie and other friends. They all hopped in a 1970 Ford Icon which was beige and white. Some in the front seats and some in the back truck bed. They headed off to an open field. It was a few hours' drive. There were no signs indicating where they were. Several other trucks had driven up to a particular open field. There was a large tent that had disk jockey music set up. Raven and her friends went inside. The place was packed. All the gals were pumped up and ready to get high and get laid. Raven had a few beers and as a result she was extra friendly. As she mingled a roofie had been slipped into her drink by one of the 21-year-old guys. Jason was seen as an object of desire. The ladies had no issue with wanting to be near him.

Tonight, however, there was one girl he had his mind set on. Raven, the brunette with the piercing blue eyes, was his greatest desire. One thing they didn't know is he drugged women all the time. Raven was no exception. She wouldn't have known since Jason was very attractive, clean cut, charming, and very charismatic. He wore black jeans and button up shirts with various patterns like flames or stripes. He always had his hair combed to the side with a touch of hair gel. He manscaped keeping his goatee beard steamed and eyebrows perfectly shaped with tweezers and makeup. He kept a pristine skin care routine. It was the perfect cover up, especially to the younger female crowd.

The effects started to kick in. Raven felt disoriented and confused and had wondered off outside of the tent away from the crowd. Her friends were inside the tent getting high and trying to get laid. Jason watched her with intent. He was filled with lustful desire, as he waited for her to get out of sight. He waited for her to pass out as she stumbled around attempting to get her footing. The moment she collapsed, Jason picked her up and took her to his 1970 Chevy C10 jet black pickup truck. Quickly and quietly, he managed to have left the rave as to not be noticed. He had parked in such a way that when he started his engine nobody would notice. Then again, the music was so loud that nobody noticed or even really cared for that matter. He put the truck in drive, and slowly pulled away and whispered, "You belong to ME now!."

He drove her to his house, got her inside, and threw her on his bed. He tied her up feet and hands and stripped her naked. He had raped her for several hours as she was tied up. When she became coherent enough to realize something was wrong, Jason had grabbed a geode and struck her head with it. He had smashed his finger in the process, breaking the skin and blood dripping from his middle finger as he continued to strike several blows as they cracked her skull. Raven's body went limp and lifeless. Panic ensued that fueled him. He grabbed his crotch as if he had a hold of his penis and screeched "THIS IS TRUE POWER!"

Jason flung her body over his shoulder. He tossed Raven like a rag doll into the bed of his truck. He drove out to up an old, abandoned fire road through the forest. He was in a hurry. It was pitch black but not for much longer. He parked next to an old abandoned red painted wooden shed. He looked down at her body, hatred flowing though his veins. This was HIS. He pulled a rusty dagger from his glove compartment. He looked down at Raven and kneeled beside her taking the blade and carving an inverted crucifix into her forehead. Grabbing her ankles, and pulling her from the bed of the truck, allowing her head to thump to the ground like a rotten melon, Jason drug her body and tossed her next to the shed. He spat on her, hopped his truck, and drove away. Her body covered in blood and semen rolled down into a ravine flush with leaves and branches and hit a large tree not far from the shed.

"FATHER, I'VE DONE AS YOU'VE ASKED! I DID SO IN YOUR NAME!" Jason yelled as if to appease his abusive parent as the sun was about to come up. Birds flew hysterically as he sped thru the bumpy mountain terrain. The silence was deafening.

He reached his house and cleaned up the evidence from his home and his truck as if nothing had happened. He laid low for the next few months. After getting a thirst for more, he felt a sense of power that would become his addiction and obsession. Over the next several years he had done this to other girls about Ravens age, taking their bodies to Huron National Forrest. He defiled them, he desecrated them. He hated them. It was all because of mother. Mother always turned away when father stepped into his room at night. Mother always turned away when daddy did the unspeakable. Mother allowed it, she turned a blind eye.

Jason returned to his job as a trucker who would be gone for months at a time. He would kidnap his drugged-up victims from raves. He would drag them back to his house. repeating the same horrendous crime and would dispose of them in the same forest but never in the same places. The news called him Rave Rapist. In 1986 a victim managed to escape as Jason had left the room. Naked, cold, and in the dark, Janine had run as quickly as she could to the nearest highway to hitchhike for help. A young couple noticed her running naked along Highway 55. They stopped their vehicle and asked if she needed help. They took her to the nearest hospital which operated 24 hours, the Manistee Community Health Center. With enough information from Janine, and from the couple who picked her up, authorities were able to narrow down his whereabouts and he was apprehended after he barricaded himself in his home for several hours with a .38 special revolver. A grenade of tear gas was tossed in his house and police were able to subdue him. He was arrested and charged with the rapes and murders of the victims, matching the same MO and evidence that had been collected and documented for the past ten years. After a lengthy trial he was convicted of several counts rape and murder in the first degree. The Jury sentenced him to life in prison without the possibility of parole.

Raven awoke. It was the year 2006 30 years since the day she was murdered. What's was this world she was in now? Why did she feel different, she was not hungry? She didn't feel human for some reason. She could see. She could speak. She could hear. How come everyone ignored her? She was right there! It was then that she realized she was dead. All Raven could feel was rage and a thirst for revenge! This monster put her here! She was going to come back, come hell or high water. It was then she realized her spirit was summoned by a group of teens doing a séance on her grave. One of those teens would live to regret it. Ravens thirst for revenge would haunt this teen well into adulthood and is the key to Ravens resurrection. That teen was Molly. Molly would give Raven the chance to fix everything.

This is that story.

2 THE CHAT

The rain had finally stopped. Living in a southwestern desert like town, the rain was always welcomed. The dryness and droughts were a normal thing for New Mexico. Katy gets up from bed after the clock alarm goes off. She puts on her robe and heads to the kitchen. Grabbing a sack of coffee grounds in one hand and the carafe in the other she begins to fill the carafe in the sink with cold water while measuring the grounds as water filled and leaked over the top of the lid. She placed the filter in the basket and dumped the grounds inside, filled the pot with the water, set the carafe under the basket and turned the pot on. She grabbed her favorite alien cup anticipating a hot cup of coffee as the aroma dispersed in the air. The coffee was soon brewed, and she poured herself a cup. Just black and fresh. No creamer, no sugar.

Her phone dings and it's a text from Molly. Katy put in her passcode to open her phone. She opened the text as it read "I was able to get four weeks off from work of use or lose time off! I can't wait for the road trip." Katy calls Molly on Facetime. "Hey what's up?" says Molly

"I can't do the whole four weeks. I'll have to cut our trip short by two weeks"

"I don't mind staying an extra two weeks with you"

"I'm working nights at the moment, but I'll be back on days when I get back, so unless you go with, you'll be by yourself for most of the time"

"I'll go with you to work, if that's alright with your boss."

"Yeah, I'll have to clear that with the boss. I'm sure you can observe. Oh snap! I'll show you everyone in the office on Facebook you'll be right at home!"

"Seriously? You don't mind?"

"Not at all, I'll just get permission. It'll be fantastic"

"Speaking of work, I need to split now and get going, I'll Facetime you later"

"See yah!"

Katy closes off Facetime and begins to sip her hot coffee. Working nights at the office wasn't Katy's favorite time of the day to be out. The city is dangerous, especially at night. Working at a hospital means no firearms. The cup of coffee soothes her.

Slipping into a hot shower, she anticipates paranormal activity she wants to experience." Is Pennhurst as scary as they say? What will it be like? Will Molly be able to hack it this time or will it be me that gets shaken up?" She thinks to herself as she finishes lathering her skin with the bath sponge and rinsing off, soaking her hair, and applying leave in conditioner She gets out and grabs an oversized towel hanging from the towel bar and wraps it around her. After getting dressed and fixing her hair she grabs a ramen cup, some fruit, a water bottle, and a small sack of ranch flavored Doritos. Katy stuffs them in her zip up lunch tote and heads out the door to her Jeep.

Traffic is starting to get light, and the sun is setting. Katy has Nine Inch Nails streaming from her phone to her Bluetooth. Music helps her focus. She drives up to the gate punches the passcode and parks in her assigned parking spot. As she walks to the entrance of building, she puts her thumb against the biometric finger plate. The door opens and she proceeds to the lab. As she sits down to her desk and places her things in a large drawer, Aaron approaches. "Katy, I need you to submit a job listing for me requesting internships. Use LinkedIn and Indeed. We are looking to find persons for pharmaceuticals with a bachelor's degree or persons perusing a master's degree, with qualifications listed and outlined in the JRPH system (giraffe) (Job Requisition and Protocols for Hiring) under internships." Aaron said as he grabbed his water bottle and filled it at the water dispenser that sits right next to Katy's desk. "Absolutely, I'll get right on that" Katy replied as she began the task.

Later at lunch Katy is filling her ramen cup with hot boiling water from the office Keurig. She sits down at one of the tables of the break room and lets the noodles sit in the hot steaming water as they soften. She picked up her phone and dialed Molly on Facetime. "Hey, girl!" Says Molly as she answers the call. "Hello there, so what time is your flight for tomorrow?" says Katy

"The ticket is for 6:09am, I've got all my stuff packed and ready to go"

"That sounds great, I can't wait to see you!"

"So, I was checking out Pennhurst and we can get a pass for $45 bucks, and we can stay late"

"Oh, that sounds great, speaking of hauntings, Aaron

my boss was out on errands with Julio, and they saw an apparition, scared Julio half to death, they've been talking all week about it"

"Whoa are you serious?" Molly said with anticipation

"Very serious," said Katy.

"That's crazy. Isn't Aaron your boss? The one who doesn't talk much about anything?"

"Yes, it is, as matter of fact he's been opening up a little bit lately. I was having a hard time the other day because I am going to Japan for a year for Arturo's orders. He is a very down to earth guy. He's much wiser than I thought."

"Wow isn't it nice to have a man listen?" asked Molly

"You know, it is nice! You know what I'll have to show you his Facebook page when you come tomorrow."

"Sounds interesting"

"So, I need to get back to work now. I'll be there to pick you up. Could you send me what gate you will be exiting the plane at?"

"My itinerary says B4 at 10:38 am at Albuquerque" Molly replied.

"I will be there to pick you up, see you tomorrow! Bye!" Said Katy "Bye!" Said Molly.

Katy ate her noodles and drank her water. She grabbed the fruit and chips and placed them on her desk for later. She finished with the job request and sat back in her chair. She took a deep breath, grabbed her water bottle, and began to refill it, careful not to spill any of the water coming out of the spout. She took a swig and felt the coolness of the water go down. It was soothing considering it was summertime and the high for the day was 98 degrees despite the rainy day. She walked over to Aaron's desk. "Hey Aaron, I finished the job request and submitted them online. Is there anything else you need?" asked Katy. "Yeah, I need you to take these invoice copies to Sam in accounting," said Aaron. "On your way back could you stop by supply and see if we got our deliveries for our research?" asked Aaron. "Sure thing." Said Katy. "After that I'll be sure to clean up the lab if that's alright. I wanted to have as many things done as I can before I get off shift, would that be alright?" asked Katy. "Absolutely, that would be great!" Said Aaron.

Katy walks over to the elevators to go to the second floor where the accounting department is to find Sam. She presses the door button and waits patiently as the numbers light up as the elevator comes down. The elevator stops and the doors open. Katy walks in and presses the number 2 button and the doors close. She gets to the second floor and turns to the left and walks down the hall, opens the door under the sign that says accounting and walks right in. "Hey Sam, here's some invoice's from Aaron." Said Katy. "Far out!" Said Sam. "Looking forward to your ghost trip?" asked Sam, "I hear that Pennhurst is scary as fuck." Said Sam.

"Yeah, we leave the day after tomorrow. We'll be flying out to Spring City early Friday."

"That's totally rad! Send me some pictures? I'm super jelly!" Sam said excitedly.

"Oh absolutely! Well, I got to get going to supply and see if some packages came in, nice seeing you Sam"

"Alrighty then! Take care Katy!"

Katy proceeds to the elevator, repeating the process she used before and proceeding to the first floor. As she exits the elevator, she notices the lobby is quiet. She proceeded to the opposite side of the lobby and went through the double doors that said, "Employees and deliveries only." She makes a left and proceeds to the receiving department. "Hello John, has anything come in for the Laboratory today?" Asked Katy, "Not today, I do have tracking saying some stuff for an experimental drug will come in over the next two days," said John. "Alright, could you forward the information to Aaron's email? I won't be here for a couple of weeks so he will need to have the details, Rodger is going to need that as soon as possible." Said Katy.

"Of course, I'll do that now"

"Thanks John. I'll probably see you in a couple of weeks

when I get back," said Katy.

"Take care!" said John.

Katy returned to the office and began to gather supplies to clean the lab. She proceeded to wipe down tabletops and dispose of trash. She dusted blinds and wiped down computer screens. Finally sweeping the floor and mopping. After cleaning the lab and putting the supplies away Katy rinses the mop and the bucket and puts them away in the cleaning closet. She proceeded to Aaron's desk. "All done with the laboratory. There weren't any deliveries today. I asked Sam to forward tracking information to your email so you can watch out for the packages." Said Katy. "Thanks, Rodger is going to be thrilled." Aaron Said. They proceeded to the parking lot with light chit chat exchanging the occasional chuckle before departing for the day.

3 THE FIGHT, THE FLIGHT, AND THE ARRIVAL

Molly was preparing her suitcase for her trip. Checking over laundry she empties the wet clothes from the washer to the dryer to have the last of the clothes fresh and dried and ready to pack. Several packing cubes were sitting on the bed. Molly grabs a small one, loading it with intimates, piling it neatly and zipping it up. She continues with toiletries and the like. James, Molly's husband, walks in, places his hand on her shoulder and gives her a light peck on the cheek. "Hey sweet pea," said James. "Hay." Molly said abruptly.

""What's wrong? Are you still upset?"

"Duh! You only care about your so-called freedom," replied Molly.

"Molly, how many times have we been through this? I don't want to have babies right now. We are too young, and we have so much of the world to enjoy before we make a commitment like this!"

"Oh?! So, you'd rather I wait until I am at a higher risk pregnancy because I had to wait for your sorry ass adventure and what for the sake of your comforts? That's just great, isn't it? Selfish prick!"

"I'm a selfish prick? Do you realize that it's a lot of work and commitment to have children? It's a pri-vel-eedge! And I am the selfish prick? Who do you think you're talking to Molly? "

"A selfish prick is to whom I'm talking! One who doesn't want to grow the fuck up and be part of a family because God forbid, he doesn't get to have his fuuuun! What are you afraid of? Huh? Like a diaper or a bottle or something? Good God I married a BOY!"

"And I married a princess toddler who lost her little binky and has to pout now in time out over a temper tantrum because she can't play babies!"

"Oh, that's really mature! Why don't you just go out with the boys like you allllwaaays do and get plastered! At this point you'd fit right in! Because you're just a BOY!"

"Molly, when are you going to grow up and get a grasp of reality? We are talking about having a human being! There's a lot of commitment in being a parent! It's not like having a baby born doll! When are you going to pull your head out of your ass? You know, now you can sleep alone! I've had enough of being treated like garbage by a child like you! I'm out of here Molly. I don't deserve to be treated like this from a snot nosed spoiled brat!" James screeched. "Yeah see right there you leave like a god damned coward James!" Molly yelped. He stormed to the front door, with Molly following behind thinking of ways to win her side of the argument and yelling obscenities. James interrupted, "Leave me alone Molly! I have had it. When you are willing to accept reality, we can have a conversation at the grownups table. Until then there's you in the kiddy section!" James gets inside his truck, slams his door, turns on the ignition and racks into reverse before clicking his belt and peeling out of the driveway. Molly stood there with anger and tears. She was going to get even. Nobody tells her royal highness she can't have what she wants.

Molly walked back in the house stomping, slamming the front door, and muttering. She continued to pack items in her packing cubes and then assort them neatly in her suitcase. Quiet tears flushed her face. Coming out freely and effortlessly. The dryer buzzed. She emptied the dryer and rolled her tops and blouses as she fit them in a larger packing cube, zipping it up, and placing it in her suitcase. Molly put her suitcase by the front door and sat on the couch and put on Unsolved Mysteries on Discovery+. A few hours later James came home. His eyes were bloodshot. James wasn't much for showing outward emotions. Tonight, he had been bawling his eyes out. This was the love of his life, and his marriage is headed for a sharp cliff. He sat next to her, putting his arm around her. Neither of them saying a word. Molly wasn't ready to make up despite the need for a long hug and a shoulder to sob on. Putting her head against James's chest was always soothing. At times it was his embrace that could get out the most intense emotions. This, however, just wasn't enough for her this time. "Should I order us a pizza?" Asked James. "Yeah" said Molly. After the pizza arrived, they each had a few slices and sat quietly watching unsolved mysteries and then heading to bed despite what James said in the heat of the moment.

On the plane, since early the following morning, Molly is quietly anticipating the end of the descent to the runway. She's been up since 3am. She's hungry, tired, and excited. The captain announces "Welcome to Albuquerque. Local time is currently 10:30am MST at Sun-port Airport. The temperature is currently 80 degrees Fahrenheit. Please stay seated until the fasten seat belt sign has been turned in the off position. Please check for all your belongings before exiting. Use caution when opening overhead bins as items may have shifted during flight. On behalf of this airline, we thank you for flying with us today and hope you board with us soon. Please continue to wear your face mask in accordance with Covid-19. Thank you."

Katy is patiently waiting at the gate for Molly to exit. "Molly!" yelps Katy. "You're here! Oh, give me a hug! It's so good to see you!" Katy embraces Molly. Katy and Molly stroll to the baggage carousel watching the bags as they entered on the conveyer belt. Molly spots her luggage. They each grab one and head in the direction of the parking structure.

"Sure, how about burritos from Tornadoes? They also have burgers, tacos, and enchiladas." Explains Katy. "I think you'll like them"

"Oh, a burger sounds great!"

"Far out!"

Katy and Molly reach her Jeep and stow the luggage in the back, and head for the nearest Tornadoes which happens to be on the way to Katy's house on base. Katy's husband is in the Air Force and is on active duty. Living on base is quiet. Katy likes it that way. Katy goes thru the drive thru, places an order for a Grande burrito stuffed with potato's, refried beans, and carne adovada, which is typically dark meat sirloin pork diced, seared, and then braised in a ripened chili pod slurry with added Mexican style spices which is called red Chile sauce. Molly goes for the All the way Burger with chili cheese fries. They head to one of the gates to get on base. Katy shows her base ID and proceeds past the checkpoint. Finally, they reach the house. "Let's eat first and then grab the bags later" Molly insisted. "Alright," complied Katy. Katy unlocks the front door and enters, Molly following behind. "Not too shabby! Nice place you got here." Said Molly.

Molly heads to the dining table and fumbles through the plastic bag of food and pulls out the meals and utensil packets, checking each one to see which entrée is what. Katy grabbed drinks from the fridge and sat down at the table.

"So, what can you tell me about Aaron, your boss how's

he doing? I remember you saying you were worried about him, something about health issues?" Asks Molly

"Aaron? Well, it's mostly Kelly she's been going thru some personal issues I'd rather not get into. Aaron is mostly to himself. He's a very caring person who can also be assertive when he needs to be. He is an excellent listener. He has been supportive of me needing to move overseas with Arturo. We are going to Korea next May. I really don't like being away from family like this. Supporting him as taken so far away from everyone that I have been feeling so isolated these days," said Katy

"I'll always be a Facetime away if you ever get lonely. Same with mama, we are here for you Katy, really," said Molly

"I know. It's different from being in person. It does take its toll. Anyway, it has made a difference to have someone to talk to in person who's been around for a while."

"Is he handsome?"

"He's not hard to look at. Here, I'll pull up his Facebook page so you can see." Said Katy as she pulled up the app and searched for Aaron. She entered his name, and it came up on the list of results. She taps his name in the list and taps his profile picture and hands it to Molly. "Here, that's his photo and his page right there."

Molly said as she glanced over the photo. Molly thinks to herself that there is something about Aaron that is mysterious and enticing. She's tingling inside. She takes note of how to get to his Facebook page by recalling what the profile picture looked like as well as his name and town location so she can pull it up later as they continue small chit chat about his attire and charm and weird sense of humor. She hands the phone back to Katy.

"OH! I got this Halloween office picture from last year! We all dressed up as Harry Potter Characters, it was a hoot!" Katy says as she hands the phone back to Molly.

Molly takes note of Aaron dressing up as Draco Malfoy and is entranced, secretly of course. Mustn't let Katy catch wind of this infatuation. They continued to make random comments about each of the costumes noting who's was well done and who's was most unique and so on.

"The one that is dressed Harry and Ron are Julio and Juan. They are like Chandler and Joey from 'Friends.' I think they are interested in each other. They hide it, yet subtle hints are suggesting

otherwise" said Katy emphasizing the word subtle by gesturing air quotation marks.

"Reeeally?" Said Molly as she chuckled "Wow I would love to see that for myself. I can't wait to meet your coworkers. Could you get my bags before we forget? I'm going to soak in the tub" Molly wanted a gentle escape so she could revert to Aaron's Facebook page.

"Sure," Katy said hesitantly. "I'll be right back." Katy grabs the bags from the Jeep and brings them into the house. She proceeds to the guest room and places the bags on the bed. Katy thinks to herself "Molly sure is bossy! I can't seem to shake her shit every time she visits me! Why is she always like this?" Katy returns to the dining table and begins to clear the empty food containers and then wiping down the table.

Molly draws the water for the bath. She adds bath oil and soap to the water to soften it. She likes her bath mostly hot, so she dips her toe quickly as she anticipates the warmth of the bath water.

She adjusts the cold water just a touch and slips inside gently. She then uses the toes of her feet to shut off the water. Then she rests her head on the back part of the tub next to the tile and relaxes. Grabbing her phone, she pulls up Aaron's Facebook. Looking at Aarons profile photo, she begins to enact meetings and conversations in her head. "How is Aaron in person anyway? Katy seems to adore him. I wonder how far I can go with Aaron without James catching me. Aaron an older man with white and gray hair in his goatee is so exciting! He's grounded, more mature, and seems to have what James is lacking." She contemplates with excitement. She sets her phone down on the shelf next to the tub. Grabbing a pouf sponge she squeezes soap in the crevices so as not to allow the soap to drip off the sponge into the bath water. She begins to cleanse her skin with the suds from the sponge reaching intimate areas and cleaning under the arms and behind the neck. She soaks her hair thru and follows with a small dollop of shampoo to cleanse the buildup of hair products. This was her once a week routine to keep her hair soft and strong. She grabs some leave-in conditioner that Katy uses and cups her hand gently to create a puddle as this conditioner is runny in consistency. She applies it to the ends of her hair first working up toward the nape of her neck.

Now she sits back to relax and closes her eyes. She begins to recall. Her first crush.

"Hello Josh," said Molly as he passed her in the school hallway. Josh ignored her and started talking to Sarah, who was the captain of the cheerleading squad. Molly was awkward as a teenager and didn't really fit in. She wore silver braces and glasses. Molly was visibly upset. She ran outside and sat down on the bench outside the cafeteria still wearing her backpack. She held her hands over her face and took a deep breath. A tall slender brunette, Raven, sat down next to Molly. She was dressed in a black mini skirt, net pantyhose, knee length high heel boots, and a midriff black top. "What seems to be the problem, Molly?"

"It's nothing forget it"

"Josh again, isn't it?" What did I tell you about him? Don't go chasing after a jock, all they want is cheerleaders and pussy," said the brunette.

"I really like him! Why doesn't he like me?"

"Now Molly we can do better than this! Pull yourself together!" said Raven as she puffed on the butt of the cigarette and flicked the ashes as they floated in the air. "There's better dudes out there, come on you're going to be late for class," said the brunette.

"Raven, I…"

Molly glanced back and the brunette was gone. She collected herself and went to class.

Molly opened her eyes. Satisfied with feeling fresh and clean, she grabs for a towel folded neatly in a white wooden bath tower that sat against the wall and placed it around her bosoms rolling the top of the towel down to secure it. She grabbed a second smaller towel to pat her hair of excess water. As she goes to get dressed a female figure appears in an old antique mirror. She notices Molly and her predicament. Molly doesn't notice as she dresses and heads to the kitchen still lost in thought about Aaron. "Thank you for grabbing my bags, Katy," said Molly. "Absolutely," said Katy.

"I was thinking about the problems James, and I are having. He is really pumping the breaks on the baby situation. My biological clock isn't going to be ticking forever. I really needed this time away from him since we have been arguing so much. He didn't even do a proper send off or offer to come with us. I don't understand why he's become so distant." Molly explains as she props her feet up and sighs. "What should I do about it?"

"Have you considered compromises? Maybe each of you give a little so that you both are happy?"

"I've tried with him. He's putting his foot down on this and it is so frustrating! We end up putting each other down and I'm so sick of him thinking I'm some little whining girl. Why would anyone not want to have a family?"

"Some people are just not ready to make that commitment. Having children is a huge responsibility and it's a privilege. Giving up the freedom of being able to do adventurous things isn't always easy."

"You sound just like James! I know it's a privilege, why is it so bad to want it? I just feel like we are pushing each other away, and I am worried about how long this marriage is going to last" Molly said as she wipes a tear from her face,

"You know I wish I had someone like Aaron. The way you describe him is appealing to me, do you think he would be interested in me?" Molly's heart was sinking. She so desperately wanted to be a mother and a wife with maturity and respect.

"That's hard to say. He's married and has a son. I know he's known his wife for a long time now, almost 30 years! What are you suggesting? Do want to attempt to break up Aaron's family for your own personal gain?"

"Ahh, you make it sound so bad! I just want a one-night stand, it can't really hurt anyone. I just want to be held by a real man! Besides, you can introduce me to him and maybe tell him how cool and sweet I am, you know, like window shopping the merchandise." Suggested Molly.

Katy gives Molly a look of concern, as she's not quite sure if she wants to get involved. She does have her reservations about James. James, in her opinion, is self-centered and arrogant. He does seem to be on the same page about being annoyed with Molly as Katy has been lately. This gets Katy to worry, even though she does understand how people like to distance themselves from Molly. After a moment to process the pros and cons of the situation, Katy realizes that Aaron is an adult and can make his own choices. If Molly goes for him, it's not her place to intervene or babysit Aaron.

"Molly, is that what you really want to do? To try and separate Aaron from Kelly and their 12-year-old son over a night of sex?" Asks Katy

"You make it sound so bad!" Molly chuckled "I just feel like I was meant to get to know him! Something about him draws me in. I want to meet Aaron and see him for myself."

"Well essentially it sounds like you have your intentions that's for sure, just know he's devoted to his wife and son. He's madly in love with her. Don't forget Molly, Aaron is a close personal friend of mine, and I don't want to see you ruin my friendship for your gain. You know he's a hard nut to crack, I've never known him to be the type to stray. He's got a lot of personal issues about which he won't talk." Said Katy.

"Katy, relax, I know what I am doing!"

"Let's change the subject here for a sec, I put in a job internship listing on LinkedIn and Indeed for a job that can be done at any of our locations. So maybe while you're there you can see about getting an interview from Aaron and maybe get a position. It'll make it easier for you to be in the office and It'll give you a chance to stick around. Its great pay and benefits galore! It'll be a step up from your EMT job that you had. What do you think? You do have a substantial background in the medical field that will benefit you greatly. Thing is you would have to move here to Albuquerque."

"Katy, I think moving here may be good for me. With everything that's going on coming here for an internship and some time to at least refresh would be a good thing, even if its temporary I'll have to quit my current job though if I get this." said Molly. "I'll get on and you can show me where the listing is, and I can apply now so that when we do get to your office Aaron would have had the chance to look it over already!"

"Let's do this," says Katy. "I'll let you use my laptop to write up a resume and you can submit it tonight"

"Far out!" says Molly. "I'm so excited!" Molly has been thinking about leaving James for some time. This to her would be a way to start out fresh. She had thought about all the legal things she'd have to do in order to make her idea of a new life a reality. She was excited! She hadn't been excited in a very long time. Molly knows the risks and is set to do whatever it takes. Even if it meant leaving her husband and attempting to acquire the man of her dreams. She was ready for her little mission.

Molly and Katy spend the rest of the afternoon applying for the job and resume to Katy's workplace. Katy's husband Arturo came home having picked up his own supper. They spend the rest of the evening watching movies and relaxing after finishing the job application. Molly never really cared much for Arturo. He's quiet and self-centered just like James. Arturo cares more for his own career, leaving Katy by herself and lonely for days or weeks at a time as he takes off to various bases to build on his career. On the outside Katy and Arturo seem like the ideal couple. On the inside, Katy's husband is no different from Molly's. Katy feels this is what she's destined to be, a childless woman. She is questioning her devotion to stick around or leave Arturo for a chance at a family, but she really loves him and wants to work things out. Molly sat on the couch, watching her sister and brother-in-law quietly in contemplation as they discussed their day and random everyday nuances. "Katy, how's Rodger doing? Isn't he up for retirement yet?" Asked Arturo.

"Yeah, here in the next three or four months I think, we are looking for a replacement for him, someone with a PHD and a strong pharmaceutical background, but he needs more positions under him before he leaves as well. Aaron has been busy with checking resumes for possible interviews. If applicants can at least get the internship, they'll get their foot in the door." Katy responded

"I see, so has he decided on any prospects yet or what?"

"Not yet. Still narrowing down"

"So have you got everything packed for the trip?"

"I will pack here shortly actually" Arturo responded. He was always a last-minute packer. As Katy and Arturo continued light chit-chat, Molly sat on the couch quietly.

"Is this all that was left for her? Is this how James was going to leave her?" Thought Molly. "No" Molly muttered to herself. She was going to get what she wanted regardless of the cost. Aaron is her ticket to a family, a relationship, and stability. She has a plan of action. "Move over wifey, it's my spot now." Molly's lips quivered in anticipation.

4 PENNHURST

It had been a long flight to Pennsylvania. Katy, Arturo, and Molly arrived at the Hampton Inn at Limerick Pennsylvania after shuffling through the airport for baggage and a rental car. Arturo headed for the front desk to check in, ensuring that they had two side by side rooms with an interconnecting door between them. The clerk handed him a pair of key cards. "Here we are sir, you will be in rooms 219 and 220, on the second floor. There is an ice machine down the hallway to the right, and breakfast starts at 6 am. Have a pleasant stay." Arturo collected the key cards, thanked the clerk, and headed out. Molly and Katy waited outside catching some fresh air. Arturo returned with two key cards. "Let's go, I'll park the car and then we can start taking our luggage up to room," he said. After parking the car and grabbing the luggage the three of them were spent. "How about something to eat?" Molly inquired. "There is a Palermo's not too far from here, maybe we could grab some pizza? I want chicken on mine!"

"You and your damn chicken, Molly. Always with the chicken." Laughed Katy.

"I don't hear you complaining when I make my famous chicken soup, dork!" Teased Molly. Katy chuckled.

"Hey, not a bad idea, I think they have delivery, don't they?" Arturo exclaimed with enthusiasm.

"Looks like they do," said Molly, "Ahh they delivery!"

"Works for me!" Katy replied, "I'm going to shower while y'all figure out pizza."

After getting the pizza, eating, and cleaning up, Katy, Molly, and Arturo sat up and did a little digging about Pennhurst. Watching several episodes from various television shows, they were intrigued and frightened. Katy was sensitive about the treatment the victims had endured. Pennhurst was a black eye to Pennsylvania, and she felt it. Molly had her own apprehensions about the place. In her mind, she felt something was out of place. But she couldn't quite place what she was feeling.

The next day they participated in the Public Paranormal Investigation tour. Having no equipment, they each used the equipment available to them. Katy, Arturo, and Molly joined a group of ten other patrons. Walking around the premises they found themselves inside Mayflower Hall. It was pitch black and the building itself was vandalized and had an abandoned feel to it. Using only night vision cameras to see they each took great care in walking around and exploring the dilapidated building.

"Molllly," Katy said trembling, "I don't feel so good right now." There was a very faint sound of a female spirit in which Molly was able to hear with her own ears.

"Shhh!" Molly replied, "did you hear that? It sounded like a woman……hey, who are you?" Molly stood still with a digital recorder device hoping to grab an EVP. "Are you okay? Do you need help?" The air was still. Molly began to review the recorder, hearing her questions she anticipated some sort of response. Nothing. They continued down one of the halls checking rooms and being very quiet. It was so quiet in fact; you could hear a pin drop at fifty feet. A loud bang erupted. It was Raven getting attention, but the group wouldn't know this right off the bat. That's what Raven was counting on. Following the direction, they assumed the noise was coming from some of the team members. Katy, Molly, and Arturo headed to the south side of the next level. There she was, lurking in the darkness as to not be seen, Raven was cunningly moving about as to not be seen just yet. Katy asked more questions using the device. "Are you trying to get away from here?" asked Katy, holding out the speaker, "Speak into this recorder so we can communicate with you," said Katy. Raven spoke very softly in the recorder. Reviewing the recording a very faint "Molllly" was heard. Katy felt a sudden presence while this was going on and stood cold as she heard the recording. "Holy shit Molly! What the hell was that?" Katy whispered. "It sounded like my name" Molly whispered back with a cracking in her voice.

Katy continued to record asking "Who are you and how do you know who my sister is? Are you trying to get out of here?" Katy asked. She replayed the recorder and there was dead silence. Raven was being methodical in her presence to the living. She moved about watching the patrons investigate the area. She taunted them with her cold negative energy. Pockets of cold air, light scratching, and pinching was Raven's forte. Her target, however, was Molly, and Raven was intent on getting everything she wanted from Molly. Some of the batteries of the cameras went out. Raven sucked the energy out of them which helps Raven's ability to do physical things to, on, or around living persons. This frustrated the ones using the static night vision cameras as they were attempting to record video evidence of paranormal activities. Some even pick up EMF readings and spikes. Raven didn't care. She continued to make subtle noises and irritate the living with temperature drops and shadow appearances. Everyone was on edge as she continued her antics. She did attempt to make several sounds from different places to get the patrons to split up. This was working. Molly had wandered away into one of the empty rooms. Raven was on her tail. This was her playground now. She was gearing up to get control of Molly.

Katy continued to ask occasional questions to engage with what she thought was one of many spirits that resided at Pennhurst. "Are you a victim of this place? Talk to us so we can hear your story," said Katy. Raven approached Katy and repeated the name of one of the buildings. Katy replayed the recorder and heard the name "Raven " It was a very faint eerie voice of what sounded like a female in Katy's mind. "Wh…wh…what's your name?" asked Katy, holding the device yet again to get a response. Raven spoke her name into the recorder. Katy reviewed it and heard the faint sound of what seemed like a woman saying "Davon". Katy had chills run up her spine as she recognized the voice, and her blood ran cold. Raven enjoyed this immensely and loved that she was closer to getting Molly alone. Katy ran down the stairs, out of the building and began to vomit, spit, cough, and hack. Arturo followed behind. "Leave me alone for a bit" said Katy, "I need a moment." Davon was the name of one of the buildings that had been unsafe to explore in as it was in a condemned like condition.

"Honey what is wrong?" Arturo asked, "what's going on?"

"Just give me a minute" responded Katy

"The voice sounded like Raven; an imaginary friend Molly had when we were kids. Except, she wasn't imaginary, mom and pop never understood what Molly was really going through " Katy explained, "Oh God no she's back! How is this happening again?!" Katy cried, "Oh God where's Molly? MOLLY! MOLLY! Where are you? Where the fuck did you go?" Katy screamed! Running back into the building, she began looking frantically. Molly didn't hear or see Katy. Katy couldn't see much, and the energy of the place was so overwhelming she came back out hollering Molly's name over and over. Raven was back on Molly's tail. She was going to stick to her, and this time for good. Molly noticed a strange shadow figure that looked oddly familiar. "Hello, who are you?" Said Molly, "Can you give me your name?" She continued. "I see your form here, come talk to me." Raven appeared as if she was human. "Hello, Molly, remember me?" The figure approached her. Molly felt an ice-cold chill flow through her body. At that moment, Molly remembered. Raven had been banished once before, but the figure had found Molly again. Raven lunged at Molly, entering her body. Molly jolted then froze in place as Raven enveloped her. Molly blacked out for a moment as she fell to the floor. Her body began to shiver and shake lightly. Then she was motionless. When her eyes opened. Molly felt normal again. Oddly, she could not understand what had just happened to her. She realized she was by herself, lying motionless on the floor. Footsteps in the distance suggested other people were frantically leaving the building. She stood up and made her way out of that rotten, foul place. "What the hell just happened?" Molly asked herself. She pulled out her cell phone and checked the time. How long had she been on the floor like that? Seconds? Minutes? She didn't know. She eventually found the exit bolting out of the building. Several members were outside already, talking amongst themselves. Dameon, one of the patrons, approached Arturo wanting to speak in private. "Hey, I saw a silhouette of what looked like a woman next to your wife over there" said Dameon, "Oh and I'm Dameon by the way."

"I'm Arturo" reaching out for his hand. "Nice to meet you. So, you saw a womanly figure? Are you serious? May I see what you got?" Arturo asked.

"It was a form, like a shadow figure, and my camcorder

caught an anomaly with this face going straight into the recorder your wife was using" said Dameon. "I have it on my video recorder here"

Dameon and Arturo looked at the footage. There was a clear face in an anomaly that appeared feminine that went straight for the recorder at the same time Katy recorded an EVP. Arturo was shocked, impressed, and scared half to death at the same time. Katy noticed Arturo talking to Dameon and approached them; "Hey, what the fuck are you looking at?" Katy asked curiously.

"Hey Katy, why are you all outside and…. woah, you don't look so good are you okay?" Molly asked. Molly looked over her sister, making sure she wasn't injured physically. On Katy's neck, Molly noticed three light scratches, just above her left shoulder. They looked ominous. "Katy, you have scratches on your neck. Does it hurt?" Katy contemplated her scratch. For her, it was just a slight burning sensation. But it gave Katy a very nervous sensation. She had been physically attacked. The reality of what had happened was palpable.

Anxiety began to rush through Molly's body. Katy turned to Molly after having just been inside the building, looking for Molly in shock and relief. She ran to her sister and threw her arms around her. "Molly, jeez sis, you're ice cold! Are you feeling alright?" Molly considered her question for a moment. Yes, she was cold, shivering in fact. But why? Outside, the temperature was at least in the mid-seventies, but she felt like she had been in a walk-in freezer. Molly rubbed her hands up and down her arms to warm up. She began to form the words to tell Katy that she couldn't remember the last several minutes while she was inside, but something seemed to prevent her from saying it.

"Here, we caught the whole thing on camera" Said Arturo, "Look." Katy grabbed Molly by the hand and looked at the footage and Katy began to cry. "I could feel the presence, it was so cold! It's like the temperature dropped a good 20 degrees in there." Arturo comforted

Katy as she was shaking and crying. "Katy, what's going on?" Asked Molly.

"Oh my god Molly! I think it's Raven! Sh….she's back!" Katy cried. "Here, look." Molly took the camera and reviewed it. Molly's face went pale when she recognized a partial face that looked all too familiar to her. She began to quiver.

Molly rummaged through her memories. She had been a teenager, sixteen in fact. One of her classmates, Missy, had swiped a bottle of Whiskey from her father's liquor cabinet one Saturday night. Molly, Missy, and a group of other girls, along with a couple of guys from the Lacrosse team in school had decided to sneak out for a night of a little fun and mischief. One of the other girls, Kayla, had brought with her a backpack with a bag of weed, a few beers, and some sort of what appeared to be a board game. Molly didn't know what it was, but no matter, she was getting shit faced tonight. Missy suggested to the group that they go hang out at a local abandoned cemetery, just outside of town. There had been an old run-down church nearby where kids would break in, graffiti the walls, drink, smoke, and perform other unnecessary acts. Nearby were several dozen gravestones, some of them dating back to the early 1800's.

"They say this place is totally fucking haunted!" remarked Missy, as she took a swig of whisky. The group sat around the old stones. They drank, some of them smoked, they joked and teased. Kayla opened her backpack and pulled out the game board, opened it and sat it on a headstone. It was a Ouija board. She produced a planchette on top of it. "C'mon, let's see if we can channel one of these so-called spirits." She said, laughing. Kayla took a puff from her joint, then placed two hands on the planchette. "Who's with me?" she asked. Molly felt a nervous tension inside of her, as if something were compelling her to join Kayla. Hesitantly, she sat down across from her and placed her own fingertips on the planchette. They looked at each other.

"Sprits we are gathered here to speak with you. Please come forth and speak with us" Kayla said. Molly felt as if some unseen energy seemed to pull the planchette in what appeared to be a circle eight figure and it stopped. R. It circled again. A. It shifted . V. Another circle, this time stopping on E. One last time, it moved, this time violently. N. The movement ceased. Nothing more came of it. The girls pulled away quickly.

"Raven." Molly thought in her mind. She pondered what had just happened and took a drink of whiskey. She felt a strange compulsion within her. The word echoed in her mind. She spoke the word out loud. "Raven… Raven… Raven…." A gust of wind rushed seemingly out of nowhere. An ice-cold chill ran down Molly's spine, and she began to get dizzy. She fell back into the grass; she closed her eyes. She began to shiver. She blacked out.

Molly shook off the memory. She looked at her sister, who had been snapping her fingers in her face to get her attention. She looked around at the group surrounding her.

"I thought I was done with that thing!" Molly interjected. "Katy I'll be fine. We can figure this out, okay. We just need to sage ourselves and say some prayers and we'll be fine!" Molly hugged Katy and they both were visibly upset. Little did Molly know; Raven was inside her once again. This time, she wasn't going to leave that easy.

After everyone settled all the patrons, Katy, Arturo, and Molly called it a night and left the property. "This trip was a bad idea," thought Molly. "I wish I could just…..." The drive back was quiet as everyone was tired and stressed out. Arturo and Molly fell asleep right away.

Katy had to continue to calm down enough to go to bed as she took deep breaths and focused on positive things. She put on her ear buds and began to listen to some calming sleeping sounds on one of her apps that help people to meditate and sleep soundly. As she had started to drift off, Katy started dreaming about when she and Molly were young teenagers. Molly had been diagnosed with schizophrenia. She was seeing people that were not there, rather she was clairvoyant, but her family felt it was a mental illness. She took medications to make the people go away. Or so they thought. "Katy, I can still see the lady," Molly told her sister in confidence. "Molly, you can't say things like that around mom and pop, they'll go out of their minds!" Katy responded.

"I know, I just can't seem to shake it and I don't know what to do about it?"

"Well don't speak of it or you'll be in deep shit you know that Molly. Ever since you went fucking around that night with your so-called friends, you haven't been the same since. If mom and pop find out…"

"Don't you believe me?" asked Molly

"I do believe you, it's just I don't want us to get into trouble." Katy remarked.

"Promise me you'll not tell mom and pop though! Please Katy don't tell them!"

"Okay, Okay, I'll keep it between us, but you got to keep it on the down low okay Molly?"

"Okay, I will," Molly said in relief.

Katy woke up and took a deep breath. She got up to use the bathroom and came back to bed. She took a deep breath and dozed off.

Katy woke up the next morning still disheartened by what had happened. "Hay Molly let's see if we can find a metaphysical shop to get some sage and palo santo," suggested Katy

"That sounds like a great idea!" Molly replied.

They spent the day traveling to Philadelphia to find a metaphysical store. Once they found one Katy, Molly and Arturo went inside to look around. Various spiritual objects, books, crystals, and incense were displayed around the shop. Molly found an assortment of sage bundles and the like and started examining the exact ones she wanted. There were various sizes. She just wanted some small travel size like ones. Once she picked out two of the bundles she wanted, she headed to the cashier and paid for them. She proceeded to find Katy. "Hay Katy, I got some, you ready to go?" Asked Molly.

"Yeah, I just want to pick up this book here, Hay Arturo, I'm going to buy this book. Molly and I will be ready to head back after this."

"Sure honey, want to stop for some food on the way back?" Arturo suggested.

"I could eat anything as long as it's chicken. I want my chicken! And after the night we had I could go for some dickin!'" joked Molly. Katy shot her an annoyed glance.

"Sounds good" Katy replied. She paid for her book, and they all headed to grab food and get back to the hotel. Once at the hotel they began to burn the bundles outside in the parking lot. They each prayed an Our Father prayer, drenching each other in the smoke from each of the burning ends. Raven was disgusted. She wanted to lash out but she also wanted to keep quiet so she could fully take over Molly. Hoping that it would work they put the bundles out with some bottled water and stored them in the sack the store had given them. Little did they know this was just the beginning. It would take more than burning these bundles to get Raven away from Molly.

5 VACATION WEEK THREE

Molly was exhausted from the trip to Pennhurst with Katy and Arturo. Molly can be overbearing when she's stuck in a plane for so many hours, so Katy was happy to have some fresh air. The flight left her drained. They each had a good night's rest and felt refreshed. It's Monday and today is the day Molly has been fantasizing about. Now she's so looking forward to the start of a new week. This last trip was very taxing, and Molly just wanted some normalcy. She has been thinking a lot about stepping into her sister's world and getting acquainted. She may have a promising new career to look forward to. If she plays her cards right.

"Katy, how do I look? Is this office appropriate?"

"Sure Molly, if office appropriate means having a skirt and blouse so short it barely covers your bits and your tits!"

"Haha!' laughed Molly. "If you want to sell yourself, ya got to show off some goods."

"You're always a bit of a showoff! Really you need to tone it down a bit and show some professionalism. You're going to be working with chemists and Dr's. I'm sure they have more important things to view than bits and tits" Katy chuckled. After Molly toned down her outfit, they each got into her Jeep and headed to Katy's work.

The drive to the office was serene. There were few clouds in the sky, and even a couple hot air balloons in the distance. Molly wasn't used to the number of trees or hot air balloons. It was fall in Albuquerque. Michigan itself was always a chilly, drab place with very little to see apart from Lake Michigan which has some scenery, so Albuquerque was a sight for sore eyes to Molly.

Katy and Molly pulled into a parking space right by the building in Katy's usual spot. It's still early so the parking lot was scarce. Most of the employees were still out grabbing their morning breakfast burritos and lattes.

'So, which one is Aaron's spot?" asked Molly. "He seems like a truck guy." Molly giggled curiously.

"He is." Said Katy. "But I don't see that he's come in yet. He usually parks right next to me" Katy led Molly to the main doors pressing her finger on the biometric plate. She held the door long enough allowing Molly to follow behind her. Molly stepped inside. She was immediately hit with the smell of morning coffee and the sound of laughter from a pair of guys standing by a coffee machine. She quickly recognized them from Katy's Facebook page as Wayne and Julio, two office clowns who otherwise really seemed jovial to be around each other. Molly introduced herself. "Hello, I'm Molly!" She said, "Heeeey, wassup girl" said Wayne, as he introduced himself. Molly noticed that he came off with a little too much false machismo. Molly sensed Wayne was covering up his being gay by putting on a manly façade so nobody would notice. Molly doesn't mind. Julio, standing next to Wayne is much more relaxed yet the nervous type when an attractive woman is around. "Hello, you must be Julio, right? I'm Molly" she explained. "Uhh…hi I uhm, nice to meet you," said Julio nervously. Molly smiled, shook his hand. As Molly continued down the hall with Katy, a young man in his early 20's Juan, had come around the corner. Molly instantly recognized him, "Oh!" She said with surprise, "You must be Juan, right?" Molly insisted. Juan looked slightly puzzled, "Oh hello, yeah uhm welcome to the office." said Juan, offering a slightly limp handshake. "How did you know my name?" he asked

"Oh, Katy showed me a photo of y'all, so I'd feel more welcome"

"You mean the Harry Potter One?"

"That's the one!"

"Ahh makes sense, well I must be going" Juan continued down the hall to start off the day with Julio and Wayne.

Katy and Molly walked their way down a bright lit hall passing several offices with their doors closed before reaching Katy's office. Katy grabbed her keys and unlocked her office door. Molly sat her bag down on a chair in front of Katy's desk and looked around. "Typical Katy." She thought as she noticed her seasonal decorations. "It's a wonder how Katy ever got any real work done with all the little art projects she made for herself." The office had a couple of nice desks with computers, monitors, and a fancy printer. Drawers and cabinets were labeled as if to say, "Katy was here" rather than what the intended contents were instead. Molly settled in a comfy leather computer chair and thumbed through a pile of documents that sat on Katy's desk as she thought of Aaron in gleeful anticipation. Soon her moment would come to finally meet this man she had sought her sights on after so many conversations with Katy and seeing his social media, Molly was ready. For now, she must look occupied so as to not blow her cover or look too obvious with her inner intentions.

Aaron, having placed his thumb on the biometric pad, made his way down the hall to his office wearing heavy jeans, a motorcycle vest, and riding boots. His office was adjacent to Katy's office. He was thinking to himself about riding into work. "Nothing like a cool morning breeze flowing over your body to get the blood moving." He thought to himself. He grabbed his keys and unlocked his office door. He sat his Swiss Army backpack under his desk. He turned to leave his office and grabbed a coffee cup from his shelf on the way out. Making a beeline to the coffee pot in the break room Aaron pours himself a cup as he reaches the pot, he gently aims the spout to his cup just right so as not to spill a drop. Adding two sugars and one cream to his cup afterward. Aaron notices Wayne and Julio giggling over a TikTok they had watched on Wayne's phone and greets them with a jolly "Good morning gents!" followed by an orchestrated swish of a scratched-up spoon in his cup and a gentle tilt to get the right sip without burning his tongue.

"Hey Aaron, you're looking fly in your motorcycle set up!," said Wayne.

"Ahh I'm not that fly! Just a dirty old biker!" Aaron replied.

"We don't be shy A-A-Ron!" Teased Wayne.

Aaron giggled, shook his head, and headed back to his office, swinging by the mail center first. He proceeded down the hall to his office. Upon arrival, he noticed correspondence in the door bin outside his office. He grabbed the handful and sat down at his desk. Aaron flipped through the mail and checked random memos. Sitting directly on top was a post-it reminding him that a potential new hire would be here today, Molly, Katy's sister from Michigan. He only knew of her through Katy's stories about growing up with her Mac, the youngest of the three sisters. He was eager to meet a new face. It's been a humdrum life for him having the same group of employees around every day. Aaron was an older man, and except for Katy, who just didn't seem to jive with this much younger crowd. Their life experiences are geared around phone screens and social media. Which was different when it came to Kelly, his wife. They could talk for hours about anything. Mostly growing up in the 80's and pop culture, and current events. They didn't have technology growing up. Doing things in an old-fashioned way was their style. Kelly, who is a lot like Katy, however got to know quite a bit of the current technology in attempting to keep on top of it for her son's sake. She had a computing degree. She could take a computer apart and put it back together with no sweat. Aaron relied on Katy and Kelly for those types of things. His idea of excelling was building complex Lego kits. He had a few in his office that Katy got a kick out of.

Aaron is a creature of habit and easily distracted in his work. Now was no exception. After reading his mail, post-it notes, and memos he checked emails and sipped his coffee. He was zoned into his work. In fact, it hadn't fazed him that Katy was now in her office, or that she had already taken the liberty of going into his office after he unlocked it, to get a few pens off his desk. He also didn't notice Molly sitting across the hall cross-legged and distracted by a newspaper article talking about a local chili festival that was to be held in downtown Albuquerque next weekend.

"Katy, I want to go to this. Take me, will yah?"

"Okay, let's go." Said Katy, as she looked up from her computer screen. Katy notices Aaron from across the hall "Oh, hey Aaron, there you are!"

"Good morning, Katy!" said Aaron as he passed the office, "I didn't notice you being here,"

"Yeah, been here for about thirty minutes." Hay, you haven't met Molly yet!" Katy said excitedly.

Molly realized she just missed Aaron as she overheard her name being mentioned by Katy. Her heart started racing. "I can't believe I didn't notice him!" she thought to herself. Molly folded the newspaper and sat it down on Katy's desk, stood out of her chair, and approached the door frame. There he was, at long last. Every bit as tall, dark, and scrumptious as she had anticipated. He stood there in his black biker outfit. His glow was so thick she swore she could cut it with a knife. He was glorious to behold. He was everything Molly imagined he would be and then some. A vibration shook through her body. This man was her mission. She was aroused. Molly walked across the hall toward Katy and Aaron as they were talking, she was weak in the knees, and she was nervous.

"Hay Molly come here," Katy said as she motioned her over "this is Aaron, you know my boss I told you about?" Katy said.

"H.h.hh….hello, I'm Molly" She stammered. Her eyes met his. She couldn't blink. She wouldn't dare. She was uneasy. Aaron turned to look at her. There stood a gorgeous young brunette, locks of straight almost jet-black hair pinned up in a hair clip and piercing dark brown eyes, gazing back at him. "Could this truly be Katy's younger sister?" thought Aaron. Katy is easy on the eyes, yet she's got a quirk about her that Aaron finds borderline comical. This woman however got his attention. "Is she really from the same gene pool? Do they perhaps have different parents?" thought Aaron. "This is not at all how Katy described her."

Aaron stood for a moment and offered his hand in return. He felt her intensity. There was something different about her. Aaron took quick notice of her slender yet curvy hips. Her mouth was shined with pink lip gloss. His eyes danced over her short black jean skirt and silky blouse. Her eyes were piercing with glee.

"Hi Molly, it's a pleasure to meet you. I'm Aaron, the department lead for supply and logistics around here." He said slightly nervously.

"Oh, I assure you, Aaron. The pleasure is ALL mine." Molly replied.

"I understand you are interested in observing what we do around here and may be interested in taking a position."

"Oh yes, Aaron. I'm very interested in taking… a position." Molly said seductively.

Aaron is oblivious to Molly's advances as Katy stands quiet knowing Molly's intentions. She felt uneasy, "And here we go!" muttered Katy with frustration. This was Molly's personality since they were children. One thing Katy knows is Molly doesn't take no for an answer. Somehow this situation was unique. In a matter of moments, Katy watched Molly turn from a sweet, perky, bouncy young woman into a primal venomous cobra in disguise.

Aaron noticed Molly made herself at home in one of his fancy leather office chairs as he directed her to his office. He sat down and began to interview her, asking the usual questions about integrity, experience, and basic knowledge of the position she was interviewing for.

"So, Molly, I wanted to go over some stuff." Aaron said as he took his seat in front of his computer screen. "So, I oversee logistics and supply. I make sure pharmaceutical supplies are ordered, received, documented, and distributed."

"What would my position be in that process?" Molly asked, as she sat across from Aaron with her legs crossed.

"Well, I've looked at your resume and I think you'll do well in the R&D department, you know short for Research and Development" Aaron replied.

"The company is developing a drug. It's a new drug that will numb patients without losing consciousness and some physical movement. It's not FDA approved. They still need to continue more trials. If it works out well, we can get it from physicians and start using it in mental health hospitals and treatment centers. It'll help replace some heavy sedation without losing mobility. It's geared toward behavioral disorders where patients have violent tendencies. This is where the position I am looking for comes in. I need someone to make sure all supplies are monitored and documented, and reports are ready for submission to the FDA from the trials. The new hire will supply the drug, then

R&D will supply the report. Then the new hire will make sure the report is complete. If anything is missing, send a request for needed documentation. Any red flags go through me. Once it's done, hand it over to me."

"Sounds interesting, I'm excited to get my feet wet!" Molly exclaimed as she leaned forward seductively.

"Great, I'll go ahead and login to the JRAF system and see your resume. After that I'll give you a tour of the facilities here in a moment." Said Aaron. After looking at her resume and considering the conversation they just had Aaron was certain Molly was right for the job.

"Molly, I think you'll be just right for this position. I'll need you to fill out some paperwork and do the standard criminal background check. In the meantime, you'll shadow me for the first week, then I'll work with Dr. Rodger Smith down in R&D. He's our current field guy; he is retiring in a few months."

"Thank you so much, I'm really excited," Molly replied. "Well let's go Molly, I'll show you around and introduce you to everyone," said Aaron.

Molly spent the day getting familiar with the company and completing company documentation for new hires. She had a private discussion with her old boss back home and quit her job during her lunch hour. She picked her phone up and called her boss's number. "This is Jack" said her boss "Hay Jack, I was able to find a job here where my sister lives so I'm putting in my notice"

"Molly this is very unprofessional of you to just up and walk out on this job. You could have at least told me in advance instead of jumping state and leaving us shorthanded as it is."

"Jack the job opportunity just landed in my lap I couldn't pass up the pay"

"Molly, you realize that you won't be desired if you want

to come back with us with this job jumping stunt your pulling, right?"

"Jack don't be so dramatic! Besides, you know how much you all really like me and my little favors"

"Molly that's uncalled for and you know it! Just for that YOUR FIRED!"

"You can't fire me I quit!" Molly yelped as she cut off Jack and ended the call. She went back to the rest of her day and felt confident in her new position.

It was a long day. Katy and Molly came back to Katy's house, but the ride was quiet. Molly enjoyed the greenery. They each got something to drink and sat down on the couches with ottomans. "So, Molly, how was your first day?" asked Katy. "It was great, and exhausting! So much paperwork and so many names of people to remember, except of course Aaron!" Molly said playfully.

"Molly, you know you're playing with fire here, right?" replied Katy, with concern.

"Relax! I know what I am doing! I am not a child, yah know!" Molly said defensively.

"Okay, but realize like I said before Aaron is a devoted husband to Kelly and a hard egg to crack"

"I know, I know," Molly sighed, "He's just so much more than James ever could be, besides a little rendezvous won't hurt"

"Okay, Molly, beware his wife. She comes by from time to time, be careful to not blow your cover if she's around." Katy warned. "Also, Aaron is my friend, Molly. He's been there for me, please don't do anything to ruin my friendship"

"Alright, alright, I'll be careful," replied Molly." I'm going to take a bath after dinner. Speaking of which, let's get some chicken?"

"That sounds sooo good! Arturo should be home soon, and we can order delivery thru the app"

After dinner, Molly ran the water for the tub adding foaming Epsom salt into the stream. She was mentally exhausted. So many prospects of the position being offered with this job. There was so much to wrap her head around, and she would need to work on obtaining a lot of certifications to do it. It's the kind of work she found challenging, and her experience will help with a more personal position that would get her a chance for a more personal encounter. That's what she wanted most. She grew excited as she fanaticized about Aaron. She slipped inside the tub and contemplated ways to get Aaron's attention. "How to do you get inside his head? What makes him tick? What is his weakness?" Aaron is going to give her the very thing her husband is reluctant to do. He's going to give her the child that James will not. He just doesn't know it yet.

"If Aaron won't do this willingly, how do I make him? A couple of roofies in his drink could work but it would make him incapacitated. I want him as my little puppet. I get what I want him to do for me. What is that new drug Aaron was talking about? Would it be strong enough to do the job and get the pleasure I want?" Molly finished her bath, dressed, and headed to bed attempting to answer all her lingering questions.

6 A WAY INSIDE

Molly's first couple of days in the office were typical "New Hire stuff." Paperwork continued beyond what the eye can see. Getting credentials for everything she'll need access to. She's tired of signing papers for benefits and company policy acknowledgments and trainings. The anxiety to get out from behind her desk and getting her hands dirty is gnawing at her. Sitting back in her chair she took a deep breath and grabbed a sip from her cup of coffee, then it hit her. "Aaron has a love for a morning cub of Joe.

Fresh coffee was his morning routine, but he had to leave his office and head down the hall to the break room to get his refills. Wouldn't it be nice if he had someone to do that for him?" Thought Molly. Ah ha! Aaron isn't here yet. Molly stepped into his office with the key Katy gave her. She swiped his Harley Davidson coffee cup and walked down the hall to the break room and filled it just an inch below the top, just the way she heard he likes it, leaving room for one cream and two sugars. As she walked into the office Aaron had just sat down and was already busy with emails at his desk.

"Here you go Aaron, I believe you like your coffee with one cream and two sugars?" asked Molly.

"Wow thank you, Molly! That's very sweet of you." Aaron yelled across the hall, teasing Katy. "Hey Katy, how come you never got me coffee before I sat down at my desk in the morning?" Aaron teased.

"Fuck off Aaron, get it you're damn self." Katy returned the banter giggling like a schoolgirl.

Aaron laughed and turned to Molly. He began familiarizing Molly with more boring company practices and policies. Molly focused on one thing, that shiny lock of silver chrome like streak that sprouted from the center of his dark brownish black hair. It fascinated her. "It looks so distinguished just like his almost fully white goatee. Salt and pepper. More salt than pepper. I want it so badly t..."

"Alright, any questions? From here we'll head down to R&D and introduce you to Dr. Roger. You'll start shadowing him today. He's been doing this for a while, so he knows the ropes well." Said Aaron.

"Oh, yeah of course you got it boss." Molly replied pretending to have been paying attention to his word and not his salt and peppered hair.

Later that morning, just before lunch, Aaron realized he

left the meal Kelly had made for him in the refrigerator at home. Texting his wife, Kelly, he wrote "Hey lady could you perhaps bring my lunch, I left it in the fridge." Said Aaron. "Sure honey, no problem. I'll be over soon." Kelly texted back. About 10 minutes later, Kelly was in her husband's office, putting the bowl of lemon spaghetti in his office mini fridge that she just bought him. He thanked her and gave her a kiss on the cheek. Somehow, the sensation she felt as he did so didn't feel like she would have expected. A shiver struck down her spine unlike any she had ever felt before. It was strange and chilling. She couldn't shake the unusual feeling. She glanced around and then across the hall to get a sense of direction, then she noticed Katy working away on the computer. "Hmm…" Kelly thought. That didn't make sense to her. Down the hall, Juan was posting flyers on a cork board. "That's strange… I don't sense it from him." Kelly thought. She had long sensed powerful emotions in people before. Sometimes it made her nervous and overwhelmed. Most times she felt it physically and emotionally. She didn't fully have a grasp with this strange sense she had, but one thing she did know, it always comes from someone. It could be somebody having a bad day, bitter mood, or even joy from good news. She couldn't pinpoint where this was coming from. Even Wayne, on the other end of the hall pulling boxes from a closet seemed jovial. "What is going on here?" Kelly thought.

"Here's those documents you needed from R&D for you, boss as well as some more from shipping." Molly said.

Kelly didn't recognize the voice and turned to see Aaron reach out to grab a small stack of documents from a very strange and unfamiliar young woman. With Molly in the room, that strange zeal illuminated from her to Aaron. Could the strange sense be from this young dark-haired woman?

"Honey, this is Molly, Katy's little sister. She is interning here for a little while to train for a new position here in the company."

"Oh hello, nice to meet you, Molly." Kelly said as she reached out an apprehensive hand to her.

Molly replied with a polite "Hello" of her own, but Kelly noticed the moment she took her hand that a strange and unrecognizable sense about her. Kelly felt nervous around her. Even though Kelly was twice Molly's size she didn't want to push it. She didn't understand what it was she was feeling, but she didn't like it. Molly looked Kelly up slightly, with what appeared to be a judgmental smirk on her face. At least that's what she interpreted, or was she misreading the situation?

Molly turned to Aaron. "Katy and I are going out to Mexican for lunch, boss. Want to come with?"

"No thanks, Kelly brought me lunch today." Aaron said.

"Suit yourself, boss. I hear their tacos are to die for!" Molly replied with a quick wink. Kelly noticed the slight advance. Was she being paranoid? This girl rubbed her the wrong way. Kelly watched her walk out the door, collecting her sister and walking down the hall. Kelly turned to Aaron, who was busy shuffling thru the paperwork he had been handed. How could he stand to be in the same room with her? Could he not feel the vibe she was putting out? What was her game? Why was she here? It didn't make sense to her. She was around her for mere minutes and in seconds could read that Molly was up to no good as if she read her like a book. How could Aaron not see that she had an agenda? Kelly had an entire scenario in her mind that led up to Molly possibly wanting to get Aaron in the sack. "Why am I thinking this way? This is nuts, just let it go" Kelly thought. "You don't want to embarrass Aaron and you certainly don't want to make a fool of yourself"

"Aaron…" Kelly said

"Yes, dear?"

"I…hmmm… never mind," Kelly replied.

"What's wrong Hun?"

"It's nothing, I just have a lot to do today"

"Okay sweetie, I'll see you later then?"

"Yeah, I love you babe"

Kelly needed to think this through. Something was way off, but she could put her finger on it. She needed time to sort out what just happened. Kelly kissed Aaron before she left. The air seemed settled. Kelly felt a weird sense of relief. She left for the exit heading for the parking lot and got back into her minivan, ready to get back to her day. She paused as she pushed the start button on the dash, causing the engine to purr to life. She had noticed a thin silver wedding ring on Molly's finger. "So, she is married. I should have nothing to worry about." Kelly thought to herself. She let her previous thoughts shift to the back of her mind. She had a lot to get done today, she needs to focus on that before she runs out of time and must go pick up her son from school. She shifted the lever to drive and pressed the gas pedal, driving off to the grocery store nearest the location of her work. Still, that nagging thought of Molly persisted as she tried to brush it off and get on with work.

An hour had passed, and Molly returned with her sister back to the office. Molly had an idea. She was going to have a little fun and test the waters. She walked down the hall to the women's room, carrying her backpack that she kept personal belongings in. Once inside, she pulled out a soft, almost silky pair of tight black yoga pants out of her bag. She removed her skirt and set it aside, revealing some very skimpy lace black panties that barely covered any of her skin, like floss between her butt cheeks. She slipped the yoga pants on and pulled them up, making sure to emphasize the undergarment shape was clearly noticeable. Her curvy feminine form was well defined, and she was going to show that off.

Molly stepped out of the women's room and headed back towards Aaron's office. Aaron was busy at his desk typing up a memo on his computer. He looked up at Molly and had a double take. Had Molly changed her clothes? He could have sworn that she had a skirt on this morning.

"Ah, your back Molly. Good, I have some materials for you to run down to Roger when you go down to R&D later." Aaron said as he attempted to compose himself.

Molly saw this as a perfect opportunity to strike. She reached out and grabbed the small pile of documents from Aaron's hand, and purposefully let a couple from the bottom slip out onto the floor.

"Woops, clumsy me!" Molly giggled. Molly turned around, spread her feet apart and bent over to pick up the documents.

Aaron was a happily married man, but he wasn't dead inside. He recognized the form of a beautiful feminine woman when he saw one. Who was he kidding? Molly was such a woman. Molly was beautiful. His eyes traced the lines of her legs, the curve of her hips, the breathtaking form of her well-defined butt. The defined outline of her womanhood between her thighs, seemed to mock him. She was very much a woman. Aaron held his breath.

Molly grabbed the two papers that she had let fall but made sure not to be too quick about it. She wanted Aaron to see what she had to offer him, her goods as it were. She slowly started to stand back up. She slid her free hand over her left calf reaching for her ass cheek, she gave it a squeeze and a little jiggle . Aaron watched Molly as Molly looked back toward him, giving him a little side-eye as she did check to see that he was indeed looking. Molly gave her butt another little squeeze. "It's all yours. Come and get it." Molly thought in her mind. Her hunch was right. Aaron was an ass-man if ever there was one. With any luck, hers was going to lure him into her arms, and later, her bed. This enticed Molly in ways she hadn't felt in years. It was like a new drug to her, this feeling of power and control. It awoke memories of a time when she learned that her womanhood, her youthful beauty, could get the attention she so desired.

She stood back up and turned around, gazing into Aarons eyes like a lioness on the prowl, and Aaron was her prey. She made her way out the door. Molly had one last trick up her sleeve. She knew how to work with what she had. She knew how to make her form appealing and she walked away by letting Aaron truly see and appreciate her soft gentle curves. She displayed her perky soft breasts as they oh so slightly giggled when she took a step. Aaron took it all In. Every inch of it.

"I'll get these right down to Roger, Aaron. I'll be back up shortly for your next set of tasks." Molly spoke softly. Molly walked out of the office, keeping one sultry eye on Aaron until she was completely out of his view.

Aaron felt his breath come back to his lungs. His heart was pounding. What just happened here? What was she expressing to him? Was that what he thought it was? No, it can't be. She has a husband back home, why would she try to seduce on older married man? There's no sense to this. Aaron couldn't deny the appeal. He couldn't deny the fact that Molly's long straight black hair looked beautiful as it swayed from side to side as she walked. He relished the thought of how her smooth soft hips accentuated every curve of her body. He began to imagine what it would be like to "Stop it, Aaron you old fool. She's so much younger than you are." he thought to himself. Still, he couldn't shake the feeling that there was something unique between them. He felt it when he was near her. A draw so powerful that it gave him butterflies in the pit of his stomach. Aaron liked her as a person. She's already proven to be a smart and resourceful young woman. She very efficient at her job and doesn't need to be told twice how to do something, but that wasn't all. She knew how to get things done. She knew how to achieve her goals. Was Aaron one of her goals? Aaron liked her. No, it's more than that. Aaron realized in his mind; he liked her.

Aaron shook his head, as if to banish the thought from his mind. He was a happily married man. He would never betray his loving wife. She would never forgive him, and he would never forgive himself for hurting and betraying his wife and son in such away. He would never live with himself after seeing the pain of such a betrayal. Aaron shrugged his shoulders and left for the office for some fresh air. This thing. with Molly, will never be allowed to be.

7 MADNESS

Katy sat at the dinner table with her husband and sister. She noticed something in her sister's eyes that concerned her. She was already ruffled over the idea that when Aaron was around, Katy basically disappeared out of Molly's world. But why so distant here and now? Molly had been chatty the whole time since she came into town, now she seemed withdrawn into another world all together. Katy remembered a time back to their childhood. A time when things were different. She remembered the times Molly would go off into a trance. Their mother always told Katy that Molly had an imaginary friend that would visit her when mom wasn't around. Sometimes this imaginary friend would influence Molly do mean things to the other kids in school. Katy despised that. She would say that sometimes it would make her physically ill, and they would have to drive her into town to see a doctor that would give her medicine to make her well again. Over time the doctor seemed to have fixed her, as Molly eventually stopped seeing her imaginary friend. Molly came back to normal just before she graduated high school. The imaginary friend had "moved away."

"So, how's life at work Molly?" Asked Katy. Molly broke her drift. "Pretty interesting stuff going" Replied Molly. "They really have some promising new medications in development that can replace old school anti-anxiety meds and offer fewer negative side effects. Paxil is out the door, as its most undesired effect is lowered sex drive. So, they have something new that doesn't have that effect. There's also a fascinating new anti-psychotic that's in trials that I'm learning about. It's supposed to calm mentally ill patients with aggressive behaviors that help them manage themselves without turning them into a zombie." Molly loved the subject of drug development. She minored in chemistry when she was in college, and she planned on taking that education further when she had the chance.

Prescription drugs had been part of her life since she was a child. She remembers the migraine like headaches she would get as a kid. Her mom took her to a doctor for it back then. The headaches would get so bad that she would forget blocks of time, 1 hour here, 3 hours there. It was intolerable for Molly. Constant pounding and feeling her head being squeezed like a citrus fruit. The doctors started using Botox to treat her episodes as they became available. She had decided at an early age to dedicate her life to medicine in some form or fashion since pharmaceuticals had made such an impact on her life. Working with Aaron was a good first step in that arena.

Aaron. The thought of him was a huge turn on. She really got his attention today, hadn't she? She began to dream about him, fantasize about him. In her mind, she imagined it. There naked bodies sweating, pressed together, rolling around in between the sheets. Or on top of them. Or wherever they ended up! She excused herself from dinner. She headed to the tub and drew a bath with her usual oils and some foaming bath. She let her self-sink in. A voice came to her. "Take him…" it said.

Molly opened her eyes and looked around. "Who's there?" she asked nervously. The voice was so clear that she was sure someone was there with her. Molly opened the shower curtain, but the room was empty except for herself. She laid back into the bath and relaxed.

The voice gave her a sense of accomplishment. She felt refreshed and energized. She knew she had to pump up her game. How? How was she going to get to a married man? How was she going to deal with his wife? That woman… she can thwart her plan. She's not an easy target. There was something about Kelly that she doesn't understand. Kelly has a bold unfiltered fierceness about her. She had to be dealt with, but how? Kelly had a suspecting look in her eye. She knows something and she can screw up this whole plan. "How do I get between Aaron and Kelly?" Molly asked of herself.

"Use them!" said the voice.

"Use what?" Molly muttered softly as she looked again around the room, curious where the voice came from, curious as to whom was there with her. Molly got out of the bathtub and wrapped a towel around herself, and her lengthy dark hair. She smiled at the thought of Aaron as she stood in front of the mirror, gazing at herself. For the briefest moment, she was startled! Raven in the mirror, what should have been her exact reflection… did not smile back. Molly looked upon her reflection in the mirror as it scowled back at her. Raven in the mirror spoke this time.

"Use them. Take him!"

Molly squeezed her eyes shut and opened them again. The scowling version of herself was gone, only her true reflection remained. "What just happened?" Molly asked herself. She headed to the guest room and got out her Metallica shirt and panties. She dried off and slipped into them. She untucked the bedding and got into bed. There was something familiar about Raven in the mirror. She looked so familiar. The quick glance wasn't enough to really recognize who was in the mirror.

The thoughts kept running thru her head, but one thing was for sure. Aaron. Aaron would be hers. Aaron belonged to her, and her to him. Molly will find a way to dispense with that wife of his and take him for herself. Those words kept ringing through her head. "Use them. Take him." What was "Them"? What or who? Molly drifted off to sleep. She began to dream about the drug in development. Something about the drug would help this diabolical goal to sleep with Aaron to attain more than just thrills. Would this drug do the trick? Would it get her the fantasy she's been having of pure bliss?

Molly walked into the office early the next morning. She wanted to have everything ready and done for Aaron before he walked in. His coffee mug would be filled, his daily reports would be filed, his desk would be dusted and tidy. The printer that Aaron constantly argued with because it was slow would be ready to go and warmed up. Little things. Teachers pet kind of things except more seductive. Molly was ready to execute the next part of the plan.

Aaron walked in at 8am as usual, saw that his morning routine was already accomplished. Molly had been in early he took it. He never asked her to do this, it wasn't in her job description. How could he say no? It certainly made his morning easier. He could focus on the daily inventories now without having to get everything ready for the morning meetings first. Then… Molly stepped in.

"Good morning boss." She spoke, looking him deeply in the eyes.

"Good morning, Molly! Thanks, uhm…. for all you did in here this morning. Really appreciate it." Aaron replied.

Molly stepped up to Aaron and began adjusting his tie. "No problem, Aaron. Got to make sure you're prepped for success. Anything for you!"

Aaron wasn't quite sure what to make of this again. His thoughts drifted back to what happened yesterday, once again gave Molly the benefit of the doubt. He thought back to something Katy had told him awhile back. "Molly is a very friendly and helpful person. Just part of her personality!" she had said. Aaron thought this is what that was. Damn, just how friendly can a person be? Molly grabbed her bag and headed down to R&D to start her day. She turned and looked back at Aaron with that seductive side eye she so loved to do.

Molly pondered what that voice said in the bathroom. Molly knew now what the voice meant by using "Them." Molly approached Roger and the rest of the development team. Roger, an older man of his late 50s, was shuffling for some paperwork at his desk. "The teams had a breakthrough, Molly! This is a red-letter day! They figured out how to work the formula without any controlled substances! It's an absolute miracle. We can proceed with clinical trials under less stringent circumstances now."

"That's amazing, but you didn't mention which formula you're talking about!" exclaimed Molly.

"The anti-psychotic one, you know the one with the number I can never remember."

"OH, THAT one." Replied Molly. "Yeah, that number needs to get a name so I can remember it better."

Molly's head began a dull throbbing. She couldn't remember the last time she had a headache. Not since she was a kid at least. Molly was usually in pretty good health. Very rarely did she ever get sick. When she did, a pot of her world-famous homemade chicken soup did the trick. This was unusual for her. She felt as though a voice in her mind was begging to cry out. As if something deep inside was trying to redirect her attention. Molly gently rubbed at her temples to sooth herself.

"You alright Molly? You look a little rough around the edges." Asked Roger, with concern in his voice.

"I'm alright, thanks for asking. Had a bit of a late night, I guess. Couldn't sleep." Molly replied.

Roger pressed on with his description of the new experimental drug he was excited about. The drug was intended to be used for patients who were prone to physical outbursts of violence. Previous drugs had a lot of side effects, such as extreme drowsiness and physical immobility. They had the intended effect of calming an out-of-control patient, but at the expense of basically turning them into a zombie that can't function under their own power. Forget about responding to instruction, the patient was rendered completely non-functional. With this new drug however, the patient was brought out of their physically psychotic state, but still had the motor function and cognitive ability to comply with instructions from caregivers and staff.

"And what's more? Its formula is completely free of any substances on the FDAs schedule of controlled substances!" Exclaimed Roger. "We can press on ahead of schedule with preclinical trials this is so exciting!"

Roger handed Molly several folders of documents, and a thumb drive containing key information on the drugs specifics. "Molly, I need to read thru all of this and become familiar with all available details. With all the work that's coming up we are going to need all hands-on deck." Said Rodger.

Molly considered what she held in her hands. On the outside, Molly saw this as a revolutionary new drug that could be far more humane for ill patients who need it than what's been available before. On the inside, something darker was at play. Something was stirring in the back of her mind that made her skin crawl. She knows what she wants. This is making her uneasy. Molly proceeded to her office to begin reviewing the material. As she passed a large mirror hanging on a nearby hallway wall, she glanced at herself. Molly raised her hand to brush a lock of her hair out of her face. To her surprise, the reflection in the mirror did not reciprocate her action. Raven in the mirror simply grimaced at her. Molly froze for a moment. An oddly familiar chill ran down her spine. It was a chill that she hasn't felt in years. The woman in the mirror from last night! It was the same one? It was! It was inside of her. She could feel it.

"Use this!" said the voice. This time Molly didn't question what she was seeing. She understood. Molly glanced down at the files in her hands. She knew what she had to do if she was to have Aaron. Molly began to see flashes of memories in her mind. She knew that girl in the mirror. As a child, Raven had been Molly's special friend. She had done her bidding before. Molly will do her bidding again. "Molly… Moooollly…." Chirped Katy, snapping her fingers at her sister.

Molly snapped out of her gaze. She glanced in the mirror and saw only her own reflection. Katy was standing next to her, annoyed at trying to get her attention. Molly turned to her sister. "Sorry, just had a lot on my mind about this project I'm working on with Roger. There's a lot of material to sift thru today."

"Yah kind of zoned out on me kiddo." Said Katy. "When you're done sifting, Aaron needs you to run the quarterly logistics report over to the finance office."

Molly was secretly delighted. She would do anything for Aaron. Anything at all to please him and gain his favor even if it meant breaking a few boundaries to do it. Molly knew that she had the ability to do it. This time, she had the help of an old friend.

Katy shuffled back to her office nervously. She had a lot on her mind now. She wasn't sure if this was what she feared since the conversation they had before Pennhurst, but she had seen that look on Molly's face before. "It can't be." Katy thought to herself. Molly's medications and therapy had worked as a child. "Molly was better now, right?" Katy thought to herself. "Raven had been banished. How did she come back? This just can't be happening again. Or can it?" Katy's anxiety on the matter was eating away at her. Was she being paranoid? Was she being unreasonable? Maybe. Should she confront Molly on this, or just let it go. Katy didn't know. All she knew was that last time Raven paid her a visit, the boy down the road from her family's home in Michigan ended up with… a few stitches. Brian was the neighborhood bully back then, always picked on whomever just happened to be within earshot of him. He was a big burly kid, overweight and he stank to high hell because he almost never bathed. He was abused and neglected at home, so when Brian wanted your lunch money, it was his. If he felt like verbally harassing you, he did it. It was his cover up. Few liked him but his little band of suck ups that always hung around him who didn't know any better about his situation at home. Then the day came he chose to pick on Molly. It was a bad choice. He had taken a wad of chewing gum and decided to squeeze it into Molly's long dark hair as she passed by him in the school hallway between classes. Katy saw it all. She saw how Molly froze in place as the bullies laughed at her. She saw how Brian chuckled as he called her "little miss gum-slut." She saw how Molly seemed to mentally vanish as something else seemed to take her place in her mind.

She saw how deep a freshly sharpened number two pencil can be buried in human flesh, as Brian fell to the floor, blood oozing from his neck. It wasn't too serious. Just enough to make Brian stop.

The coldness of Molly's eyes…Katy snapped back into the present. She shook her head. "No, can't be" she thought. Molly was better now. Molly is ok now. Those days are long gone now. Or so she thought.

Across the hall, Aaron sat at his desk typing up reports to be emailed out by the end of the day. There was a knock on his door frame, and he looked up. Molly was standing there, looking at him with a sense of want in her eyes. Aaron looked her over. There was no question that this woman was a sight to see. She was wearing skintight shiny blue leggings, and a tank top that hugged her skin oh so flawlessly. He considered her as she stood there. The curve of her hips, the shapeliness of her athletic build, the gap between her thighs. For the briefest moment… he imagined what it would be like to…

Aaron had been distracted all day. Frustrated even. He was very much in love with his wife, Kelly. They had a wonderful marriage and a wonderful son together. Everything seemed perfect on the outside and it was! However, the bedroom things were different. Kelly suffered from general anxiety and depression disorder. There were times when she was able to make it thru the day like a trooper. There were days she couldn't get out of bed. It was hard on her. It was hard on Aaron to see her like that. The doctor had come up with a penistail of medication that finally gave Kelly a sense of being human again. Almost anyway. There was one drawback that Kelly and Aaron didn't see coming. Kelly had completely lost her sex drive. Absolutely nothing remained of it. She felt no pleasure, no physical sensation at all when they made love. The desire had seemingly packed its bags and walked out the door. To add insult to injury, the change came. This was hard on Aaron because he wanted one more child, and bam menopause. Kelly was a hot mess on a regular basis. To make this worse nothing was going on in the bedroom anymore. Aaron tried his best to understand where she was coming from in all this, but the frustration was real. Aaron was feeling the pressure to get what he wanted. Taking care of his own needs was only a temporary measure. He also craved the passion, the pleasure of being wrapped in a woman's arms, feeling the heat and sweat and two bodies embraced in the throes of love. He wanted this so much from Kelly, yet it was completely absent, and this hurt Aaron, deeply.

"Got a minute, Aaron?" Molly asked. Aaron gestured towards the chair next to him. Molly passed in front of his desk, with the slightest hint of sweet perfume about her. She gently sat down; eyes constantly fixed on him. Aaron felt something. An excitement seemed to flow between them as he glanced at her. He gazed into her dark brown eyes, followed the lines of her long brown flowing hair. Her soft round cheekbones seemed to give her an air of sweet innocence. He felt a tingle flow thru his body. He hadn't felt that in so very long that he forgot how much he missed it.

"So, what's up Molly?" Aaron asked, running his fingers thru his chromed goatee as he pondered her "Not much, really," Molly replied. "I was just taking a break from those reports I was running for Roger. He's been running me ragged. I was also thinking about what to do for dinner tonight. There's this cool new sports bar downtown that I want to try. They're supposed to have this amazing new flavor of pineapple glazed wings which Taylor down in finance had told me about. I was thinking about stopping after work to try them. Hey, you like wings. You should stop by!"

Aaron pondered her offer. He did love his beer and wings and Kelly wouldn't be home until later tonight anyway, so he wouldn't have much to do for dinner anyway. What would be the harm of stopping by a sports bar after work with a colleague anyway? Kelly had been rather busy at work lately, hadn't had much time to spend with him. He wouldn't mind hanging out with Molly for a bit, maybe get to know her on a more personal level. She really was a fascinating person, and he hadn't had much time to get to know her on a deeper level. He was curious about her growing up in Michigan. He was curious about…well… her in general. Plus, he needed someone to talk to and relate to. He hadn't talked with Kelly in so long. This was his chance to talk about his frustrations. This time, to a neutral party.

Aaron turned to look at her. "You know what, you're on Molly. I'll meet you there when I get off. Save me a seat at the bar."

"Awesome! I'll even order you a beer for when you get there. I should be there by 5:30."

Molly glanced at her reflection in glass cabinet behind Aarons' desk. She smiled slyly. This was her chance. This was her opportunity. She needed some insurance first. Molly was going to make sure this chance with Aaron was a sure bet. Molly knew exactly what to do, but she would have to play her cards right. It was time to go down to R&D and see her new friend, Meredith. She had what Molly was looking for, an insurance plan of sorts. Molly's smile brightened as she realized she needed to turn on the charm. Raven in the reflection did not smile back.

8 LOTUS

Meredith Love was a young girl. Just out of school, she began working at Origin just a few months ago. She didn't exactly care much for being a receptionist for the R&D department, kind of found the work a little boring. Shuffling paperwork, answering phone calls, typing up emails… no, Meredith preferred a little more excitement. She preferred to party, and she did so every weekend, sometimes during the week. At least the pay was better than she expected for a young woman just starting out. She is well versed in local party, and she knew all the major partiers in town. She also knew where to get a little something to… spice up the night.

Molly had Meredith figured out from the moment she saw her. She recognized that sullen look on a Monday morning, dragging her feet to her desk after a hard weekend of partying. She had been that age herself too not all that long ago. She remembers the all night keggers, night clubs, and the morning hangovers that made her feel like she just wanted to die. Those days were behind her now. She didn't care much for drinking anymore. Sure, an occasional beer or glass of wine would be fine in the appropriate situations, the partying was over. Molly knew her type. She if anyone would have access to what she needed Taylor would be able to get access to her little "party pills" the kids are into these days. If Molly played her cards right, those pills placed in Aaron's drink in a timely manner would do the trick and get his guard down.

Molly envisioned a plan in her mind. Everything would fall into place. The sports bar was the perfect environment for her game to play out. The waitresses were the key. The bar was one of those trendy "breasteraunt" joints where ladies in skimpy clothes to bring in customers, thirsty for a beer and a little eye candy to boot. This week was special! It was lingerie week, and even Molly couldn't resist sneaking a peak at girls from time to time. What a perfect way to get Aarons guard down, get him in the mood, and what's more convenient? The hotel across the parking lot was the perfect place for them to retire for a few hours after a fine meal and… stirring conversation.

Molly could hear the tiny voice in the back of her mind, egging her on. She closed her eyes, she listened. She turned and looked at her reflection in the office window. Raven looking back at her did not smile back. She glared at her. She pointed her finger to the door. Molly knew what she had to do. Molly obeyed.

Meredith sat at the receptionist desk to the R&D department typing up a request form frantically for shipping containers that Roger had requested from her. Meredith heard food steps approaching from down the brightly lit hallway to her right. She flipped thru her dirty blond hair to make sure it looks presentable just in case it was her boss approaching. She hadn't had much time this morning to make herself look her best for work. Then a young attractive, dark-haired woman stepped around the corner and approach her. It was the new research assistant, Molly. Meredith really didn't know Molly all that well. She had certainly noticed her around. Her soft cheeks, her warm smile, the way she swayed her hips when she walked. These things caught her attention, and now Molly was in front of her, resting her elbows on her desk and her chin on her right hand.

"Hi, Molly!" Meredith said shyly. "Something I can do for you today?"

"I just had a bit of a personal matter that I was wondering if maybe you might be able to help me with." Molly said, while twirling a lock of her thick dark hair. "Can you keep a little secret between us?" Molly eyed Meredith seductively up and down her body. She lowered the tone of her voice to just above a whisper. "I'll uh, make it worth your while."

Meredith eyed her curiously yet intrigued. She smiled back at her. "Sure, what do you need?"

Molly looked around the otherwise empty room, then leaned in closer to Meredith. "Yah know, when I was younger, I was a bit of a party girl too. I always enjoyed a little pick me up for the all-nighters. There's a party I am thinking of going to this weekend, and it looks like it's going to be a trip. I wouldn't mind boosting things up, and I haven't dropped any E in a long time so, I don't know any sources here, being from Michigan and all. Got any lines?"

Meredith looked nervously around her. She never thought anyone knew she would know stuff like that. She guessed like-minded people can pick each other out. She lowered her voice to a whisper and said, "Look Molly, I don't want to get in trouble for this, so I'll hold you to it to keep this on the down low."

"Of course!" Molly replied in a whisper.

Meredith looked around again the still empty room.

Marie, the cleaning lady had just made her way down the hall opposite her to hit up the next set of offices. She whispered to Molly "Look, E is old news. Nobody's slinging that shit around here anymore. There's something new, now." Meredith reached down into her purse and pulled out a small clear bottle. Inside where 5 little yellow pills, each on seemingly engraved with the image of a unique flower on it. "It's called Lotus. It'll keep you going for hours. It'll to put you mind totally on the other side of reality, man. They're sub-lingual, so slip one under your tongue when you get to your party. It'll dissolve in seconds, and you'll be in seventh heaven. Be careful, just one at a time. Then wait about an hour after you come down for another one. Otherwise, you won't remember fucking thing and you'll be sick to your stomach."

Meredith slipped the bottle under a small stack of paperwork. "Here, take these. I've got more where those came from. Remember, it's our little secret, and never more than one at a time."

"Thanks, sweetie! I'll make it up to you when I can." Replied Molly. Meredith looked up at her and smirked. "You can start by running that paperwork over to shipping for me. The rest…we shall see." Meredith winked at Molly with a sly smile. Molly knew what she wanted. She had caught her peeking at her from time to time. "So what?" Molly thought. So, she would have to sleep with her at some point, big deal. Molly thought she was kind of cute as it was, and Molly had always been just a touch curious. This situation was a win-win for her.

Molly made her way out of the reception area and down to shipping as promised. She handed the dock worker the pile of documents and signed a form for their delivery. Molly was pre-occupied. Aaron was the only thing that mattered now. Her plan was falling into place more easily than she thought. She had him in her grasp now. Tonight, she would make her move. Molly was going to get what Molly wants. She always has. She always will. When Molly returned to her office, she sat down and logged into her computer. As the black screen began to boot up, she noticed a brief flash of her reflection in the monitor. For the brief moment, she saw Raven. Although Molly wore a light, sly grin, the woman in the reflection did not. Cold, black eyes looked back at her. Raven's face was always straight.

Aaron closed the door to his office and locked it. He was tired and frustrated. He had just had a disagreement over the phone with Kelly. She had decided to push back their upcoming weekend getaway back by a month due to a project she was leading at work. "Damn." Aaron thought. He was really looking forward to it. For now, he just needed to clear his head. Maybe Molly was right. "A cold one after work with her isn't a bad idea." He said as he thought out load. Kelly never minded him hanging out with female friends anyway. She knew Katy and was on good terms with her. What's the difference with Molly?

He stepped outside the office building, unlocked his truck, and climbed inside. It was hot in there. Aaron was hungry. Yes, this was going to be a great idea. He started the engine turned the A/C on max and pulled away, headed towards "Big Lou's Sports Bar and Grill." The joint was trendy, with scantily clad waitresses almost as far as the eye can see. The patio was pumping with music and cooled with several lines of water misters. Aaron stepped inside and looked around. Just as he expected, Molly was sitting on the far side of the u-shaped bar in front of him. He came around and approached her. He noticed she had changed her clothes before coming out. She wore a black spaghetti strap tank tap, with just enough sports bra visible on the sides to be noticeable. She also wore a very short pair of what he would have called volleyball shorts. They almost looked too small for her. As she stood there, she turned and faced him. Aaron took it all in. Her smooth curves, her sweet friendly smile, the way her shorts revealed her womanly form.

Aaron refocused and approached her. She greeted him with bright lit eyes and grin from ear to ear.

"Hey, you." Molly said in an almost sing song voice. "I just ordered you a beer." It was Molly's standard issues greeting for him, but this time there was something more… intimate about the way she said it. She ran her eyes up and down his body, taking him all in. He was wearing his black leather biker vest today. Molly liked it when he did that. She moved closer to him as he waited for a tall IPA, one of his all-time favorite beers. A small feather from his pet bird Flappy, seemed to have found itself stuck to his right sleeve. Molly took it upon herself to pluck it away and let it fall to the floor. Aaron studied her for a moment. Molly seemed to be in a very natural element. Just behind her, the green trees and shrubs seemed to highlight her form as well as white butterflies that seemed as if they were dancing around her. Molly's eyes had a certain glimmer to them. She looked upon Aaron with a new light, with a sense of intent, like she was on a mission. Aaron felt a strong connection flowing between them. It was something he hadn't noticed before, he noticed now. Had this always been there? Was there something else at play here?

The bartender, clad in very revealing black lingerie, placed the beer Molly ordered in front of him on top of a square napkin. The glass had been chilled and had looked frosted. Aaron pondered her dark red hair and smooth curves of the bartender for a moment. He felt a flow through his body. It was as if something deep with had been poked and prodded back to life. His thoughts began to wander for a moment. His attention turned to Molly, who was standing just inches from him. He wondered how she would look in similar lingerie. He pictured how she would look in that silky black thong, how a lacy bra would hug her perky breasts and hold them up just so. Molly looked up at him as if she knew exactly what thoughts were flowing through his mind as if she could read him like a book. She inched slightly closer to him with a friendly smile. Aaron could smell a touch of sweet perfume permeating from her.

It was enticing to him, as if the scent were meant to enhance an excitement still growing inside him.

"You know Aaron, it's good you decided to come out this afternoon. I feel like you've needed it. You've been so stressed out lately, I've noticed. Maybe I can help you unwind a bit?" Molly said in a soft, soothing tone.

Molly was right. Deadlines on several projects at work were getting closer and tighter, and life at home was having its challenging moments. Kelly had been stressed out to. At moments they found themselves snapping at each other over the slightest of things. Sometimes, stressors from ages past kept resurfacing. It was tough on both, and it was starting to show. Molly was right. Had it shown in him so strongly?

"Unwind? Yeah, I could use some unwinding, Molly. What did you have in mind?" asked Aaron.

Molly looks down for a moment, then back up into his eyes. She brightened her smile and spoke. "You know, I've noticed something lately. I kind of feel like there's something between us. I feel like, when I'm near you, I feel you. The real you, you that's deep down inside. I like that side of you. It makes me feel good." Molly edged a bit closer to Aaron. She gently ran a finger over his hand that was sitting up on the bar. As she did, Aaron felt an electricity. It was like nothing he had ever felt before. It dug deep into his soul, it enticed him. It called to him. "What was this thing?" Aaron thought to himself. Who was this woman to him that she could so easily entice him, put these thoughts into his mind? Aaron thought of Kelly. Aaron loved his wife; he could never go through with what the images in his mind. He focused himself. He quietly pulled his hand away from the bar, as he took a swing of beer from his glass.

Molly looked into the mirror on the wall behind the bar. Beyond the reflection of assorted liquors that she could see stared the reflection of Raven who had been haunting her for some time now. She gazed back at her straight faced and determined. She spoke. "It's time, Molly. Do it. Take him for yourself." Molly looked down into her purse. The bottle of pills was there, Lotus. She casually reaches inside and opened the bottle as Aaron took another sip of his beer. She pulled out two tiny pills and casually hid them in her grasp. She stuffed the bottle deeper into her purse, right next to a key card she had earlier obtained from the hotel across the parking lot. Now all Molly needed was a distraction. She looked behind Aaron. The red-haired waitress she caught Aaron looking at earlier was bent over a table as she sat down drinks for a group that has recently ordered. She eyed the smooth lines of her hips. Molly looked back at Aaron.

"Wow, she's cute. I always thought redheads are hot." Molly said to Aaron, hoping he would pay attention. Aaron looked behind him. Yes, Aaron noticed how the view of the waitress from this angle would capture anyone's attention. Aaron put his glass down as he pondered the woman. In an instant Molly casually swept her hand over the rim, letting the two tiny pills drop soundlessly into the beer. The music was loud enough that any sound would have been unnoticeable. Aaron maintained his gaze as the waitress and slowly turned back to Molly. The thoughts of what a woman like her might feel like in a more intimate setting raced thru his head. By now, the two pills had dissolved to the point of being completely unnoticeable, even to Molly. The task was complete. Molly need only wait as Raven in the reflection smiled viciously back at her. It was the first grin of any sort of Molly had noticed from Raven.

9 EMBRACE

Aaron turned back to Molly and took a large swig of his beer He noticed her expression was more intense this time. There was something odd about it, but Aaron could not place what it was. He took a final drink from his glass, as he motioned to the bar keep bringing him another. The bartender brought him another ice-cold beverage and he began to drink it down. He had been hot, and thirsty. The suds tickled his lips oh so slightly. He noticed after a few minutes that the buzz felt a little bit different than he was accustomed to. This batch of beer must have been particularly strong this time.

"So, Aaron, I was thinking. I feel like the relationship between us has… potential for more. I like you Aaron, a lot." Whispered Molly.

"Molly…" replied Aaron in a flustered tone. "I like you too, but I'm married, and you're married. We can't be going down that road. Those are forbidden waters!"

Molly sighed. "My husband is a child. He's not ready to make the steps he agreed to take a few years ago. I need more Aaron. A real man, the man of my dreams. I need you, Aaron."

"Molly, Kelly and I have been together for so long…" Molly cut him off. "That doesn't change the way you feel for me though, does it?" she asked. "I've seen the way you look at me, Aaron. Don't deny it. Don't think I haven't noticed it. I never see you looking at the other girls like you do me. Marcy at the front desk is a complete looker and you never once shot her a glance. Amy in project management? Shit, she eye-fucks you every time you walk in the room. When I walk in the room, I see the desire in your eyes."

Molly shifted her stance towards Aaron, fully squared off towards him now. Aaron was feeling oddly woozy at this point.

"Aaron, I feel the energy between us. Let's build on that. We have a lot to offer each other, baby." Molly suggested.

Aaron considered her for a moment. She was pressing him in a way he never saw coming. He felt her game and looked back to the moment he first met her. She was right. He didn't notice then what he sees now. There it is, clear as crystal. Molly leaned closer in.

"I'm going to make you a sweet little deal, Aaron. I'm going to put that deal right here on the table in front of us, all wrapped up in a neat little bow." Molly gestured toward the bar top in front of them. "I want you Aaron, and I always get what I want."

Aaron was confused. Why was she saying this? He's a married man, she knew this. She has a husband of her own back in Michigan. What was she leaning towards? More importantly, why were her words so convincing. Why was a part deep down inside of him considering her offer? For some reason, in a very unusual sense of emotion for Aaron, he began to not care about the certain pitfalls that would come of this. He began to feel a sort of emotional numbness to which he was not accustomed. His thoughts of Kelly, which were usually always on his mind were beginning to fade. Why? Normally a couple of ice-cold IPAs would never have this effect on him. It was as if anything else around him didn't matter. His focus was now completely fixed on one thing. Her. Molly. Right in front of him. Her eyes seemed to dig into his soul.

Molly reached her hand out to his elbow, sliding upwards gently to his shoulder. She began to caress him. That energy, it was stronger this time. It invigorated him. Molly pulled herself closer to him, her face only inches from him. Why wasn't he withdrawing? He didn't want to. He didn't resist. He couldn't resist even if he tried. He could feel the warmth of Molly's breath against his face. She pulled closer. Their noses brushed against each other. Their foreheads pressed together.

"Aaron…" Molly whispered.

Molly pressed her lips to his. Aaron felt a surge inside of him. He liked it. It felt good. Nothing else in the world existed but her. He kissed her back with passion. Molly let out a slow moan. Aaron placed his right hand on her hip. He let go of his beer and placed his left hand on her cheek. He pulled her into him. Passion and energy flowed between them. Molly was exhilarated. She had him. She wrapped her arms around him, not caring that the random strangers in the bar might be watching them. She felt the fire throbbing in her and their lips pressed passionately together. Aaron could not understand why he was helpless to resist, and yet he didn't care. He liked this. He wanted this. He wanted Molly, wanted to taste her. Aaron pulled slightly away from her, to look at her. Up and down, left, and right, he knew every inch of this beautiful woman's body was his. He wanted it. He wanted to be inside of her.

Molly reached into her purse and pulled out two $20 bills and placed them on the bar. She eyed the very curious bartender. "Keep the change sweetie." Molly said to her. "C'mon Aaron, Lets go get a bit better acquainted." Molly grabbed Aaron's hand gently as she glanced at the mirror behind the bar. Raven was in the reflection (Raven that was possessing molly) was smiling devilishly. She pointed in the direction of the hotel. "Go now," said Raven. Molly obeyed as she led Aaron, who was solely focused on only Molly now, away from the bar and out the door.

Aaron didn't know where he was now, and he didn't care. The numbness of his mind was deafening now and yet he could still feel her as she led him to across the parking lot, into a lobby of some sort and down a hallway. She produced a small key card from her purse, inserted into the lock and opened the door. She turned and looked into his eyes as she guided him thru the door frame. The door closed. They paused for a moment to examine each other. Aaron's numbness surged thru his body. He knew nothing of where he was. He cared about only one thing. The only thing that existed in his hindered world. Molly. Only Molly existed now, and as she removed the skimpy tank top from her body, and peeled away the black sports bra, he was greeted with the sight of her perky, soft breasts as they seemingly beaconed to him. He reached out and caressed them. They were warm to the touch. Her chest was heaving with each breath.

"I belong to you now, Aaron." Molly whispered. "I belong to you, and you… belong to me."

He slid his hands down to her hips and pulled her into him. Their lips came back into contact as they began to kiss feverishly. Tongues seemingly wrestled as their bodies began to move in harmony. A tiny voice in the back of Aarons mind began to scream at him to stop. His body was no longer under his brains control. A team of wild horses could not pull the pair apart. He felt the surge of sensation in his penis as he became erect. He pressed himself against her. He slid his hands under her yoga pants to pull them down. The pants complied with his desire, revealing her soft smooth buttocks that had been calling to him for weeks now.

Molly reached out and placed her open hand on his chest, smoothly drawing it down him until she reached his belt buckle. She unfastened it and undid his pants. She reached inside his boxers and exposes his erect shaft, stroking it gently and seductively, all while maintain lip lock in an animalistic kiss. Aaron felt her quiver with delight as she did so, and soon his girth was revealed to her. She continued her grasp as her hand and caressed it slowly. Molly dropped to her knees and began slowly sliding his thick shaft toward the back of her throat.

"This is it." Molly thought, as she ran her tongue gently up and down. She looked up at Aaron. He looked down into her wanting eyes. In Aaron's clouded mind, the voice screamed at him. This was wrong. This was unacceptable. This… was unforgivable, and yet Aaron could not resist. It was as if the combined inebriation of a 12 pack of beer and a fifth of whiskey was swirling in his brain. Desire. Desire drove him now. Desire… and something else that he had never felt, and he couldn't fight it back. Not now, not like this. He was numb and yet had never felt more alive.

Molly stood up and pulled him toward the bed. Aaron pushed her down on it, lifting her legs high and almost ripping off her remaining garments. He grabbed her knees and spread her legs wide. He considered her for a moment. Before him was the smooth shaved flower that was to be his goal. She had taken great care to prepare herself for him. It beckoned to him, moist and pink. Quivering with anticipation, Aaron flung off his shirt crawled towards Molly who had already glanced well at his manhood fully revealing his muscular chest and shoulders to her. He hovered over her as she spread her legs around his waist and pulled him into her. He slipped inside and she gasps. He began to thrust her slowly. Her tight pussy grasped his penis as he thrusted. He lowered himself onto her, feeling her soft breasts press against him kissing passionately and moving as one flipping over to ride on top. As Molly slipped up and down his shaft Aaron looked up at her. His inner self is screaming, he senses the danger as the room began to dance and spin in his eyes. Something was wrong. "Who am I? What am I doing? Why can't I stop this!? Why do I feel this way? This is wrong!" He wants to scream but he can't. He's in prisoned. Trapped on the outside as Molly had taken control of both him and she. He's enslaved. Her moans had become louder, her movements more intense. Molly gripped Aarons hands as the pressure build inside of each of them. For a moment, Molly turned and looked into the dresser mirror adjacent to them. Raven in the mirror was pleased. Her eyes were black as the night is dark. Her grin was evil and sinister. Molly, for a moment, knew that something was coming out of this encounter. She felt the energy in her pussy. She felt the tingling in her womb. Molly thrusts harder getting Aaron deeper inside her. The intensity exploded in her. Molly squeezed Aarons hands. She had climaxed in a way that James couldn't. She screamed out in ecstasy! She squirted hard as her come ran down her legs and soaked Aaron's testicles. She looked back into the mirror. Raven in the reflection urged her to continue. Aaron MUST finish. Molly MUST take ALL of him. NOW!

Aaron was energized and his adrenaline was at its peak. Even as the voice in his head and his heart were bellowing out warnings of danger, Aaron grabbed Molly and tossed her on the bed with her face buried in the pillow. He set her body with her ass in the air. He spread her legs apart, He was ready. He plunged deep inside of her and pounded furiously slapping his balls against her vulva. With each stroke, more pressure built inside with every deep thrust inside of her, feeling every single drop of his come explode deep inside her pussy. Sweat was running down his face.

Aaron dropped down on the bed beside Molly, panting and sweating. Aaron tried to catch his breath, but something was wrong. The edges of his vision seemed to be closing in. He felt pressure like a hammer to his head. He felt the heat rise as he started sweating more and more. His stomach was turning and twisting like never before. What had happened to him? What was this sensation? The room got darker quieter. He couldn't hear or see Molly anywhere. Blackout.

Molly looked down at Aaron as he lost all consciousness. She had achieved her goal. She had him, yet something wasn't right. "What have I done?" thought Molly. "Is this a mistake? Is this man mine to have?" She looked over to the mirror. Raven was gone. Molly now saw her own reflection. Her eyes went from jet black to a dark candy apple red. Molly sensed a feeling of completion. She had done her job. The reflection smiled back. Mission accomplished. Molly pulled herself of the bed and approached the mirror. Feeling a sense of anxiety like she had never felt before, she studied the reflection. The reflection spoke. "Thank you, Molly." She spoke. "It's my turn now. You owe me a debt, Molly, for what I did for you. You must allow me to do this"

Molly looked down at the reflections right hand. Something shiny was protruding from it. It looked like… could it be? Molly thought she recognized a knife, a Victorinox butchers' knife. Sharp. Precise. Molly turned around to see Aaron, unconscious, still breathing. "What have I done?" Molly asked herself "It's time." said Raven.

10 BLACKED OUT

Miles away, Kelly sat at her office computer. "This project is kicking my ass!!!" Kelly muttered. She wanted so badly to go home and curl up under the covers in bed. She has been tired of working so many late nights, never really knowing when she would get home. She loved making dinner for her family, it relaxed her. Lately, she just couldn't keep up. The demands of her job were stacking up every day. She noticed how it was affecting her family. Aaron and her, had become more distant. She didn't have the time to sit down and just talk tom him anymore. She loved the sound of his voice, the warmth of his embrace. Yet now when she got home, he was already sound asleep in bed. She would have to wait until morning to discuss anything that needed talking about. Groceries, bills, their sons' school grades… it all had to wait. Kelly was frustrated, but she has been down this road before. Kelly continued typing her email.

Then, something struck her! It was something she has never felt before. What was this? Something was wrong! Kelly had been learning to deal with her ability for only a few years, and this sensation was completely new to her. Something had gone horribly wrong. She felt it. She sensed it. Aaron. He was in danger! Of what? Kelly's anxiety had kicked into high gear. She could not pinpoint a source. Something lingered in her mind…

Her! That little bitch that she had been feeling so strongly over the last several weeks! Whatever Kelly was feeling was sourced around her! Why? What was her deal? What was significant about this woman, a woman she saw as a little whore? Kelly began to panic. She knew something was wrong. She could not think of why. She knew she didn't like Molly when she met her. She didn't know what specifically she didn't like about her. Molly was a devious person in her mind from the onset. She just plain didn't trust her from the moment she met her. What is this sudden surge of energy? Why here and why now? That fucking little bitch! Why did she feel so much hatred and anxiety over her? She didn't like that she was her husband's protégé. She didn't like that she made every effort to be in his presence. "What is this little cunt up to?" Kelly asked herself. Why did Kelly feel some much anger towards her? Kelly knew something was wrong. She just did not know what it was.

Kelly wrapped up her work, grabbed her keys to her van. She proceeded home, wrestling thru Albuquerque's streets. She was angry. She had no source for the anger. She didn't know what was driving her anxiety. When she pulled into her driveway, and Aaron's truck was in its normal parking spot. Aaron was home. She saw no other cars that were unusual to her. She unlocked the door and stepped inside her home to find her husband face down on the couch, snoring loudly. This was unusual to her. Sure, Aaron always came home and had his beers to relax. This was not unusual. Kelly was used to it. He had a very challenging job, and the stress was a huge factor in his life. He never really had the opportunity in his younger years to deal with his stress. Kelly had always felt bad for him for this. She loved him with every fiber of her soul, every day she saw him come home tired, mentally drained, and physically exhausted.

Kelly poked at him as he was sleeping on the couch. He stirred; his body turned slowly to face this disturbance. His eyes opened. Before Aaron was the caring face of his loving wife. How did he get here? He pondered for a moment. How did he get home? His memories were a cloud of confusion. He looked up at his wife, her flowing locks of deep red hair.

"Honey, uhm, are you OK?" Asked Kelly.

"Uhm, how did I get home? Did you pick me up or something?" Asked Aaron, cautiously.

"Did you go out with your friends tonight?" Asked Kelly. "Did you have too much to drink?"

Aaron sat up and thought about his situation. He couldn't remember. He searched his mind, looking for answers to a question he couldn't source. "I… had a drink with a few friends from work… I think." Answered Aaron. "But I…"

There was a sound coming from the bathroom. The toilet flushed; the door opened. Molly stepped out drying her hands with a towel.

Molly approached Kelly.

"Oh hi, Kelly" chirped Molly. "I hope you don 't mind. A few of us decided to have a few snacks and drinks after work. Things got a little crazy. We're approaching the end of our experimental drug project and we decided to step out and celebrate. Aaron Had a few to many, and I decided to drive him home. Sorry, I really needed to pee, and Aaron said it was alright. I'll be rolling out now." Kelly looked at Molly quizzically. "Ah, OK. Thanks" Kelly replied. Kelly had nothing to base her sense of inquisition on, but she was grateful anyway.

"Where's your car?" Asked Kelly.

"Oh, it's back over at Big Louis's" Replied Molly. "I'll call an Uber and go back. I only had one drink, several hours ago. I'm good!"

"Oh no, I'll run you back over. It's not far." Replied Kelly, feeling grateful, yet still curious. "It's no issue. I'm grateful for your bringing Aaron home. When he gets around his friends at a bar, he can get..., Stupid."

"Oh, ok! Thanks Kelly!" Replied Molly.

As Kelly grabbed the keys to her van, Molly looked over her mockingly from behind her. She knew the truth of what really happened. Molly felt... powerful over it. Deep inside her insides, she felt a new energy growing. Yet, she could not explain what she was feeling. But she knew one thing, she... had succeeded. She had taken Aaron.

Aaron looked over the top of the couch as Kelly and Molly proceeded to the door. Something didn't feel right. He couldn't remember where he had been earlier. He knew something had happened and had no idea what it was. Kelly gave him a cold judgmental glance as she walked out the door. Molly... The look she gave him... He couldn't figure it out in his state of mind. As Molly stepped out the door after Kelly, she looked back at him. The smirk on her face was unmistakable. Molly had been up to something. She had done something. Aaron just couldn't recall anything after his second beer. Had they been that strong? Had he done shots? Even if he had done shots, he still should have some memory of the night. Something, anything should still be there. There was nothing at all! Aaron considered other ideas. Perhaps at his age, his health was declining? Did he have a small stroke? Did he have a heart attack? Aside from the tremendous headache and sense of wooziness, he didn't feel much else. What had happened this afternoon? And why were his pants unusually loose?

Kelly and Molly drove down the street in Kelly's van. The bar where Molly's car still sat wasn't too far away, so the trip was no hassle at all. Kelly was suspicious of Molly's actions. She didn't have to bring him home, why did she bring him home? Kelly hated it when Aaron had too much to drink, except that happened very rarely, and she had only once seen him completely passed out. This get together must have been rowdy. Why, she thought? Sure, Kelly remembered how things got in the earlier years of their marriage, when Aaron was still in the Air Force. He and his friends could sure throw a few back with ease. Those events rarely happened, and when they did, they still stayed upright at the end of the night. Kelly was somewhat thankful to Molly, but something… still troubled her. Molly's' … energy… seemed off. Maybe it was in Kelly's mind. Maybe she had misjudged her when she first met her. She had been a good friend to Aaron tonight, making sure he got home safe. That is all that mattered now.

"Listen, Molly, I appreciate what you did for Aaron tonight. I can't imagine him coming home in that state." Kelly remarked. "How…" Kelly began to ponder. "How much did he have to drink anyway?"

"Started with a couple beers. Then some jackass from the shipping department started buying shots of tequila. I guess tequila doesn't agree with him." Molly replied.

Kelly nodded to that statement. Yet Aaron had always hated tequila. He never liked the taste and always avoided away from it. Kelly thought on that for a moment. Something didn't add up. Why would Aaron do shots of a drink he can't stand? She brushed off the idea. If he's not buying, he's not going to complain. Still.

They pulled into the parking lot at "Big Lou's Bar and Grill." It was almost empty now, except for Molly's dark grey Toyota sitting in the parking lot. They came to a stop. Kelly thanked Molly again one last time as Molly opened the door. Then, Molly's purse snagged on the shifter handle on the vans console. It fell from Molly's grip and tumbled to the passenger floor. A few things fell out and Kelly, who was closer, reached down to grab them for molly. It wasn't much, just some lipstick, a bottle of fancy perfume, her wallet, and a key card. Kelly picked them up and handed them back to Molly, who swiftly put them back in her purse. She noticed the name of a hotel on the card in a quick glance but thought nothing of it. Molly thanked her and turned away as she walked off to her own car. Kelly shifted her van into drive, still pondering her husband's idea to have Tequila. Aaron despised Tequila. As she looked around for approaching traffic, Kelly noticed the Hotel across the parking lot. She recognized the name from the key card she had just handed back to Molly. "Hillman Hotel" was known as one of the fancier hotels in the area. It was pricey, and Kelly had never stayed at one, yet she had seen pictures online of their rooms. Very romantic looking, Kelly thought.

As she drove home, she wondered why Molly would have a key card for that hotel. Had she had some need to stay there? She knew Molly had been staying with her sister Katy, had they had an argument or something? Aaron would have known if they did, but he never mentioned anything. "Oh well…" Kelly thought. There was one more detail that picked at her brain. The perfume, "Blue Diamonds," that was some expensive stuff! Kelly always loved how it smelled, but at one hundred fifty bucks a bottle, she was never going to buy it. "Molly must be doing well for herself if she's going to wear that to an after work get together at a bar." Kelly thought. Kelly disappeared down the street on her way home. Kelly had questions for Aaron.

Molly adjusted the rear-view mirror of her car. As she investigated it, Raven in the reflection gazed at her with a slight grin. Raven's dark eyes reflected no emotion, but she gestured down towards something. "What does this mean?" Molly thought to herself. Down? "What's down that I need to see?" Molly didn't know what Raven was referencing, but when Molly looked back up, it was her own reflection this time. Molly shrugged as she started the car and drove away. She pulled up to her sisters' house, turned the car off and went inside. Katy had been waiting up for her. It was well after midnight.

"Well, there you are, sis!" Katy said. "You've been out all night. I was getting worried."

Molly turned to look at her, then turned back to gaze out the window. Katy had noticed a certain look in Molly's eyes. It was like looking into a deep dark chasm. They were dark, almost as if she had someone else inside her. She recognized those eyes. She had seen them before when they were children. Molly had done something tonight. Something was not right. Katy knew that her sister had gone out for an afternoon bite with Aaron. Except afternoon bites don't last past midnight. What had Molly done?

"Where have you been all this time, Molly?" asked Katy, sheepishly.

Molly turned quickly to Katy. "You're not mother, Katy. Don't worry where I have been" Molly spoke sharply.

Katy was shocked at Molly's response. Then she remembered well her outbursts of attitude. Was her friend Raven back? No, it can't be. She suppressed that long ago.

"What happened to Aaron? Molly? What have you done? You fucked him, didn't you? You raped him!" Asked Katy. She had begun to sense that Aaron was somehow involved in whatever Molly had been up to that night.

Molly quickly turned and approached Katy. The smell of fancy sweet perfume followed her. "My Aaron is just fine, he's home now, resting. I made sure of it."

"Your Aaron? You mean our boss, Aaron?" asked Katy

Molly spoke sharply. "My Aaron and I have a new arrangement between us, Katy. Call it a new deal if you will. A sweet little deal. We've elevated our relationship and now he's going to be with me." Molly said.

Katy looked upon her sister with utter shock. She

couldn't believe what she had just heard. Katy knew what she had done. How did this happen? Katy had known Aaron for over 12 years! He's never been the cheating type! He's always been loyal to Kelly. This didn't make any sense. For Molly to arrogantly assume Aaron would do anything like that to his wife, of his own free will was Ludacris.

"Of his own free will, my ass…" She thought. Katy thought back to their youth when Molly was still being visited by her imaginary friend, Raven. Molly was known to take mischievous steps to appease this so-called friend. What had Molly done this time?

"Molly…" Katy said as she stepped toward her sister. "What did you do?"

Molly turned slowly to her sister. She approached her slowly. "I did what needed to be done to have him." Molly spoke in a low voice. Molly slowly tilted her head to the side in a sinister manner. "And now, I have him right where I want him." Molly began to walk away as Katy stood in complete disarray.

Katy took a moment to center herself. She then went to her cell phone and started to look thru her contacts. She knew what she had to do. She had to warn James. He had to know that his wife's friend had come back, with a vengeance. She picked out his number from the contacts list and hit the call button. A few moments later, a sleepy voice answered on the other end.

"Hello?" Said James.

"James, its Katy. We need to talk."

"What's up? Where's Molly, I haven't heard from her?" asked James.

"It's about Molly, James. Remember that moment I talked to you about years ago, at your wedding? Well…" Katy paused for the next part. "That moment has come. Raven is back."

James audibly paused for a moment. "Alright, I'll be on the first flight out in the morning."

James hung up on his end. In his mind, he knew that this day might come. He knew what he would have to do.

Kelly came home after dropping off Molly to pick up her car. Aaron was still lying on the couch where Kelly had seen him. She pondered him for a moment, concerned for him. It wasn't like him to go out with his colleagues and party so late especially during the week. Something was going on. She sat down beside him and placed her hand on his shoulder.

"So, what happened tonight, Aaron?" She asked.

"I… I don't know hon. All I remember is that I got to the bar, Molly was already there. I joined up with her at the bar and she had ordered a beer just before I got there. We started chatting about work and I finished my first beer and ordered a second. After that, I think I started to get lightheaded. I felt a weird kind of buzz and then… here I am on the couch."

Kelly thought for a moment. Molly had been here, using the bathroom. "Do you even remember Molly bringing you home? Do you remember her needing to use the bathroom?"

Aaron thought for a moment. He didn't remember anything about that. His head was still pounding from whatever had happened. He tried to recall anything and came up empty handed. He put his hands on his head and ran his fingers through his hair in frustration.

"What about the tequila? Molly said somebody was buying tequila shots. Maybe that did it?"

Aaron thought about it. There was never any tequila involved that he could remember. He wouldn't have any of that stuff anyway, he hated the taste. It was horrible like panther piss. All he remembered is the two beers he had. Had he ordered something else? Aaron had to investigate. "I need to check my bank account and see what I charged. I don't have a receipt on me, but I bet if there were extra charges it would account for anything I had," said Aaron. He slowly shuffled over to the computer in his home office, sat down in his gaming chair, and pulled up the internet browser. After signing into his banking, he pulled up his most recent transactions and began to review the charges from the bar. Nothing! There were no charges made on his card. How would he have paid for his drinks without using his card? Aaron didn't typically carry cash, so that wouldn't have been a thing. His other cards were for emergency use only, so he wouldn't have used them either. Did Molly pay for his drinks? He didn't remember her offering to buy him any. He didn't remember leaving the bar or paying for the drinks. He closed his browser and got up making his way toward the bathroom to relieve himself. He unzipped his pants and began to pee. To his surprise, his shaft was drenched and slick. Had he passed out so bad that he had pissed himself? His clothes certainly weren't stained or wet. They didn't stink of urine but a personal scent he couldn't put his finger on. So why this? There was something more about it. Arron noticed a dab of makeup on the base of his shaft "Is that lipstick? Couldn't be? Where did this come from" Aaron puzzled, "this doesn't make sense." The whole time Aaron pondered the situation. He could not connect anything. Going over every moment. He turned on the facet to the bathtub and turned the knob to turn the showerhead on. He stepped in grabbing a poof and cleansing himself. He continued to notice the scent on him as he washed himself. Questioning himself and where it and the lipstick came from. He finished his shower, dried off and dressed for bed. He dozed off quickly on top of the bedding. Kelly soon joined him rubbing his back and worried about what happened to him. She felt helpless, yet she suspected foul play after the mention of tequila, yet how could she prove it? Is she just exaggerating?

Aaron began to dream. He found himself in an open field of green grass. There were lines of trees in the distance, green bushes surrounding him, and then, there she was. Molly, standing before him with her eyes shut. Curious, Aaron approached her. There where small white butterflies fluttering around her. She remained motionless. "Molly?" asked Aaron. She did not respond. He moved closer to her curiously. A strange distant disembodied voice called out to him. "Aarrrooonn." The voice said. It sounded like Molly, but younger, more childlike. "Aaaaronnnn…" The voice summoned. He approached Molly. , without warning, her eyes shot open. Staring back at him were no longer Molly's dark brown eyes, these eyes were pitch black with no white showing as if her eyes were giant marbles. Aaron was startled and he jumped back and began to fall backwards. Molly reached out to help him, as if to help him up. The dream faded.

Aaron woke up distraught and sweating. Breathing heavily, he thought "What did the dream mean? Why were Molly's eyes so black?" Aaron could not understand. The dream did leave one burning question. Did Molly have something to do with this? Only one way to find out.

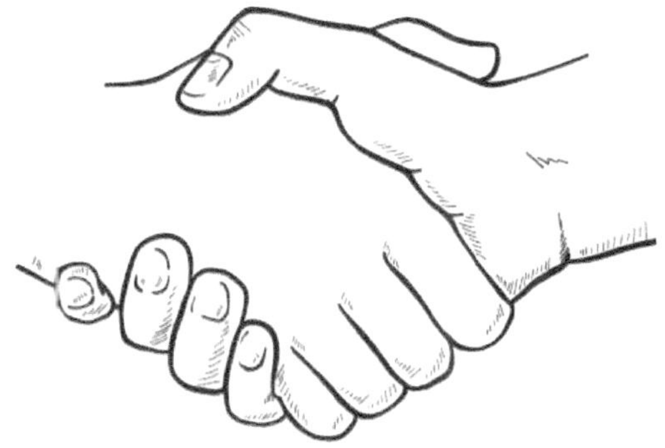

11 SWEET LITTLE DEAL

Aaron woke up the next morning with a slight headache, but nothing more. He remained confused about the night before. He still had very little memory of what had gone down. Everything seemed to be a blur to him after that second beer. Molly was there with him. That much he knew. Had others from the office been there too? He didn't recall seeing anybody he knew, though Big Louis's is a popular after-hours hangout for many of the staff, so it was possible. Did they party? Did he get hammered? Aaron had been super drunk before in his life, but still he had memories of happened then. He only remembered the two beers, so this made no sense to him. This time he was drawing blanks, nothing came to mind, he couldn't understand why. There was one thing that seemed to stick out. Somebody had a snake tattoo on the small of their back. Who was that? Were they showing it off? Why is that the only detail that seemed to stand out the most?

He started his morning routine after the short pause and proceeded to work. Molly would be there. Aaron had many, many questions for her. He was going to get the full story from her perspective. Molly would have to shed some light on the situation. He pulled up into his normal parking space, headed inside to his office and attempted to unlock his door. To his surprise, it was already unlocked. This was not his normal routine. Nothing was normal about this at all. He opened the door and stepped inside.

"Hey you!" Molly said as she winked at him. "Molly, I uh didn't know you were in here. What brings you in so early?" asked Aaron.

"I figured you were going to have a rough morning, so I came in and started the day early for you. You uh…. had a very hot night." Replied Molly.

Aaron considered that for a moment, then sat down at his desk. Molly picked up a file with the morning reports and brought it over to him. As she passed behind him, her short black skirt bushed oh so slightly across the back of his neck. As she reached around him to place the files down, she gently placed her left hand on his shoulder, with the oh so slightest of caresses. As she did, that strange energy seemed to flow throughout his body. "What is she up to?" Aaron thought to himself. Had something about their relationship, their friendship escalated last night? He turned around to look at her, consider her.

"Molly, I need to know what happened last night. I need to know what's between us." Aaron spoke softly. Molly glanced at him with a sly smile, then brushed her hand across his back as she crossed over to the front of his desk. She bent over the front of his, tilting her chest down to reveal a very noticeable cleavage.

"Let's just say I offered you a little something extra, sweet little deal Aaron." She leaned in closer. "You didn't disappoint."

Molly winked as she stood back up. She ran her hands down her skirt to smooth it out, then turned around to adjust the thermostat. As she bent down slightly to make the changes, her short blouse rose oh so slightly to reveal the skin of the small of her back, and… a tattoo.

It was a small snake, coiled in the shape of a figure eight. The memory. Aaron remembered it. He had seen it before. How? And when? And under what circumstances.

"Molly… again, what happened last night?" Aaron spoke sharply this time. He needed answers.

Molly turned back to look at him, this time with a sterner gaze. "It's going to take some time for you to get accustomed to a few things, Aaron. Rest assured, you and I share a deeper bond now. We've become closer in our time together last night. I think you'll like our little arrangement." Molly turned and walked out the door. Before she walked down the hallway to her desk in R&D, she turned back at him, and gave him a smile that looked a little to seductive… and sinister. Aaron sat at his desk, puzzled. What had he done?

Molly sat down at her desk and was immediately approached by one of the young women in her department. Haley, a short slim yet bubbly young blonde appeared at Molly's desk. "Hi molly, what's up?" Asked Haley.

Molly turned to Haley. "What's up Haley, how's it going?" Haley looked at Molly quizzically.

"So… I was just curious. Uhm, I don't know how to ask this but me and some of the girls around here went out for drinks at Big Louis's last night. We uh…" Haley paused. "We saw you there with Aaron last night. So… are you dating the boss now or something? I thought he was married?"

Molly looked up at Haley. "Well, I guess the cats out of the bag. It's really no secret that Aaron has been flirting with me for some time. I think it's so cute! Well, he ended up asking me out last night for some after work drinks. I indulged him." Molly smiled "As for his wife, well, between you and me they are on the rocks." She whispered. "I don't think they will last much longer. I'm very interested in what he has to offer."

Haley looked at Molly with shock on her face. "That's funny, Kelly comes by sometimes to bring him lunch. They always seem happy together. I wonder what's going on?" Haley asked.

"Well, looks can be deceiving, Haley. You never really know what's going on behind closed bedroom doors. Or what's not." Molly replied.

"Wow, I didn't see THAT coming!" Exclaimed Haley. "Well, I got to get back to work. See you around."

Haley walked away. Molly pondered her as she did so. "Well, this could go easier than I thought." Molly thought to herself.

Later that morning, Katy stepped into Aaron's office, who was typing away at his computer.

"Good morning, Katy." Said Aaron, casually. He turned his attention back to his computer.

"Hey Aaron, say… you got a minute? I wanted to talk to you about something."

"Sure, what's up?" Aaron replied.

"It's about my sister. Look I know she can be super friendly and helpful, but… well… Just be careful around her. She has a history, a past. She wasn't well as a kid. She got better and all, but I'm worried she is having those issues again. I think she might be up to something. With you, specifically. I just want to watch out for you."

Aaron pondered her words for a moment, then turned to her. "What kind of things did she do in her youth, Katy?

Was she every kind of sketchy?" Aaron asked? "Did she ever do anything to make you feel unusual?"

Katy pondered her response carefully. She wanted to tell him everything, but she didn't want to say too much. "Let's just say Molly sets her eyes on what she wants, and the has always gotten what she wants." Katy sighed.

Katy thought back to the previous night's conversation with her sister. She knows she was after Aaron, and she know she was up to something. Katy wants to

"Just watch out around her, Aaron. She lies a lot and tends to deceive anyone she desires" Katy said, as she walked back to her office.

Katy walked into the cafeteria and sat her lunch bag down on a nearby table. A group of women a few feet away were clearly gossiping about something. One of them, a burly older woman in her mid-50s, Gertie, glanced back at Katy with a look of surprise in her eyes. Then she turned back and giggled amongst the other women. Molly entered the room. All eyes were on her now. The group quickly hushed as the Molly strolled by, airing a sense of confidence and accomplishment. She sat down next to her sister. Katy looked back at her nervously.

"So, sis, I was just thinking. I just wanted to let you know some things are going to change around here." Molly said. "I'm going to be spending more time with Aaron now. I won't always have a chance to come do lunch with you. I'm thinking Aaron and I need to spend some quality time together."

Katy looked at her in a weirding out kind of way. "Are you seriously thinking he's going to allow that? What about Kelly? She comes down from her work all the time to have lunch with him." Molly looked deeply into her sisters' eyes. "Well Kelly's just going to have to wait her turn, isn't she." Molly stood up and walked away. The group of gossipers watched as she opened the double doors and stepped out.

Katy considered what she had just seen and heard. It was happening again. Just like when they were kids, Molly was pulling her strings. She was manipulating her again, and Katy never did find a way to stand up to her back then. She was always intimidated when she was like this.

One of the gossipers, a young woman from finance named Candy approached her. "So, is it true, Katy? Is what everybody saying true?" Katy turned to look at her. "What are they saying, I keep out of the gossip galley." Said Katy.

"They say Molly is dating Aaron now, and that Aaron is going to leave Kelly for her." Whispered Cindy.

Katy looked back at her. In her heart, she already knew that was wrong. Hearing it spoken out load by an outsider seemed to make it more real.

"Look, I happen to know Aaron and Kelly are on good terms. There's no reason Aaron would do that to her." Katy replied. "If Molly thinks that they are together, it's only in her little entitled princess mind."

Candy raised an eyebrow. "I don't know, Katy. She looks like she got him wrapped around her little finger to me!" Candy turned and walked away.

Molly walked up the hallway to Aaron's office, passing several glass windows to other offices. She glanced at the reflection in the windows. Raven stared back. "It's time, Molly." Raven said as a voice in Molly's head. Molly knew what this meant. Molly reached into her purse and retrieved a small vial she had swiped from the laboratory, earlier that morning. Inside it, a serum of some kind. Something that will make Aaron a little more agreeable.

She arrived at his office. Her hunch was right, he was in a meeting. His ever-present water bottle was right where he always left it on his desk. All Molly needed now was a repeat of her previous nights' success. She approached his desk, unscrew the lid, and swung it open. She opened the vial and placed a few drops inside. She closed it again, looked up and around, then smiled as she walked away.

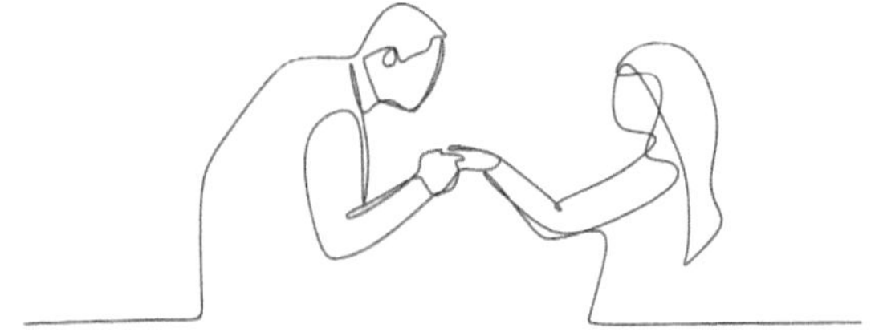

12 GIRLFRIEND

Aaron returned to his desk from a flurry of obnoxious antics at the morning meeting. These things were always so boring, and always left him thirsty. This morning left him rather parched after last night which was unusual. He picked up his stainless-steel water bottle and unscrewed the top and he put it to his lips and took a long satisfying swig gulping several times. The cold water felt satisfying. Finally, some hydration. He returned to his work and began typing up some new reports. About thirty minutes passed by, and he noticed he began to feel woozy. Perhaps a late bloomer hangover from the night before. He felt like his head was in the clouds. He had hoped it wasn't another round of his pass out from the night before. He pressed on.

Wayne and Julio entered his office a few minutes later. "Hey boss," said Julio. "Do uh, do you mind if me and Wayne take off a couple hours early? We got some stuff we got to take care of together."

Aaron looked up at the. "Sure, go ahead, take the day. I'll see you all tomorrow."

Wayne and Julio smiled. "Thanks boss, see you later." They turned and left out the door.

Aaron paused… "what did I just say?" Aaron asked himself. Normally he would never allow both his supply guys leave at the same time. He always needed at least one, as they both had sets of keys to the supply room. "Oh well." Aaron thought, un-characteristically.

Wayne and Julio passed Molly at her desk as they went to retrieve their jackets and belongings. Molly looked up at them and smiled. "So how did it go? What did he say?" Asked Molly.

"We good to go, Ma'am. Hey thanks for that suggestion. We never thought we get a chance to go see a rap festival in Santa Fe. We would have missed all the best artists if we had to wait to leave until after work. You da man, Ma'am."

"Sure, no problem!"

Molly nodded as the two grabbed their gear and walked out the door.

Molly's little experiment had worked. Aaron, in no way would have agreed to let even one go this early on the day, let alone both. She had him right where she wanted him. She unlogged from her computer and stood up. Raven grinned back at her from the reflection in her screen. She walked out the double doors and up the hallway. Her coworkers, each one entranced with her smooth body lines, watched as she made her way out. She arrived at the door to Aaron's office. She stood in the doorframe at him, with one arm leaning on it.

Aaron was standing by his office conference table, charting out logistics plans for tomorrow. He turned around and saw Molly, standing there.

"Are you ready to learn about our sweet little deal? Are you ready to learn what we've done? Asked Molly.

Aaron pondered her for a moment. Normally, he would

have instantly pounced at the chance to hear it, finally. Now he felt numb, non-caring almost, yet still interested. Molly approached him, stood within inches of him, reached her hands out to his shoulders and grasped him firmly. She pulled herself into him and pressed her soft red lips to his. She now slid her hands down his back. Aaron was not resisting. He liked this. It felt good to him. He returned the kiss with equal passion as he tossed his paperwork aside and embraced her.

A few minutes later, they gently broke their kiss as they looked into each other's eyes. She slid her hands down over his butt and squeezed.

"And now you know, Aaron." Molly spoke softly. "I'm your girlfriend now and its official, and you, you are my loving boyfriend."

Aaron thought about the previous night. "Did… did we make love last night, Molly?

"Passionately, babe. You really gave me your all." Molly ran her hand over her belly and looked down at it.

"And, if we're lucky… maybe a little surprise!" Molly said as she looked back up at him.

In the back of Aarons mind he knew this was all wrong, that it can't be. The numbness and weird buzz in his head persisted. What was going on with him? Why can't he fight this? Why doesn't he want to fight back? He just wanted to go home to Kelly, yet he had no control over himself, and he didn't understand why, yet.

Meanwhile, several passers-by making their way up and down that central corridor had a chance to glance into the open door to Aaron's office. They saw what they needed to see. The rumors were true! Aarons WAS seeing Molly now! That's impossible! Everybody who knew Aaron, knew him as a kind and caring man, and very loyal to his wife. What would make him do this, and so out in the open too?

Within minutes the hallways were buzzing with gossip. Watercoolers had become community chatrooms.

Eventually the news made it to Katy. Her jaw dropped. She couldn't believe what she was hearing.

"Molly!!! WHAT HAVE YOU DONE?" screamed Katy in her mind. She wanted to cry. Aaron was one of the few people who cared about her as a person and treated her like a sister.

Several miles away, Kelly, in her own office was sitting quietly at her desk, signing some paperwork for her clients. Then panic set in. Anxiety, Fear, something was very wrong. "Aaron…" Thought Kelly. Something had happened to Aaron! The nervousness rattled Kelly's brain. She had no Idea what was going on, just that something was off. Something wasn't right. She thought for a moment. She picked up her cell phone off her desk and dialed Aarons number.

An iPhone began vibrating on Aaron's desk. Aaron, still under the influence of the serum, didn't seem to care. He looked down at, saw "Kelly" on the screen, and simply looked on. Molly saw it too. An idea popped into her mind. She glanced in the mirror behind Aaron's desk. Raven was there, scowling.

"Answer it." Raven demanded.

Molly picked the phone off his desk, swiped the screen. "Hello?" Molly answered is a sultry tone.

"Hello? Who's this? Wait… Molly? What's going on? Why are you answering Aaron's phone? Where is he, I need to speak with him immediately, Molly."

"I'm afraid he's a bit indisposed at the time, Kelly. I'll be handling all his calls from here on out. I'll be handling… many things." Molly said in a smooth tone of voice.

"What, but this is his personal phone. You don't handle his personal business, Molly. That's a boundary you don't cross with people unless they are family you little bitch now hand him the phone right now!"

Molly chuckled to herself. If she only knew what she was

planning. She will. Soon.

Molly looked up at Raven in the mirror. Raven produced a devilish smirk. "You're going to find there will be a wide variety of changes around here, Kelly. I'm overseeing the final details with Aarons even now."

On her end of the line, Kelly's mouth dropped. "Molly give him the fucking phone right fucking now!"

Molly replied with a smirk. "I'm sorry, but there is a change in leadership around here. Certain positions needed filling. Aaron saw fit to fill those positions. Now I'll have to say goodbye for now. We are in the middle of negotiations."

Molly hung up and turned to Aaron. "There now, you see the things I can handle for you?" Molly stepped closer to Aaron, whom was still in a fog. "Just like I handled your big throbbing penis last night?"

A memory flashed into Aaron's mind. It was faint, but it was there. Yes indeed, he now remembered a small detail. He remembered Molly getting on top of him and riding him in such a way.

Kelly knows something was indeed very off. She needed to see Aaron. Molly was cutting her off. She needed to see him right now. Grabbing her keys, she closed her office door and dashed out to her van. Starting it, she began to drive away, straight to Origin Corp. She felt something was off. She didn't care what Aaron was in the middle of. She would confront him about this.

Kelly pulled into the parking lot and dashed out the door. She sensed danger, but why? She walked thru the revolving door and up to the reception desk. Meredith looked up at her. Meredith was now in the know about the rumors, so the sight of Kelly was of concern to her.

"Kelly! Uhm, hi. What can I do for you?"

"I need to see my husband immediately, Meredith. It's urgent."

Meredith looked at her with concern. She knew that this could get complicated, but it wasn't her business to intervene. She handed Kelly a visitors pass, just as she always had. Kelly was trusted around here. People knew her, and she knew the lay of the land. "Kelly, I'll let him know you're here and on the way. As Kelly made her way past the entrance corridor, Meredith looked back at her with concern. She turned back and picked up the phone, dialing Aaron's extension. Molly answered.

"Yes?" Molly asked.

"Uhm, please let Aaron know that his wife is here to see him. It seems urgent."

"Very well." Molly replied.

Molly hung up. Meredith was concerned. She knew Molly and Aaron worked closely together, but when did she become his personal secretary?

Molly turned to Aaron. "Babe, Kelly's here. Remember what we talked about." Molly said while pointing a stern finger in his face. Molly turned around and walked out the door, but not before turning back and giving him a seductive smile.

Aaron at this point seemed to be coming back around. He knew one thing. This was going to end badly.

He paced in his office, waiting for the woman that he knew he loved yet failed to protect was moments away. Molly had made her way to the R&D doors just as Kelly rounded the corner to the main hallway. Kelly saw her leaving but made no mind. Aaron was all that mattered now. She arrived at his office and entered.

Kelly felt relief to see him standing there. She looked at him. She watched him pace around his conference table. He stopped and looked over to her. There was something… off. He had a guilty look on his face. She could feel the shame, the embarrassment emanating from him. Why? What had he done to be embarrassed…

Kelly approached him, and before even saying a word, she smelled the scent of expensive perfume on him. She saw the hint of lipstick on his collar. Her heart sank. She felt the foul play. It was hitting hard. Had Aaron kissed her? If he did, why? This is nothing like him. Nothing at all! In the 30 years they had been together, Aaron had never once been unfaithful.

Kelly's mind raced with a thousand thoughts all at once. She stepped closer to Aaron. She reached up and placed her hand on the side of his head. She could feel the confusion. She could feel the shame, the remorse. She could feel… the lack of feeling. No, something was wrong. He wasn't drunk, she could feel that he was under the influence of something.

"Aaron, did you kiss that woman?"

"Yes." Aaron replied, looking down to the floor like a whipped puppy.

Kelly stepped closer. "Aaron, did you fuck that woman?"

Aaron paused and began to shudder immensely. A tear rolled down his eyes. He let his head down.

"I…I. .I think I did. I don't remember it, but I think I did. I think my girlfriend and I…"

"YOUR FUCKING GIRLFRIEND?" Kelly screamed! Rage began to course thru her veins. Her body temperature began to rise. The fury flowed thru very soul!

"Since when did that little wench become your FUCKING GIRLFRIEND? THAT LITTLE FUCKING CUNT!"

Kelly's rage toward Aaron was at a boiling point. Aaron and she had many arguments over little things over the years this was anger that tore her vary essence.

"YOU! And YOU!! I FUCKING HATE YOU, YOU GODDAMN PIECE OF SHIT!…"

A voice loudly interrupted them. "It's not his fault! ITS NOT HIS FAULT!" Yelled Katy from the doorway.

Kelly turned to see her standing there, panicking. "Please give me a chance to explain!!! MOLLY IS NOT WELL! SHE NEVER HAS BEEN!"

Kelly felt something in Katy in that moment. Katy's eyes were telling her a story, it was then she knew she had to listen. Kelly focused her mind and let herself breath. She then opened her eyes and looked coldly at Katy. "Talk. Because you brought that little shit stain here, I find you equally guilty Katy"

Katy took a breath, a deep one. "When we were kids, Molly had a condition. Many thought it was schizophrenia. Not all the symptoms matched up, but it was the closest diagnosis the doctors could find for her. She did things. Bad things. She hurt people, in bad ways, both emotionally and physically. In fact, even now, there's a young man in Michigan why may never be able to speak right again, after Molly jammed a sharpened pencil in his neck."

Katy took a breath. Kelly listened on with interest.

"She always said she had a special friend that only she could see. This friend demanded things of her, made her do things for her. It made her steal things, manipulate people, ruin peoples. Lives. It took many years of medication and therapy to fix her mind, but as we got older, the medications began to kick in. She was normal for a long time after that." Katy reminisced for a moment, then a thought came to her. "Molly hasn't been the same since… Pennhurst. Our trip to Penhurst! I wonder if being in a place like that triggered something in her, reminded her of her unseen friend?

"And does this unseen friend have a fucking name Jesus Christ Katy what the hell?" asked Kelly, sarcastically.

Katy thought for a moment. It wasn't a common name, but there was something familiar about it. She knew it started with a D. What was it? Katy thought on. She recalled a popular rock song that she had heard where the name was used. She remembered!

"Raven! Her friend's name was Raven!" Katy exclaimed.

Something in Kelly's mind began to stir. As ridiculous as Katy's story sounded, somehow, she knew it was true. Her feelings of anger and pain began to subside. No… they didn't subside, they shifted focus. Kelly knew whom she truly needs to confront. Molly. Molly was her target now. Kelly was about to rip into her in more ways than one. Kelly turned toward Aaron, who was moping like a child who just got chewed out by his parents. She stepped toward him. "I'll deal with you, dumb ass motherfucker later, Aaron."

Kelly turned toward the door, enraged with a new kind of fury. Meredith was standing there.

"Please, I need to apologize. I overheard everything." Cried Meredith

"What the fuck do you want?" Kelly said, rage burning in her mind.

"I think this may be my fault." She said, poutingly. Meredith stood there, hands folded, and tears in her eyes.

"What do you mean? What's your part in all of this?" asked Kelly, while Katy looked on.

Meredith paused for a moment. "Molly came to me the other day looking for some… party boosters, something to uhm, well, you know, get you a little high. You know, get a little fucked up, so you can party all night long. It's called lotus, hasn't been out on the market for too long, and its real popular… and real dangerous if you overdo it. I had warned her. I thought it was for herself, I didn't know she might use it on someone else. I think Aaron was raped, Kelly"

Both Kelly and Katy stood there in confusion and shock. Had Molly date raped Aaron? Had she gone so low as to put his life at stake? And what about now? What had she used to get him so loopy this time?

Kelly looked at Aaron. "How many beers did you have last night?"

"I, I only remember the two." Aaron replied, weeping loudly.

"Was there any time when Molly had access to your beer that you wouldn't have noticed?" Asked Katy.

Aaron shrugged. "Maybe? There were a lot of distractions last night, I think. I…I….I just don't know anymore." Aaron began to sob uncontrollably and looking at Kelly with as much remorse as he could muster as his senses were coming back to him. He wanted to embrace her

Meredith had an idea. She had a lot of friends down in

the lab that owed her some favors. "

Kelly, would you mind if I took him down to the lab for urinalysis and a blood draw? We may be able to find out what and how much he was given." Kelly took a deep breath and considered the option. This woman may have been part of the problem, but she may be part of the solution. She considered it.

"Alright, take him. So long as you don't try to fuck him too along the way."

Meredith understood her sarcasm. She was in fact part of the reason this happened. She felt responsible. Meredith walked over to Aaron and gripped his arm, leading him out of the office and to elevator that goes down to the specimen testing lab. "Hey, Kelly do you want to come along?" Suggested Meredith. As Aaron slowly stepped out, he looked back at his wife. He wanted to die. "No, I'll wait here.

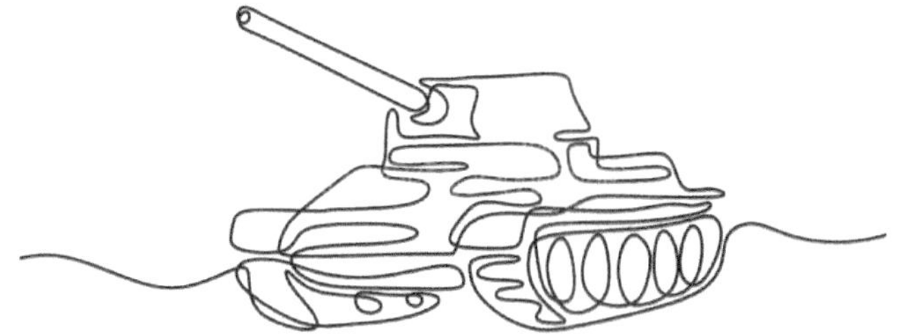

13 WAR

Kelly turned towards Katy. There was still fury in her eyes, but she knew the true adversary. She knew there was only solution to this problem. Molly must go down, and hard. Kelly didn't enjoy physical violence, but she sure had a mouth on her. Molly, however, was about to get both. Kelly turned towards Katy and looked her sternly in the eyes. "You and I aren't done here. Your hands aren't clean in this." Katy looked up a Kelly, whom was a good foot taller than her and far more muscular. Katy relented. She knew she failed her part in stopping this. She moved to the side to clear the path. She knew what was about to come. Yet it didn't feel like Katy's place to intervene, still she felt responsible for not discussing anything.

Kelly stormed out of Aarons office and turned down the hall towards R&D. She double stepped with a sense of power intent towards those double doors. There was staff in the hallway, most who knew her and tried to greet her as she passed by. Kelly ignored all. The staff knew something was up. The thing was the rumors had already infiltrated most of the offices in the facility. They all looked on in quiet curiosity as Kelly, whom had no real affiliation with this company, was basically given free reign of the place.

Kelly reached the double doors that led to R&D. She stood before them for a moment. Then, with a ferocious push, she slammed them open. Roger was standing there. "Oh! Ms. Kelly, how are you? What are you doing down here? This is restricted area!" Kelly paid no mind. She liked Roger, he was a sweet old man, but he was irrelevant right now.

At the far end of the room stood a group of staff about five deep. She studied them, and there she was. In the center of the group, acting like the most popular girl in school, was THAT BITCH. Kelly approached.

The group went silent when she got to them. They all knew, based on the rumors, that trouble was coming. The others slowly backed off, apprehension on their minds. Many questioned if the rumors were true. Many questioned if this was the end of Aaron and Kelly.

Kelly stood behind Molly, silently, waiting for her to turn around and face her. Molly noticed the expressions on the face of her colleagues. She knew something was up. She slowly yet smugly turned around and faced her new threat.

"Hi Kelly, I thought I might run into you today." Molly said with a sly smile.

Kelly looked deep into her eyes, took a step forward. Without warning her right hand flung out like a bolt of lightning and slapped Molly's left cheek so hard she leaned to the side, Molly doubled back, but quickly regained her composure. "You little whore! Who the hell do you think you are assaulting MY husband like that? Did you think I wouldn't figure it out? Your little posse let me in on EVERYTHING. What your tiny hubby can't give you dick, so you go around whoring yourself to innocent men like MY husband for sex? He would NEVER willingly fuck a trashy skank like you!"

Molly looked at her with rage in her eyes but maintained her composure. She knew this was coming. She was not prepared to face the fury of this fiery redhead.

"HOW FUCKING DARE, YOU! HOW DARE YOU DO THIS TO MY HUSBAND! HOW DARE YOU DO THIS TO ME! WHO THE FUCK DO YOU THINK YOU ARE YOU WORTHLESS WHORE!" Kelly yelled, with the energy of a thousand raging bulls feeding her pushing her.

Molly took a deep breath and stepped closer to Kelly. "I'm his soul mate, Kelly, and I've come to give him what you can't, and he is going to give me what James won't."

Molly continued. "My plan was to claim my prize from the moment I first met him. You failed him, Kelly. You can't give him what he wants or needs. You're not worthy of him. I AM!" Molly exclaimed.

Kelly's rage tripled inside. In her bones, she wanted to take every blunt object she could find in this place and bash her skull in, and she was tempted to do it.

"Listen to me you trash filthy whore! I have thirty years with this man. You have NOTHING. I knew there was something up with you from the moment I first met you. I should have kicked your ass from day fucking one you worthless no good lying shit sack! What about the whole Aaron? You're after a façade! Youi don't care about him! I do! You don't have the capacity to care for him!"

Molly simply smirked at her. Kelly was enraged by the disrespect. This added only more fuel to her fire. It reminded her of the disrespect she experienced in her youth. She always felt like she had to work harder, try harder to get what she wanted. Aaron was her prize, not Molly's. She was tired of the struggle; she was tired of being stepped on by others. Nobody was going to take Aaron away from her, especially this little tramp, these vermin, this… snake!

Molly looked up at Kelly. "You know, I think this slap constitutes assault and battery. I think I'll get security on the line. Molly turned away from her and started walking to the phone. "Assault and battery?" Kelly thought. "I'LL SHOW YOU ASSAULT AND BATTERY YOU LITTLE FUCKING BITCH!"

Kelly followed behind Molly with a swift pace, grabbed her hair and pulled her back towards her. Others tried to hold Kelly back. Kelly was so full of adrenaline that she fought off anyone who came at her. Molly stumbled for a moment. Kelly pounded Molly square in the face over and over. She loosened her grip and Molly fell to the ground smacking her head hard into the floor tile. For the moment she was dazed, but she attempted to get up to swing back. As Kelly saw this coming and blocked with her right hand then counterstriking with her left, she grabbed the Molly's other wrist with her right, to restrain it. Molly looked up at her with absolute rage, blood oozing from her nose. Kelly was on top of her now and grabbed her head slamming it into the tile making it bleed and punching her face. Molly was dizzy and swollen. Blood was oozing from her nose and on her blouse. Kelly grabbed her throat while she was on the ground and began to squeeze. Molly winced in pure fear. Kelly prepared herself for the final head butt blow, but she flipped her hair around and caught a glimpse of her and Molly in the wall mirror. Something jumped out to her in the reflection. Although Molly was struggling on the ground, pinned under Kelly's weight, her reflection in the mirror seemed to stare back at her, laughing, grinning. A surge of energy shot thru Kelly, something she had never felt before.

Kelly looked at the reflection from one of the decorative mirrors as it began to chuckle, with stone cold black eyes, staring at her. She released her grip in a panic. "They are mine now, hahahaha!" Molly said. It wasn't Molly. It was a scary demonic voice coming out of her. Kelly felt the intensity inside her. She looked up into the mirror as Molly continued to fade. Black eyes stared back at her. It laughed. It came out of the mirror. Showed itself. Grinning with sharp teeth and black gums. Looking like a skinny goth chick with high heal boots, black lipstick, and jet-black eyes. It began to morph. Greyish black scaly skin began to appear. Sharp pointed nails emerged. Kelly looked back down at Molly, bleeding everywhere from her nose and the back of her head and beginning to pass out. Kelly sensed a plea for help, a plea for forgiveness. The plea was sincere. Molly was in pain, not only of the physical kind, but something much deeper.

Tears rolled down Molly's face and she spoke "She's haunting me, Kelly! Ever since I was a child. She Haunts me now. I want her gone. I can't take this anymore. I got rid of her then! She's back! She found me at my weakest. Help me! PLEASE HELP ME!" Molly passed out from the pain and the blood loss. She wasn't used to physical conflict. She laid helpless on the floor. The remaining staff, whom Kelly fought off stood still and frightened.

Kelly started envisioning what Molly was saying. She felt an overwhelming physical pain inside her. She could see Molly was telling the truth with this strange ability she couldn't figure out. She could sense Molly was under control of something and she could see that something. It scared her half to death. She began to get choked up. She got off Molly and offered her a hand to pull her up.

Katy knew something was going on down the hall, in the R&D department. Fear held her back from going in there. She approached the double doors. She reached for the handle. Her phone rang. It was James. She pulled back and answered it.

"Hi Katy, I just landed. Can you pick me up? I need to see Molly ASAP."

Katy composed her thoughts. "I'll send you an UBER right away. Things went south over here. Molly needs you, badly."

As Kelly helped Molly slowly pull herself up from the floor. Molly wiped blood from her nose. She examined it. The pain was unbearable. A part of her was angry. She wanted to hit back. The feeling subsided when she glanced in the mirror and saw only her own reflection this time. Raven was gone, at least for now. She turned to look at Kelly, who was still trying to understand what had just happened.

"I don't know what to say, Kelly." Molly sighed. "I can think of a thousand fucking things you can say, like Who the fuck is that? What does she want? Why is she turning you against everyone? Look at me Molly! She's controlling you!"

Molly stumbled and shuddered. The knock to her face and her head hitting the floor really did a number on her.

"What was that thing in the mirror, Molly? And what does it have to do with FUCKING MY HUSBAND?"

"Raven. Its name is Raven." Molly replied.

"Who the fuck is Raven? What is it? A Demon or what?" asked Kelly.

Molly closed her eyes, lowered her head. There was a tingling sensation inside of her. Then a pain, as if someone, or something had grabbed her insides, and it was there again, only stronger this time. That sinister urge was back. Molly felt a blackness to her soul. Raven was here, and this time with a vengeance.

"Talk to me Molly! I want answers!" Kelly demanded as she held her down.

Molly opened her eyes and looked up at Kelly. Kelly was horrified at what she saw! Those light blue eyes that defined Molly were gone. Instead, they were replaced with complete blackness. Molly…Was it still Molly? Raven? Whatever this thing before her no longer seemed human. Its skin dripped with sweat. It bared teeth at Kelly that grew sharper and longer. It hissed at her, angrily. Its hands splayed out as if to resemble claws. It assumed a striking pose.

It lunged!

Kelly was no martial artist, but she was a survivalist. In a split second, she swept her forearm across her chest to block and deflect this… things… attack. She the thrust her other palm out at the creature's chest with enough force to knock the wind out of its lungs.

Raven doubled back, almost collapsing. Kelly moved in. Whatever this thing was, wasn't quite physically strong enough to make an effective blow. For the moment, however, it was in complete control of Molly. It's fury and desire put up a formidable opponent. Kelly didn't want to hurt Molly knowing she was possessed by this demonic presence. She was able to pin her down to keep her from hurting herself or anyone else.

Meredith crashed thru the double doors from the hallway outside. She approached Kelly and offered her a small vial of some unknown blue liquid. "Give this to Molly NOW!"

"What the fuck is this?" asked Kelly.

"Trust me, just get it into her mouth so it can absorb into her system. This will ward off that thing temporarily"

"Here hold her arms down and I'll give her the vile"

Meredith held Molly's hands down as Molly's voice changed as she fought back. She moved her head from side to side trying to fight Kelly and the vile. "Molly, I know you're in there! I'm trying to help you!"

As Molly went to respond and her mouth opened Kelly poured the blue liquid as fast as she could into Molly's mouth. Molly passed out.

14 JAMES

James collected his luggage and headed toward the exit of the airport terminal. The air was hot and dry. He wasn't accustomed to this. Michigan was normally cooler than this, more humid. Living next to lake Michigan was a very different experience. The dry heat was something else to James. As he looked around, he noticed the iconic shape of the Sandia mountains in the east. He was fascinated. He had been around mountains plenty of times is his 27 years of life. For him, the Appalachian Mountain chain was green and majestic. The Rocky Mountain chain was a whole new experience, as he had never been any further east than Illinois.

James was feeling disconnected from his wife. It had gone on for weeks. She desired children. A family. She had been pushing him beyond his limits. Sometimes at night, she would weep silently, alone in parts of the house where James wouldn't notice. Molly thought James had been asleep. He wasn't. He would silently approach the corner of the hallway to wherever she was crying and stand against the wall. James didn't feel ready and was conflicted with desire and regret. He had invested so many years in his work in the field as a rancher. He loved the fresh air, the hard work, and the feeling of plowing fields. He cared for cattle all his life and had been able to hire hands to help him on the farm. Especially when he wanted to elope with Molly. James loved to travel the world to explore sights unseen. He fantasized about all the places he wanted to see. Having a child would take his freedom and his travels would be tarnished by parenthood. James knew why he was here. He knew the truth of Molly's past. He felt it deep in his bones. He didn't truly understand it. Molly had been treated for schizophrenia as a child. He didn't see the symptoms personally. He was aware of her attachment. He was raised to be non-religious, so he had very little knowledge of anything supernatural. He was raised to believe that what isn't seen doesn't exist. So, anything having to do with spirituality, or the existence of the Father, son and the Holy spirit was never discussed or believed in within his culture.

A grey Dodge charger pulled up, with an Uber sign flashing in its windshield. At this point the heat was sweltering to him. He couldn't wait to feel the cool breeze of air conditioning flow over his skin. The passenger side of the car rolled down. He double checked the app on his phone to ensure this vehicle was meant for him. It was.

"Hey homie, are you James? I was hired to pick you up. You look like my guy." Said the driver.

"Yeah, I'm James. My sister-in-law wanted me to get over to a place called Origin Corp, a pharmaceutical company out on the north side of Albuquerque. Know of the place?"

"Yeah, vato. I'll pop the trunk. Throw your bags in, I'll get you there. Names Martin' by the way."

James tossed his bags in the trunk of the car, and he stepped in the back passenger seat. He was instantly amused by the small metal stamped Zia symbol dangling from the rear-view mirror. On the dashboard where small red and green chili's pinned all over the place. He looked at his driver. He was a portly Hispanic man, somewhere in his mid-fifties,' from James's estimate. The car smelled like food, one that James didn't recognize. It made him hungry however, as James hadn't eaten since he left Detroit.

"Hey, man! Something smells good! What is that?" asked James.

"Pinche gringos, hahaha!" exclaimed the driver. "I just pounded macarra pinche chili rellenos on the way here, homie. There's some badass fuckin' food trucks in El Centro, where I dropped off my last ride, Ese'." Martin' said.

James had no idea what some of the words were that he was saying. He wasn't accustomed to anything but English. Why would someone use two languages at once? Whatever, his appetite was raving. Whatever a chili relleno was must be pretty good. He desired one but knew that Molly was his only true priority. He must get to her.

"Hey gringo, where you from anyway? You don't look like you're from around from Burque,' Ese'?" asked Martin.'

"Uhm, I'm from Michigan. Small town just outside of Manistee. It's right by lake Michigan. My wife and I have 80 acres of land out there. We have sheep and grow wheat out there. My wife is studying pharmaceuticals here. She was an EMT but is looking to advance her career in medicine." Replied James.

"So, she wants to make drugs, eh! Joder si'! Mierda, She's in the right town for that! A few years ago, we had a vato that made some good shit out from an RV. Don't know what happened to the fucker, but damn that shit was good.”

“Yeah… not those kinds of drugs. She wants to help people. She's a sweet woman, has as good heart. I think she's in trouble, and I need to get to her now she may be hurt!”

“Aqui vamos, Ese'! I'll get you where you need to go, gringo!” exclaimed Martin.

James was lost with Martin' and his rhetoric. He blew it off and concentrated on Molly. He watched as Albuquerque passed him by, building by building. He watched as the shape of the Sandia mountains changed and the colors were a vibrant blue, grey and black as the sun reflected off the granite stone of its western face. He was mesmerized by it all. He knew now why Molly was so excited to come here. He now understood why his sister-in-law had made this place her home. This place had a magic all its own. It was beautiful.

Martin' pulled his car up in front of a large, elaborate building, decked out with many sorts of trees and shrubbery. James exited the car and collected his bags. He handed him a moderate tip for his services.

“Gracias, amigo.” Replied Martin.’ “No dejes que el chile te cobra, pendejo!” replied Martin' as a drove away.

James had no idea what Martin' had just told him. Was it a sign of appreciation? He didn't know, but with bags in hand, he began searching the parking lot for any sign that Molly or Katy where there. It didn't take long, Katy's black jeep stood out from the crowd. He knew she had a bad habit of not locking it, so he took a chance. He approached it, opened the back passenger door, and placed his luggage in it.

He pondered the massive facility in front of him, and then noticed a police car and a pair of ambulances parked in the fire lane in front of it. His heart sank. Something wasn't just wrong; something had gone horribly south. The anxiety in his bones had him trembling. He feared the worst. Could it be? Could Raven… be back?

James approached the entry of the massive facility. His heart was pounding, sweat dripping from him skin. Katy was sitting on a concrete bench in a small grove of trees not far from the doubled revolving doors, leading into the facility. James ran toward her in a panic. Katy looked up and pounced off the bench and ran to him. "James, oh my god, I'm so glad you're here!" exclaimed Katy.

"Katy what's going on here? Where's Molly? Where's my wife?"

Katy looked up to James with fear in her eyes. There was only one way to get the message to him. There was only one word. There was only one way. A tear dripped down the right side of her cheek. She began to stutter, to mumble. "Ra….Ra…Rav…Raven." Katy replied with as much energy as she could muster.

James looked at Katy horrified. He knew exactly what this meant. He wanted to forget the memories of their youth when Molly battled Raven before. He thought the medication would solve the issue. He hadn't been much of a believer in the supernatural in his youth let alone having any religious beliefs. To him, it was all just a fancy hallucination, a vivid imagination gone awry. He bought into the diagnosis of schizophrenia back then. He trusted science, he trusted what could be seen and measured. There was a moment that caused him to question everything, in their youth. He remembered Molly, as a teenager in high school, in a fit of rage one afternoon where she had been fighting with one of the girls in the cheer leading squad. He didn't know what the argument was about, only that the two girls never really got along. Missy had grown up with privilege and she was a bully to Molly. Her parents were successful lawyers who had major clients in Detroit. They looked down on people like Molly because she was raised out in the country, on farmland and didn't have sophistication. James remembered Missy had started in on Molly hollering "Hay guttersnipe! You forget to shower?"

as Molly passed her in the hallway as she was heading to her next class. Molly would usually ignore her and speed walk away, avoiding confrontation and fighting. This time Molly had enough of that damn name "guttersnipe." She was sick of her entitled snotty remarks. She stopped, got a chokehold her heavy book laden backpack and swung it as hard as she could towards Missy's face. Missy fell flat on her ass and slid down the hall. Everyone, including James, were in disbelief as it was not typical behavior for Molly. She never defended herself. It was then that he saw in the reflection of the window to the classroom next to her... someone else. Someone in the place where Molly's reflection should have been, something that just didn't seem natural, someone that wasn't Molly. It startled him. He looked away and looked back. She was gone.

The memory faded and James refocused on Katy.

"What the hell going on here, Katy? She won't call me. I haven't been hearing from her. She won't answer her phone or text, she won't email, not ever her favorite facetime chats." remarked James "She's avoiding me like the plague."

At that moment, a slow drizzle of rain began to fall. Katy's long blonde hair began to soak and drip. It didn't seem to faze her. She looked to the ground, and then spoke.

"James, Molly came here with a certain intention. She... she has a thing for our boss, Aaron. I think she may have done something horrible to him. I think she..." Katy trailed off.

An ambulance and two police cars pulled up. EMTs exited and pulled out a gurney, then rushed inside the building. Meanwhile a pair of police officers dashed inside after them. James looked on at the scene, confused.

"What the hell is going on here? Katy! Talk!" demanded James.

"There was a fight. Aaron's wife showed up a little bit ago and confronted Molly. They argued, and somehow, things got physical. When I made my way inside, Molly was lying on the floor, bleeding and unconscious. Kelly is being held in the security office being questioned."

James listened in amazement. Who is this Kelly woman and why start a fight with his wife? Who is this Aaron guy, and what happened with him?

"you're not telling me what I want to hear Katy! Tell me what I need to know!" James spoke sharply.

"I think Molly… may have somehow forced herself on Aaron. I think she may have slept with him, James."

James looked at her with shock in his eyes. Molly, his wife, had betrayed him she had slept with another man, and he had so many questions going thru his mind. James looked toward the building, furious. Who was this other man that she was seeing all the sudden? He had to confront him. In James mind, there was about to another beat down. Skinny as James was, he didn't care what he was about to do. He balled up his left fist and started advancing toward the doors. Katy reached out and grabbed him, pulling him back.

"Wait, James. It's not his fault. He didn't do this willingly!" Katy exclaimed.

James turned to her, looked her in the eye. "You can't tell me that he didn't have anything on his end to do with this. No man just goes and fucks my wife without intent. That son of a bitch…"

"James, I don't know exactly how she did it, but she drugged him. She seduced him and got him in bed."

James looked at her even more confused this time. "How can a man be drugged and still be able to function? None of this made sense!" James thought to himself. He turned back to the door and continued his advance. The doors swung open and a young woman, in handcuffs, was being escorted out. It was Meredith. James was even more confused now. Who the hell was this woman and for what was she being arrested? Another man, an older man, stepped out from behind them. It was Roger. He was holding his face in shock. He looked terrified.

Katy pulled away and approached him. "Roger, what's

going on in there? What's the situation?"

Roger composed himself. He wiped sweat from his brow, even as the rain kept coming down. He turned to Katy and James. "Molly is being taken to the hospital. She's in and out of being conscious" said Katy. Meredith over there has been arrested for possession of illegal substances. I'm not sure what's going on with that, but I think she turned herself in to the police. Kelly is still being questioned in the security office by the police. As for Aaron, he's pacing franticly outside his office, waiting to see what's going on with his wife."

Roger recentered his thoughts. "Katy, I don't know how to say this, but that wasn't Molly back there. That wasn't the sprightly young go-getter that I've come to know, and I don't mean that figuratively, either. That was someone… something else. It was as if she was…"

"What? Possessed?" James interjected. He thought back again to the moment with the book bag.

The doors opened again, and EMTs pulled out the gurney with a Molly in it, strapped down. James dashed over to her. As they pulled her down the pathway to the ambulance, James approached but was quickly waved off by a third EMT holding a tablet. "It's ok, I'm her husband. I need to know what happened!." The EMT supervisor approached him.

"She got into quite a physical altercation, and it looks pretty serious." We need to get her to the ER for evaluation and toxicology. We think she may have been drugged. We are taking her downtown, to St Mary's hospital. You can follow us and meet us there."

The EMT's loaded molly into the back of the ambulance, closed the doors, and after a few minutes, drove away. "C'mon James, let's get in the Jeep. I'll take you there." said Katy. Once again, the doors opened, and a second gurney was being led out to an unnoticed ambulance on the backside of a small maintenance storage facility in front of the main building. Katy looked on. It was Aaron, and he wasn't looking so good, himself. What happened? Had he been involved in the fight to? The last Katy saw of him, he had been taken down to the lab for evaluation.

A woman in a dark grey business dress came out to speak to Roger, who was still standing there, collecting his thoughts. This woman was Danielle, head of the human resources department. She was a tall woman, with long black hair tied neatly in a bun, and thin rimmed reading glasses over her eyes. She approached Roger and Katy. James looked on, anxiously.

"Roger, the police need to take some statements from you in a few minutes, when you're ready." she said.

"What happened to Aaron, Danielle? Is he sick?" asked Roger.

James turned to the gurney in shock. That was Aaron? That was the man who…

"Aaron is having a possible allergic or drug reaction. He may have been poisoned. He was getting blood work done in the labs he started vomit profusely and he was really lethargic. We called the ambulance right away. They were the first to arrive."

"Poisoned? How? And with what? And by whom? And for what purpose?" asked Roger.

Danielle, oblivious to the presence of James, turned toward Roger. "Look, I don't know what's going on, but I've been hearing rumors, and you know how they spread like wildfire around here." She leaned in closer to Roger, glanced side to side, then spoke softly. "I heard that Sam, you know the guy in accounting, swears up and down he saw that Molly girl put something in Aaron's water bottle. He had just been passing by Aaron's office looking for Katy and happened to glance inside as she did it. I don't know about you, Roger, but that girl has always given me a funny feeling. Couple that with all the other rumors going on about her, makes for a pretty sketchy situation."

"Well why didn't he say anything?" asked Roger. "One would think if you saw someone put something in somebody's drink, one would speak out!"

"I guess that's Sam, for you." Said Danielle. "He's the type who would see a pile of papers scattered on the floor and leave it for someone to pick up. He's always been kind of a prick, I think."

James listened in on the conversation, feeling completely invisible. "Katy, get me to the hospital, right now. I've got to find out what is going on around here. James turned toward Roger and Danielle, who were now in deep conversation. James raised his voice slightly and pointed an accusing finger toward them. They turned to finally notice him. "My WIFE does NOT go around POISONING PEOPLE. Get that through your thick skulls right now!"

Roger and Danielle turned to look at him in shock not knowing how to respond. James walked away heading to the Jeep with Katy following behind him. They got in and sped away to catch up with the ambulance. James sat in quiet contemplation. Molly… She wasn't capable of this. Not his wife. "She's not that type of woman." He thought to himself, over and over, repeating those words. Each time he repeated them, somehow, deep in his soul, he didn't buy them.

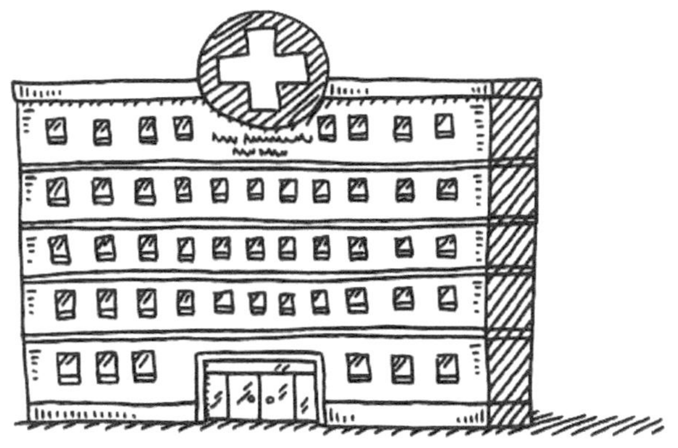

15 HOSPITAL

Molly opened her eyes. The room was brightly lit. It had been a few weeks since the fight. Her possession from Raven kept her unconscious. She was unaware of where she was at or what happened. Which occurs when possessions take place, even if they are temporary since the spirit is control of the mind and body of who they possess. Looking around at her surroundings Molly noticed the IV in her arm stinging a little. The vitals monitor at her side beeped at a steady pace. She turned to her right and felt a familiar hand on her shoulder. She focused her eyes and turned more. James!

"What was James doing here? When did he get here? She hadn't seen or heard from him in some time. Why now? The door opened, and her sister walked into the room. Katy sat down next to James but offered no greeting. What was going on here?" Molly thought to herself.

"James? Katy? What is this? Why am I in a hospital room? What happened? Was there an accident or something?" Molly said slowly. Katy looked nervously towards James. They offered no reply. James got up to hold her hand not knowing what to do, "Molly, you got into a nasty fight. You have a head injury from it. You may have a concussion." James then went outside the room and called the nurse in letting her know Molly was awake.

The door opened and a nurse stepped in. she was an older woman in her sixties with short grey hair. She studied Molly for a moment, reviewed her vitals and made some notes on her clipboard. She checked the time. It was 6:05 pm.

"How are we feeling today. Looks like you've been in a bit of a tussle. I'm glad to see you awake young lady"

Molly thought for a moment. Had she been in a fight? Why and with whom? She was drawing blanks.

"What happened? Why am I here?" asked Molly.

"Well, Molly, you got in a nasty little skirmish. You have a few lacerations and swelling on your face, and we are monitoring for a concussion. We got some labs back looks like your blood work is good" replied the nurse as she wrote down more notes. Finishing up the nurse turned and said, "The doctor will be in soon, if you need anything use this remote to call me okay."

Moments later Dr Sandoval came in, "Hello, I am Dr. Sandoval. We will keep you here for a little longer for observation. We ran some blood work, and it looks like everything is good. I'm not sure that you know this yet, Molly, you're pregnant. We will need you to increase your calorie intake. I have started you on prenatal vitamins. You'll need to get with an OBGYN and schedule regular visits okay. Looks like the baby is doing okay. Any questions right now?" Molly looked at James and back at the doctor "No, I. No"

"Okay now that you're up we need to get you something to eat. I'll have the nurse bring you some food." The doctor left the room.

Molly glanced a glaring star at Katy. "It was Raven, Katy." James shot an angry stare at Molly. "Fuck you Molly! You can shove your little imaginary friend right up your ass. Hell, you'd probably like that wouldn't you! 'Oh, it was Raven' FUCK YOU!"

James turned toward Molly. "I'll have your things in Michigan boxed up and put in storage. Be on the lookout for papers Molly. Divorce papers. Consider us done. I've taken a lot from you, but this shit, I won't take anymore! We. Are. Done!" James's voice was crackling. He was shaking furious.

James knew that her friend wasn't imaginary, yet his anger towards her right now was raging through him like a raging bull ready to toss her in the air. James was oblivious as to the control that Raven had over Molly, and he didn't care. This was the ultimate insult to him. Complete slap in the face if he ever saw one. No fucking possession could ever excuse her for this, in his mind. He'll be God damned if he's going to raise somebody else's kid hell he didn't even want his own damn kid in the first place. What was she thinking?

James turned toward Molly. James lowered his voice almost to a whisper as to not draw attention, pointing his finger at her and motioning back and forth, "I won't sit here and deal with you and you're fucking infatuation with whoever you damn well please. I won't put up with your manipulative bullshit anymore. You've had your way with me long enough, and this bullshit nonsense excuse of some ghoooost haunting Raven garbage you spilled isn't going to cut it. If it's true that you drugged this Aaron guy, well I can't… I just can't…Enough is enough Molly. Enough is Enough."

James grabbed his coat off the chair. He glared at Molly.

He couldn't stand to look at her. He didn't know whether to scream or cry. He stepped toward the door, and while not even giving Kate herself a second glance, out of the hospital room. He was gone. Gone for good.

Three weeks prior

The day it all happened; Aaron was laying down in a hospital emergency room bed. The doctor, sitting at the swivel desk beside him began reviewing charts and noting numbers of various lab results. Mind you this was the day everything happened. Three weeks prior.

"Aaron, you seem to have had high levels of methylenedioxymethamphetamine in your blood stream, are you a user?" asked the doctor

"English, Doc. I'm a little out of it and don't have my desk reference right now."

"MDMA, Aaron. Ecstasy. The compound I'm looking at doesn't seem to quite fit the bill in what I've seen in patients before. I see here you take blood pressure medication; did you take any today?"

"Yeah, I take Atenolol. Took it this morning like usual."

"Interesting. There's something else here. I'm seeing trace levels of Ethanol and 3-quinuclidinyl benzilate." Said the doctor.

"Wait, isn't that the stuff they put in so called truth serums? How did I get that in me?"

"This isn't something you find at your local corner drug store, Aaron. I understand you work at a pharmaceutical company. Do you have access to the substances that make up this drug?" asked the doctor.

Aaron thought for a moment. Aaron wasn't a chemist, he delt with logistics and supply. He never directly handled any chemicals that went in or out. The chemists in the labs had access to many things not available to the public.

"I don't handle any substances in person, Doc. That's R&D's department. I do order a supply for them. I don't have actual physical access to them. So, no, I really don't."

The doctor considered his findings for a moment. He

concluded.

"Aaron, do you work with anyone who does have access to these chemicals who may have done something to you?"

Aaron already knew the answer to that. Of course, he did. He handles the supply requests from R&D every day. Whatever substances they needed, Aaron could research it and source it for them. It was a challenging process sometimes, as many requests are only found overseas. Who introduced him to these substances? For what reason?

"Molly!!! Son of bitch!"

"Excuse me?" asked the doctor.

In a flash of memory recall, a complete scenario formed in Aaron's mind. "Molly worked directly with supplies for R&D. She had access, albeit with some very high levels of control, to almost anything she needed. Was it Molly that had done something to him? Can't be." Aaron thought, she would never do that. "Too much integrity right?"

"I'm going to suggest Aaron. If you are not an active user of MDMA, and this serum is showing up in your labs, you may be a victim of a crime. If necessary, I can suggest a host of available resources that can help you address the situation."

Aaron thought for a moment. It was like a complete puzzle was forming in his head. The doctor interrupted his thoughts.

"It's apparent you've had a severe drug interaction. It counteracted your blood pressure medication. It explains the blackout you described. The Serum… interacted with the residual chemicals left over from that experience and sent your body into, what shall I say, purge mode. That is why you vomited. The body, as you know, tries to cleanse itself. It may have caused further damage. I'm going to set you up for a liver ultrasound for now, as that is the most vital organ for cleansing the system. If anything comes up, we can do a biopsy. This combination of chemicals can wreak havoc on your liver. I also want you to monitor any cravings. Even one dose of MDMA can trigger an addiction, whether you took it intentionally or not. Furthermore, I would like you to seek counseling. This event, even if done covertly, will have lasting effects on you. You need to protect yourself."

Aaron sat on the bed, his fury growing. Molly. What the fuck did Molly do?

"I don't see a need to admit you into the hospital long term, so I am going to prepare some paperwork and let you go home. If any symptoms reappear, come back immediately. I'll give you discharge papers that will have all the symptoms to look out for."

"Got it Doc."

The doctor shook Aarons hand and left the room. Thirty minutes later, Aaron found himself standing in front of the main doors to St. Mary's. He was at a loss. How does he get home? Is there even home to go to? Kelly was in her own predicament, with the police. Even if she could come pick him up, would she? Aaron's heart sank as the reality of the situation came crashing down on him. Aaron had slept with another woman. Regardless the circumstances, it still happened. Kelly was heartbroken and furious.

Aaron was hungry and tired. He picked up his phone and inquired about getting a ride home. He would figure out food once he got home. Moments later his ride showed up and took him to his work so he could pick up his bike. It was a quiet ride. He tipped the driver. He headed to his Truck and got inside. He sat for a moment before putting his key in the ignition. "How did this happen?" He thought to himself. "Even if I were sexually assaulted it would be so hard to prove. I don't know if I can even do anything about it." He put the key in and turned the ignition to start his truck. He turned off his radio before putting the gear shift from P to R and then in D leaving the parking lot.

Aaron returned home. The ride was quiet. It was still raining off and on. Kelly hadn't showed up yet. He sat in his study, pulling up food delivery and finding something to eat, while looking at YouTube videos.

It was later than usual.

Kelly sat in a gray cushioned office chair in the security office, surrounded by camera monitors on the walls behind her and to her right. She was nervous, slightly bruised, and emotionally broken. How had things deteriorated for her so quickly? What had she done? She had never faced inner rage to the degree she did, this afternoon. Two security officers sat at the end of the long table, across from her. She remembered when they entered the room, frantically separating her from Molly, that thing she had become. The officers had approached her with haste, pulled her hands behind her and applied binding straps. She remembered the discomfort of them, how they dug into her wrists. She had never been apprehended before, never arrested. It was a humiliating feeling for her, and Molly, as she lye there on the ground, bleeding, what was with her? Kelly remembered sensing something inside of her. Yes, in that instant she sensed a baby but that wasn't what concerned her, at least for now. It was something else. Something that wreaked of pure evil, torment, anger, and pain. She focused inwardly as the murmuring of conversation echoed in the background between the security officers and police, who had arrived minutes earlier. She didn't focus on their conversation, only on her own thoughts.

"Ms. Eastman, Ma'am. Ma'am…" The policewoman, officer Susan Menendez shook her shoulder. Kelly looked up at her. Her concentration focused on her now.

"Ma'am, you seem to have friends around here. You got a lucky break, believe it or not." The officer sighed. "This could have led to serious assault charges, and various property violations in accordance with state and county law, as well as violations of company policy. The senior staff around here has chosen not to press any charges against you. Talk about a lucky break, they seem to respect you around her. As for Ms. Jenson, she was taken to the hospital and being treated. She has also been interviewed by other officers. She also has decided not to press any charges. Not sure why, you sure gave her a beat down. We could under state law take actions of our own, between you and me Ms. Easton, I don't feel like writing up paperwork tonight over some cat fight. It's a pain in the ass, and our jail is overcrowded with druggies and hobos as it is. We're going to let you off with a warning. The security officers here are to escort you off the property, and you're not to return. If you do, we'll be back, and this time you won't be as lucky."

The officers typed up information on their tablets, turned around to the security officers, told them something Kelly couldn't hear, then stepped out the door and left. "What just happened here?" Kelly thought to herself. The tall Hispanic security chief, Fil, stepped over to her and offered her a hand to get out of the chair. Kelly had known fil for as long as Aaron had worked here. They had been on good terms with each other, always had friendly conversation at the holiday parties. He offered a sympathetic smile to her as she stood up.

"Look Kelly, we know you around here. We know this isn't like you. We know something more is going on between you and Ms. Jenson, but that's none of our business. Look, go home and get some rest. Figure stuff out. Let things cool off."

"Aaron? Where's Aaron? Is he ok?" asked Kelly.

"Last I heard, they got him to St. Mary's downtown. That's all I know; you may want to head there after this and find him. I'll make sure his office is secured." He said.

"Thanks Fil, I really appreciate it. You have no idea what this means" Kelly replied.

"Take care of yourself, Kelly. Maybe when things cool down, yah know." Said Fil.

Kelly nodded her head. Together, they exited the security office, walked down the hallway and out the front door. Fil waved at her as she made her way to her van. She felt numb. She was exhausted both emotionally and physically. She stepped into her van and started it. What to do next? No matter what had happened, deep down she still loved him, and she also knew something else, that something more was going on here. It was something far more sinister than she had led to believe. It didn't excuse what happened, not by a long shot, but she knew Aaron. She had known him for over 30 years. This wasn't like him. This wasn't him, why would he do something like this? He was always affectionate, honest, sincere. What is going on? However, it was time to go home collect herself and then figure out what to do next. Kelly texted Aaron asking where he was, he responded he was at the house. She responded by telling him she was on her way and then Kelly left heading for home. As she got to her house and pulled into the driveway, she noticed Aaron was indeed at home. She entered the front door. "Hello?!" anticipating a response from Aaron. He was at this study on his computer, scrolling thru various music videos and sipping a tall glass of ice with a little bit of tea. "Hello, love." Aaron sighed. Kelly sensed Aaron's demeanor and walked towards his study as he sat pouting to himself about the turn of events. Kelly approached and leaned against the door post. "How are you feeling? Any better?"

"I'm okay. The drugs are wearing off a little. The junk in my system I mean, Hon, I'm so sorry for..."

"You're sorry? You're SOORRREEEYY? Aaron sorry isn't going to cut it this time. Do you have any idea what I am even remotely going thru right now? Not only did you get your ass to a skank bar and sit with a MARRIED WOMAN, but you also allowed your best fucking judgement to go right out the God damned window and for fucking what? Someone to talk to about our most personal fucking issues? Those issues are NONE OF ANYONES FUCKING BUUUSIIINESSS! So, you just ignore fact that I am your wife and that I am the one you should be talking to because you got stressed? Let me guess, you want me to show you some understaaaanding, yet you can't even respect OUR privacy let alone respect me? Hay, I get stressed too just like everybody else, you don't see me airing our dirty fucking laundry because something didn't go right the day befooore! Do you think I asked for this? Do you think that this bullshit I am going thru is any fucking easier for me? Well, you got another thing coming Sherlock! You see, I get wanting to confide into someone, but why the fuck would you confide in some filthy butt floss wearing whore? Rodger would have been a better person to talk to, but NOOOO you had to follow electric fertile hussy hips! What in God's name were you thinking? Did you even think about our son, my health, your health, our finances, this house, our responsibilities, our reputation? Speaking of which what the fuck were you thinking? Better yet, I don't want to hear it, because nothing you can say right now will even matter at this point. You can't even keep your pecker in your pants. When you decide to put that away and start being a fucking man, then maybe I'll consider talking to you!" Kelly's face was red as she turned away. Aaron's face was flushed with salted tears and unmanageable regret. He loved Kelly so much as his heart was drowned with love and excruciating embarrassment. How could he even convince her of anything now?

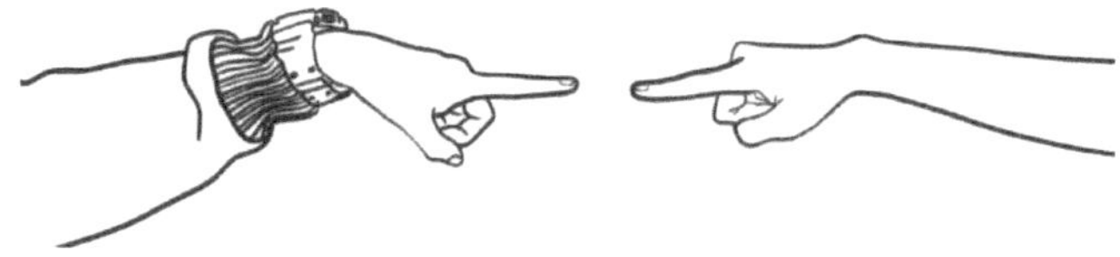

16 AFTERMATH

Three weeks after the fight Aaron had stepped out of St Mary's to get some fresh air. He had just come out of an appointment for his mental health since had been drugged. Soon, a young man with dirty blonde hair stepped out and stood by a shrub not far from Aaron. He was a shorter, scrawnier man than Aaron. His denim coat hung loosely on him. He looked angry. He pulled out a pack of cigarettes smacked the bottom of it. Jolting a few out of the pack the man put the pack up to his lips grasping a cigarette with his mouth and setting the pack down on a concrete ledge. He cupped the open end of the cigarette with his hand and pulled out his zippo lighter. He ran his thumb several times getting a flame. He puffed the butt of the cigarette and made an ember at the end. Aaron was a former smoker. He didn't much care for the smell, however the rush after the fresh smell of a lit cigarette enticed him.

"Hey, buddy, mind if I bum one of those?" asked Aaron.

He picked up the pack he set down, pulled one out, and handed it to Aaron. He held out a lighter, again flicking it several times for a flame. Aaron put his hand over the open end and stuck it to the to the flame to light it making his own ember. Aaron noticed the young man seemed disturbed. As they stood there and sucked the smoke in and exhaling out, Aaron asked "Thanks man, Hospitals suck, don't they?"

"Yeah, I always fucking hate these places. Nothing but pain here." Said the man. Keeping his gaze on the sidewalk.

"Got family in here?" Aaron asked.

"Yeah, a bitch ass cheating whore of a wife and my dingbat pushover sister-in-law," Answered the man.

Aaron was intrigued. "I get yah, buddy. I got something similar going on. Only I was on the other end of it." Aaron replied.

The young man, still not looking up, considered his comment. His thoughts were racing, still focused on his wife's actions. "What, did you ever fuck another man's wife?"

Aaron considered his reply for a moment. Thoughts and memories had begun flashing through his mind. He considered the sun as it set over the mesa to the west of him.

"More like, another man's wife fucked me. In more way than one. Hoooolleeeey shit!" Aaron replied. His mind was distant. Aaron took another puff of the cigarette. Holding it in and letting the smoke curl and twist its way in the air.

The young man puffed his cigarette to the end. Lifting his foot, he smothered the end before tossing it in the garbage. Still focused on the sidewalk he said "We all fuck, and we all get fucked. I guess that's just how life works these days. One minute you find yourself busting your ass, trying to provide a life for your wife. The next minute your she takes off trying to build some new career in a different state, then starts fucking her God damned boss. Shitting on everything you've worked for." The young man stood for a moment in quiet contemplation. He walked off, silently out to the parking lot. Aaron watched as he opened the door and reached into a familiar looking black Jeep Wrangler grabbing a tote bag and walked to the sidewalk next a bus stop. Moments later a bus pulled up. The door opened. He entered and it drove away.

"Who was that guy?" Aaron thought as he turned his gaze in the dying light, towards the Jeep. He approached it. He recognized the license plate. It was Katy's. So, if this was Katy's Jeep, then that means she was here for some reason. Why? Was she sick? Aaron considered for a moment. In a flash, a feeling of dread fell over him. Molly was still here, wasn't she? Something else was going on.

Aaron turned to go inside the hospital and find Katy, she might still be here since Molly was still here. Katy might know the details. He walked thru the doors to the main lobby and looked around. The walls were painted southwest like colors. The smell of the café permeated. Addicts and homeless people were crowding the ER. Then he noticed the ER front desk. He walked toward it regardless thinking of how to form his question when abruptly the elevator doors opened. Katy stepped out, holding a cell phone up to the front of her face. Aaron thought "She is Face Timing someone again? Holy lord will she ever fucking learn to keep conversations private? For the fucking sakes!" Aaron approached her. He could hear the conversation that she was having, it was Arturo on the other end.

"Ok, I'll get back with you when I know more… No, I don't know where James went, he just up and left… OK, I'll call you back later." Katy ended the FaceTime.

"Katy! You're here!" Aaron called out. Katy turned around, surprised. "Aaron!" she said as she approached him.

"Katy, what the hell is going on around here? I was just leaving from a follow up and there was a guy outside who grabbed a bag out of your Jeep and hopped on the bus. Where's Molly?" Aaron asked.

Katy put her hands up to slow him down. She took a deep breath. "Aaron…" She paused.

"Molly came out of the coma from the fight. She's going to be okay. Her and James got into it and well,"

"I need to see Molly, Katy. ASAP!" Aaron interrupted.

"Ok, I'll take you to her. Aaron there's something she must tell you. You're not going to like it. Be gentle with her though, she's literally in a delicate state."

Aaron looked at her in uncertainty. He followed her back to the elevator and down a brightly lit hallway on floor three. After making several turns, they arrived at room 304. Katy paused, took and breath and opened it. They stepped inside. There, lying on a bed was a very visibly bruised and shaken Molly. She looked up at Aaron as he stepped in.

"Molly! What the flying fuck happened to you?" Asked Aaron in hurried concern.

Molly was speechless. She stared sheepishly back at him. A new feeling began to flow though her. Raven. The presence of Raven was starting to seep back in as she entered Molly's body. Raven knew Aaron was there. He had triggered her upmost attention.

"Aaron, your wife… she knows about us now. She knows we belong to each other now." Molly spoke. Aaron looked at her, now clear headed, but still confused.

"Molly, I don't have a full understanding of what's going on here, but there is no US!" Aaron approached her. "I don't know what you've done to me, Molly, but ends NOW. Kelly is my wife. I love her. I would never ever…"

Molly sat up in her bed and looked deep into Aarons eyes. "You did, Aaron. WE did, and now, we have something to show for our newfound love." Molly replied in a sinister voice. "Aaron, I have something wonderful to tell you, for US!" Molly leaned in closer. "Aaron…" Molly chirped as she smiled. "Honey, we're going to have a baby!'

Aaron felt a rush of panic flow over his body. His heart sank. Something deep in his mind exploded in a rush of sudden memories flooded his mind. He remembered. The embrace, the kissing, the thrusting, the dripping sweat, and exchange of passionate sex flowed thru his mind like a deadly curse. This woman was out of control! She had no boundaries, no respect, no common sense whatsoever!

17 AARON TELLS KELLY

Aaron paced around, his head in a fog, in the ER waiting room. He had texted Kelly to come down. What was his next move? What will he tell Kelly when he got home? What will their life be like now? Will Molly keep the baby? She sure didn't seem like an abortion was an option for her. What would this mean for him? So many questions flowed through his brain. The doors to the patient area opened, Katy stepped out and approached him. "They are going to finalize her paperwork and set her up for release, probably within the hour. I'll get her home. What about you? If you want a ride, and can handle the tension, I'll take you home." Aaron considered it for a moment. A ride, stuck in a jeep for 15 minutes with her, with Molly. After what she's done, after what they have done, how could he stomach it? She had… raped him. She had done this to him, and now, she was pregnant with his child? How did all of this happen so quickly? How had his life gone down the tubes so instantly?

Aaron had a surge of energy, a mystical energy, flow through his body. He sensed a presence nearby. Kelly. Aaron and Kelly had always had a strong spiritual bond, like most other married couples. Because Aaron and Kelly possessed highly elevated spiritual abilities, the bond between was much stronger than most. He was always able to close his eyes, focus on his wife, and feel her as if she were standing right next to him. It didn't matter where he was. It didn't matter where she was. She was always there, right beside him. That energy, that sensation flow through him now. Kelly. She was here now. He could feel her. He sensed her approach. The doors to the ER slid open, and Kelly, with her long locks of flowing red her walked thru. She hadn't seen him yet, although she was looking frantically around the room for him. He looked upon her lovingly, yet sorrowful. He couldn't bring himself to call out to her. The pain of what happened ate away at his heart like a ravenous beast. Eventually her eyes found him. She stopped in her tracks for a moment, then approached him. Aaron couldn't speak. She stood before him, as beautiful as the day they first met. They considered each other for a moment, and quickly without expectation, Kelly threw her arms around him. She pulled him into her. She kissed him deeply. Aaron was amazed she wasn't slapping him silly.

"Aaron, I've had a lot of time to consider what has happened a few weeks ago. I'm still hurt by what happened, but I still love you and I'm not giving up on you. I'm not giving up on us. I've learned a lot about what happened, I've overheard the rumors at the office. I know it's not true. I feel it, Aaron. Molly, that thing, orchestrated all of this. I know she drugged you. I feel it in my gut what the vile woman has done. Molly will get hers, Aaron. You and I may have a lot of damage to repair, but the circumstances of how this happened changed my perspective."

"Kelly…" Aaron interjected

"That little bitch will pay, I saw and felt something else going on here, Aaron. Molly… that wasn't Molly back there Aaron. I sense something inside. Something horrible. Something…"

"Kelly… Molly… is pregnant." Aaron said.

Kelly looked deep into Aaron's eyes. She knew that what Aaron had just revealed to her must be the most painful thing he had ever told her. She felt that pain in him. Aaron looked back into her eyes, but the shock and anger he expected to see there didn't materialize.

"I'm sorry, Aaron." Kelly looked to the floor for a moment, then back up at Aaron. "Molly's desire for you is true, that's' on her, and I hate her for it. But at the same time, the more urgent need must be dealt with. The baby, we need to protect it."

Aaron looked at his wife in shock. This is not at all the response Aaron expected to hear. Where was the outrage? Where was the anger? Where was the yelling and screaming, he expected to come from her?

"How do we do that, Kelly?" asked Aaron, sheepishly. Aaron thought for a moment as realization of what was being said hit home. Was Molly possessed? If so, why didn't Aaron, who himself was a moderately powerful clairvoyant, not sensed this himself. Was this possession so elusive? Did it have its own designs on Aaron? What was the path being laid before them?

Kelly looked around the room for a moment, then back at Aaron. "I have an old friend from college, Aaron. Her name is Haley. Haley Higgins, she was my dorm mate. She studied spirituality and demonology in her free time back in those days. I think she works as one of those ghost hunters for some TV show now. I've seen her on their time and again. She has a lot of knowledge in this kind of stuff, and she owes me a lot of favors." Kelly made an uneasy chuckle Aaron considered the gravity of what was being suggested.

"What, are you suggesting exorcism? I know a few things about that from when I was in Catholic school. Not just anybody can do that, the church must be involved. It's not a game."

"Haley has connections, she's seen a lot of things in her day. I don't know exactly how she could help, but I still have her number. She's our best shot." Kelly replied.

Aaron thought more on the situation. What was happening here? Kelly had literally just hours before had been berating him in his office, stormed out to confront Molly, and from the looks of things, gave her a proper beat down. How was it now that she is looking to help Molly? Aaron realized however this wasn't about Molly, it was about the baby growing inside of her. A baby he only just found out about an hour ago. A baby. "There's a baby involved in all this mess now." Aaron thought to himself. What kind of mess had he gotten himself into?

The doors to the triage room burst open. Out stepped Katy, carrying a purse that didn't belong to her. A few moments later, Molly exited, looking more than a little banged up. Kelly turned to look at her, look at the work she had done to her. Molly slowly raised her head to meet her. She froze in her spot, not expecting to see the woman who had caused this. A rush of fear flowed through her like a raging river. The two women gazed at each other, not speaking. The tension in the room was thick enough to be cut with a knife. Katy looked back and forth between her sister and Kelly, fearing another outbreak. It didn't come. For the moment, Raven didn't show her presence. For the moment, this was Molly in her truest form. Kelly felt it. Kelly stepped forward and confronted the true Molly this time. Molly stepped back, accidently backing into the wall and kept her eyes glued to the ground. She was afraid to face this woman again.

"Molly, what you have done here... unthinkable.

Unforgivable." Kelly spoke in a calm stern voice. She took a stepped closer to Molly. Molly quivered in fear. Kelly reached out and grabbed Molly's chin and held it up like a small disobedient child being disciplined. She lifted her head and looked sharply into her eyes. "Now you listen here, Molly, and you listen good." Kelly spoke with authority. "You and I have unfinished business, but there is another matter that comes first. I know about the baby. I know. For now, the baby is the priority, and that… vile thing that inhabits you needs to be banished. I know the influence it has over you, but I also knows it's playing to your true desires, so don't think you're in the clear because of it. You're NOT." Kelly said glaring at Molly.

"Raven will never let me go. I invited it in with some stupid Ouija board when I was a teenager. I thought I got rid of it. It's hunted me down, and now it has me." Molly whispered slowly under her breath.

Kelly grabbed Molly's shoulders and gave them an authoritative squeeze, being ever cautious not to make this look like another assault.

"Molly Jenson, I despise you. You're a despicable excuse for a human being. For the sake of MY husband's baby, I'm going to help you, and you're going to take that help, and when we get that figured out, you're going to leave us the fuck alone. We will deal with this first."

Kelly could feel the quivering in Molly's' body. She let her go and took a step back. She took a deep breath as she looked back and forth between Molly and Katy. "You'll be hearing back from me soon. Very soon. Both of you." Katy, who had been standing there dumbfounded, slowly nodded her head. Kelly turned to Katy and approached her.

"You'll start with sage, there's a metaphysical store not far from the mall. Go there and speak with Brandy, the blond girl behind the counter. Give her this specific list. She'll know what you need." Kelly produced a small notebook and began writing a list also including palo santo. She tore of the page and handed it to Katy. "There's incense on that too, make sure you get those specific ones, and when you get home, place salt at the base of your doors and windows AFTER YOU burn these until you can hardly breathe with all windows and doors open." Katy looked at her confused, she wasn't too familiar with this metaphysical stuff. No matter, she wasn't about to argue with this raging redhead.

Kelly looked back and forth from Katy to Molly one last time, and then gave Molly one final glare. She turned away and called for Aaron to follow her out to the van. After what felt like the longest day, they were going home. They walked out the door. They were gone.

Katy and Molly walked of the hospital after her discharge. They didn't speak. They entered Katy's Jeep, started the engine, and began the drive home. Katy turned up some weird electronic death metal music that she used to distract her. Molly sat in quiet contemplation as they drove home. She began to think of the events of the day. How did she get to this point? She started they day excited about being Aaron's new girlfriend. She had worked hard to plan this out. Then all the sudden she's getting her ass beaten to a pulp by a furious angry redhead in Molly's own workspace. Then… what happened next? She couldn't remember. She didn't know what led her to end up lying in a hospital bed with her sister, and her husband, who was supposed to still be back home in Michigan, and now he was gone. He left her. The idea rang in her mind. James was gone.

"Fuck James, he was always a childish loser to begin with. I don't know what I ever saw in him anyway."

Molly blurted out.

Katy turned to her and shot her a nasty glance. "I fucking told you this was a bad idea, Molly. You've been pulling this shit since we were kids. You're the fucking little princess who gets treated with kid gloves and I always got the shit end of it. Now look what its cost you." Katy replied, angrily.

Molly shot her an angry glance. "It wasn't fucking me in fucking control, KATY!" replied Molly. "Raven is back and this time she…"

"SHUT THE FUCK UP, MOLLY!" Katy yelled, as the Jeep began to swerve. The angry metal music was beginning to fuel the fire and rage that had been building up inside her today. "You've been pulling this bullshit since we were kids, and mom and dad let you get away with it because you're the prettier and smarter one. Kelly had a point. Your lust and greed is on YOU. Your desire for Aaron is on YOU. That's your fucking fault. Raven only gave you the tools to act on your urges. It used you because you are a selfish, entitled, weak little rotten BRAT!" The scowl on Katy's face was one of pent-up rage. Katy turned to her and stared her in the face when they came to the next stop light. "AND YOU'RE FUCKING PREGNANT NOW!? AND YOUR HUSBAND FUCKING LEFT YOU? WHAT THE FUCK ARE YOU GOING TO DO NOW?" Katy yelled with a sense of pent-up fury.

"Katy, please, I've lost so much today." Molly whimpered. Tears began to roll down her eyes. She could feel her soul breaking down.

"Fuck you Molly! I've had enough of your pity potty bullshit!" Yelped Katy.

Molly had never seen her sister this angry at her before. She never once had stood up to her. Just like James, Molly had always known how to manipulate her older sister. She could always sway her to her will. Today was a day of reckoning, it seemed. For the moment, she had never felt so alone. Her husband was gone. Aaron seemed out of reach. Even her sister seemed to hate her.

"And what about Aaron?" Katy asked with contempt. "He's been such a good friend to me since I started working there. Our freindship will never be the same, and you know I don't make good friends easily." Katy began to cry as they pulled into the driveway of her home. She pulled the key out of the ignition, stepped out and slammed the door shut. As the two women began to walk up the cobbled stones that led to the door of Katy's house, Katy paused and turned back to Molly.

"You don't have a home in Michigan to go home to anymore, Molly. James owns everything. You have nothing left to claim there. I'm going to be honest with you, SIS! Arturo and I have no intention of hearing a baby cry all night for months on end." Katy thought for a moment, as a slight sheet of rain began falling down on her.

"I'll give you time to figure your shit out. You WILL be finding your own place. You are not going to bring that shit into my own home. This is on YOU now. Get your shit together. Find a place of your own. I don't care if you stay here or go back to Michigan. I don't need your fucking manipulative bullshit in my house. Get the fuck upstairs and go to bed. You have a lot of shit to think about, and I wouldn't put much faith in you staying at Origin much longer. Aaron has every ability to fire your ass and send you packing."

Molly thought for a moment. A tinge of Raven began to flow though her again. She glared at her sister.
"Then he would be the fucking , wouldn't he? Firing the mother of his child? Putting her on the streets? Letting them suffer?"
Molly felt a surge of electric like oppression flow through her. Molly took several steps closer to her sister. Raven was back. Raven was in control again.
"We wouldn't want that now, would we?" asked Molly,

with a new sense of confidence. "Aaron would never let me go. He will never let me go."

Thunder struck in the distance. There was a lightning storm brewing over the Sandia mountains. The outline of its hulking shape looked ominous. Evil. Katy looked at her sister with a new sense of fear. She knew that Raven was the one who was speaking. She felt the urge to kick Molly out of the house at that very instant. She could not do it. She thought back to words that their mother had always told since they were children. "Family sticks through thick and thin, kiddies!" Katy relented.

"Just fucking go to bed, Molly." Katy said, as she sighed.
Molly passed her up as she made her way to the door, stepped up on to the covered patio. She paused for a moment and turned back to her sister. There was a new sense of power that Molly felt inside of her. Raven was influencing her mind, controlling her. Lightning struck nearby, close enough to send vibrations through the house. Katy saw the reflection in her sisters' eyes. The reflection however wasn't natural. Molly's eyes were completely black. No pupils, no whites, only cold black stone.
Katy walked up the steps, in front of her sister. "Molly, there's lightning. Get inside. C'mon" Katy spoke. She wasn't sure if what she what had seen in Molly's eyes was real or just an illusion of the night sky and lighting. Molly didn't move an inch. As katy stood before her, in a stance of confrontation, Molly reached down and ran had right hand over her thighs, then ran it in circles over her stomach.

"This, Katy, is true power. This is how you get what you want." Molly fingers began to tug at her tight, at her clothing, revealing her soft skin. She rolled her black eyes at her sister. "This… is how you control your man." Molly spoke, with a sense of seduction.
"Aaron is MY man. MY man. MY MAN!" Molly

emphasized, as she yelled. There was a flowerpot of marigolds growing next to the door. Molly began to pace franticly, then kicked the pot over into the dirt outside of the patio. She began to scream into the night. She screamed out for Aaron. The scream didn't sound human. There was something… un-earthly to her voice.

Molly continued to pleasure herself, running her hands between her thighs, slowly. Katy was appalled and absolutely outraged! What the hell was she doing? Her own sister, rubbing herself on the porch of her own home? It was raining and lighting struck flashing a light that showed a strong reflection in the window, next to the porch. Katy noted the reflection of both her and her sister. For a moment, Katy saw Raven. It was brief, yet clear. Raven had completely replaced the image of what should have been Molly. What she saw now was dark, and evil. It looked back at her. There was an evil, toothy grin. Katy knew that this had to be stopped. She stepped forward toward what she thought was her sister. She raised her hand and slapped her so hard and fast and pushed her head to the side.

Molly stood, motionless, staring at her sister. She stepped forward. "You're a coward, Katy. You're too weak to step up and take what you want. The child that grows inside me, is my prize. I earned it. I worked for it, and Aaron will now forever be tied to me, to us. Our child, and I'll never let him go."

Katy thought back to her youth. She remembered her own anger when she saw how tortured her sister had become. The endless nights of crying, the screaming, the tortured nightmares, the memories that had not been her own. The memories of a young girl named Raven who, in the spring of 1976, was drugged, kidnapped, raped, and beaten to death by an unsuspecting attractive appearing man. A man who left her body desecrated. A man who performed satanic rituals on his victims graves. A psychopath.

Katy had gone into her parent's garage at the time, grabbed a sledgehammer, and hopped in her father's truck. She drove down to the cemetery where her sister had fooled around with her so called friends for a night of drinking and conjuring. She searched until the sun began to go down. She knew what she was looking for. She found it. Before her stood the dilapidated and vandalized head stone of Raven DeBardot. Now she saw the source of the evil. Her grave had been cursed! Etched in the stone over Ravens' grave, an inverted pentagram. Someone sick did this. Was it her killer? Katy didn't know, but she knew one thing. The evil monument must come down. She felt it in her bones. She took the sledgehammer and struck a definitive blow with all her might. The weather-stained headstone came crashing down. She struck again, directly on the pentacle. It shattered. From the distance, lightning struck. Thunder rolled. Rain began to fall. She didn't know why she felt that this course was action was the way to go, but in her bones, she felt an energy. Miles down the road, Molly, whom had been sleeping on the couch, awoke. She lurched and sat up quickly. Molly had been freed. Raven was gone.

Katy came back to the present. A tear ran down her face. She feared what her sister was encompassed by. She feared the control that Raven had over her sister. Katy was powerless, this time she had no overgrown headstone to smash with a sledgehammer and force this tortured spirit out of her sister. This time there was only Molly. The headstone had been a talisman of sort, entrapping the spirit of the tortured soul. Now, Molly had become that talisman. Raven had been seeking her out all this time, following her, looking for energy for which to bind herself to her. The evil of Pennhurst had given Raven that energy, and at Pennhurst, Raven had Molly exactly where she wanted her. Katy felt this truth right down to her bones. She feared she had lost her sister forever.

Katy and Molly entered the house. Katy stopped in the middle of the living room and turned around to her sister. "I won't put up with this, Molly. I won't put up with your games. Not again. Not anymore." She circled around the couch, mindlessly adjusting the blankets that covered it. Arturo stepped in from the kitchen and looked at the two women, standing there, face to face.

"What's going on?" Arturo mumbled, as a chewed on an apple. He looked back and forth between them.

The dark, sinister look in Molly's eyes told him everything. Something bad was about to go down.

"Molly, I won't have Raven here. Not in this house. Not this time, and I won't be having a baby here, crying all through the night, keeping everybody up." Katy took several steps towards her sister. "You have one week to pack your things and find your own place. "I won't play Ravens game again."

Molly looked coldly at her sister; she tilted her head to the side.

"Fine! I can find an apartment by the end of the week. I'm going to make a nice cozy little life myself, Aaron, and our baby, and you won't get to be a part of that." Molly replied coldly.

"You arrogant little bitch! Do you really think Aaron is going to want anything to do with you after what you and your little friend have done? I'll be surprised if you'll even have a job to go to, tomorrow!"

Molly chuckled. "Do you really think Aaron would be so foolish as to throw the mother of his child out on the streets? No..." Molly stepped toward her sister. "I have Aaron exactly where I want him. You see, I'm the better deal now, Katy. I was always the better deal, and I'm going to give him this child and so many more." Molly turned and stepped to the living room window and gazed out of it. Arturo stood stupidly as the scene unfolded before him.

"And as for Kelly, well…" Molly turned back and gazed at Katy.

"You're absolutely insane!" Katy yelled. She began to pace. "Aaron will have you fired and banned from the campus altogether! You have no idea the power that man has! You have no idea the sway he has with the execs over there!" Katy exclaimed. "It's a wonder you're not in jail now for what you pulled on him!"

Arturo looked on at the pair as if watching a soap opera. He remained speechless.

Molly circled around her sister. "And that power belongs to me now." She began to rub her belly, gesturing to the child within her. "Never forget… sis… I ALWAYS get what I want." She turned and began to walk away towards the stairs to her room. She stopped and turned back to her sister. This time the blackness in her eyes shown back at her like vast pits of blackness. "Raven ALWAYS gets what she wants." Molly turned to Arturo as the apple core he had been holding in his hand fell to the floor. She considered him for a moment, said nothing, then walked up the stairs and shut her door.

Katy let herself plop onto the couch. She put her face into the palms of her hands, as her long blonde hair fell to the side. Arturo came and sat down beside her. He placed a loving arm on her shoulder. "What the hell is all of this? When did a baby become involved? What's up with Aaron? What the hell happened today? Who the hell is this Raven? Why didn't you tell me this before Katy?" Katy took in a deep breath. She sighed. She turned to her husband. "Art, honey, it's time I told you something about our past, something that goes back to our childhood. This is going to be a hard pill to swallow but bear with me." Katy said. She took in a deep breath. "Art, Molly is possessed. A spirit once possessed her she summoned in a graveyard, back when we were teenagers in Michigan. Its name is Raven. Raven tormented her then and it's tormenting her now." Katy stood up and began to pace. "Ravens headstone was cursed, and defiled by someone, maybe her killer. So, I destroyed it. I thought Molly was freed from Raven. It made it worse. Raven followed her for years now. She showed her ugly face at Pennhurst. Proving me wrong about her possessiveness. Arturo listened on in shock! He wasn't questioning it. He knew it was true. The recorder from the trip they had taken didn't lie. That thing was in control of his sister-in-law now, and he had looked into it's cold, black eyes.

"Now I don't know what to do. I don't know how to help her. She can't stay here. I don't know what she's capable of. There may be no saving Molly from Raven this time." Katy sat down again. She began to sob. Arturo threw his arms around her.

18 STALKER

Molly was back at work. She was talking with one of the chemists. "What the fuck do you mean he took a few weeks of leave? Who the hell does he think he is?" Molly cried out, as she learned from her coworker, Jill, that Aaron had taken some time off.

"Whoa, chill Molly! He's the boss, not you! Just because you're sleeping with him now doesn't mean you control him!"

The staff all knew now what had happened between Aaron, Molly, and Kelly. News spreads like wildfire here. Many were divided as to who the was the aggressor. Some believed Aaron had been hitting on Molly since day one, most believed it was Molly who started it. All believed that regardless, Aaron and Molly were an item now, in their eyes.

Molly plopped into her office chair, crossed her arms, and pouted like a child who lost her binky. Molly had to come up with a new plan, and fast. While she sat there sulking, and contemplating a plan, she thought of how to get to him. "That's it!" Molly thought to herself. If Aaron won't go to her, Molly will go to him. She doesn't care what Kelly thinks. She will be pushed aside, one way or another.

A voice in her head began to speak. It was Raven. "Make her leave him!" Raven said. Molly turned to the mirror next to her desk. Raven was there. "Make her think he wants you more than her." Raven said. Molly began to realize something, two things. For starters, Ravens ability to speak to her was getting stronger. Her connection to Raven was strengthening. She felt her more, saw her more, felt her more. The other realization… a plan.

Raven looked at the clock, it was almost 4 and time to leave for the day. She logged off her desktop, threw an empty bag of chocolate chip cookies that was lying on her desk in her trash can, collected her purse and stood up. She was determined now. This time, this new plan will work. She knew what to do next, but she needed to be cautious. She looked at the desk calendar next to her, her idea needed to be enacted today.

Molly walked out of the lab, down the hallway and out to the parking lot. She opened her car door and stepped inside. Anticipation ran through her veins. She started the car and began the journey to Aaron's house. Molly had a good sense of intuition. Something told her now was the time act. The drive was short, only ten minutes. She entered Aaron's neighborhood and found a place to park, several houses down the street from Aaron's house.

Molly got out of the car and began to walk toward the house. She stood close behind a wall of shrubbery that separated his house from the neighbors. She peeked over. "Good, Kelly's car isn't here, and there's Aaron's truck!" she thought to herself. She took a good look around the area. Nobody was outside. Molly collected her thoughts and remembered conversations she and Aaron had in the past. If he was home, he always had the back door unlocked. Molly remembered that he was always was back and forth between his house and the separate garage in the back, usually because he was working on his truck or bike. Molly's intention was to get inside.

Molly's plan was simple. If the back door was unlocked, as Aaron said it usually was while he was home, then that was her key. All she needed to do was ensure Aaron wasn't present. She would slip in, remove her panties, toss them somewhere that Kelly would find them, and slip out. If Kelly found the panties, she would suspect that she and Aaron had slept together again. That would make her furious enough, hateful enough to kick him out of the house. He would be hopeless. That would make him damn near homeless, and Molly would be there to save him, with open arms! Molly knew that they had cameras watching the property. She also knew that there were blind spots. Aaron always wanted a new camera overlooking the side yard entrance. The current one had shorted out a few weeks ago, and Aaron hadn't had a chance to replace it. She had seen him view it on his phone several times while bringing him documents and coffee. Sure enough, one could easily skirt the outer wall of the house, duck behind the row of rose bushes that Kelly maintained, and get to the back door, sight unseen. A new sense of courage hit her, and she made her move.

Making it to the back patio, Molly peaked through the window. Seeing as nobody was in sight, she put her hand on the doorknob anticipating an unlocked door. She very gently twisted and pulled the door open. She stopped, carefully listening for anyone around. She noticed loud snoring coming from one of the bedrooms. "Ah Aaron must be asleep!" Molly thought to herself. "This is too easy!"

If Aaron were asleep, she could pull of her plan a little more convincingly. A sudden urge hit her. She wanted to see him., hear even, maybe even… feel him. She slowly moved down the hallway towards his bedroom, where she can hear the rough, tired snoring echoing. Inch by inch she made her way, until she was at the doorway. Molly was beginning to believe, Aaron belonged to her now. She peeked her head around the corner of the door frame. There, lying on the bed, was the man of her dreams. He was out like as light. Molly sensed that she could dumb a five gallon of ice water on him, and he wouldn't wake up.

Molly was getting aroused. Molly slowly entered the room. She stood before the bed, looking upon whom she was convinced was her man. Her breathing began to quicken. Swiftly, with one hand, she pulled up her skirt and grasped the side of her panties. She began to pull them down and remove them. The black thong panties slipped down and fell to her ankles. She stepped out of them. Her arousal was at an all-time high. "Time to pet the kitty!" Molly thought to herself, enthusiastically. She reached her hands down thru her skirt and began to finger herself. One finger at first, she started with. Soon she added a second, and a third. The sensations escalated within a matter of minutes. Her body quivered! Thin come erupted from her, dripping down her leg and on the floor. She looked down upon Aaron who was still sleeping, lustfully. She took the thong and wiped herself dry putting her scent even more on the fabric, just for Aaron. She stepped to the side of the bed, as Aaron continued to snore. She looked down upon him, taking in every inch of his masculine body. She craved him so badly. She bent down, leaned into him, smelled him. She reached her hand out and ran a finger through a lock of his greying hair. She lowered herself and kissed him on the forehead.

"Soon, my love." Molly spoke softly. She ran her finger over the sleeve of his black tee shirt, in a way as not to wake him. Her desire for him brought strong emotions. She quivered again. She stood back up and began to gently fold the black thong panties she held in her hand. She placed them softly next to Aaron's chest. Molly gently ran her finger over his arm hair. She let the moment sink deeply into her mind, she was invigorated. She stood back up and began to back away. Molly looked around and saw that the closet door was open. She turned to it and approached. Inside, a neatly aligned row of black tee shirts seemed to call to her. Molly reached inside and selected one. She pulled it off the hanger and studied it. It was a Harley Davidson shirt, one of Aarons favorites. On it, a young brunette sat straddled across the seat of a dark red motorcycle. Molly liked it. It excited her. She would keep this as her little love token. She folded the shirt tightly and swept it under her arm. Next to her, she noticed a pair of earrings sitting on a dresser. She studied them for a moment. They were small gold loop earrings, with three small dark blue golden orbs attached. She picked them up. She liked them. Molly slipped them into the pocket of her white blouse as she made her way toward the back door.

As she approached it, she heard the slamming of a car door in the driveway in the driveway. Kelly had come home early from work. Molly needed to think quick! She wasn't close enough to the back door to make a quick exit. She looked around the living room and noticed a tall bookshelf in the corner, with enough of a gap between the back of it and the earth tone wall behind it. Keys could be heard turning the lock of the front door. Molly quickly moved to the bookcase, and shimmied her way behind it, concealing herself. She peaked around the corner as the door opened. Kelly entered and set her purse down on a table next to the door. Molly watched as Kelly began to undo her pinned up hair, letting fall over her shoulders.

"Aaron, I'm home." Kelly said lazily. She wasn't feeling as perky an excited to see her husband as much these days. Considering recent events, she wasn't very enthusiastic about anything she did.

The snoring from the hall ceased. She heard shuffling. Aaron spoke. "I hi Kelly, I was just taking a nap. I needed a little shut eye." He replied. Kelly didn't respond. Molly watched as Kelly made her way to the kitchen, opened a cabinet, and pulled out a wine glass. She proceeded to open the refrigerator, where she had pulled out a wine bottle, she had placed there earlier that morning to chill. She opened it, filled her glass, and took a sip.

Molly looked upon Kelly with contempt in her heart. She despised this woman, who was her obstacle in her way of taking her place at Aaron's side. Hatred filled Molly's heart. She began scanning the room, looking for any blunt object she could use to strike at Kelly, should she be discovered. Kelly began to make her way down the hallway to the bedroom.

"That's right, bitch. Go find the little present I left for you on the bed." Molly thought to herself.

Kelly had intended to go check on Aaron but decided to turn and go to the bathroom instead and freshen herself up. Aaron sat up, wiping the sleep from his eyes. He swept his legs across the bed, inadvertently knocking the thong to the floor. He looked down and picked it up. He studied them.

"That's funny? I don't remember Kelly liking this style of panties. She never was in to but floss. Why would she have them now?" Aaron wondered. He stepped over to the laundry basket and tossed them inside. He began to wonder, began to walk away but stopped, and turned around. He looked down at the sexy black panties.

"No, it couldn't be…" Aaron considered. "Kelly would never…"

The toilet flushed, Kelly opened the door of the bathroom and stepped out. She dried her hands with a towel, then stepped over to the laundry basket and tossed it in, covering the panties. Aaron looked at her, curiously. He studied her attire. It was a typical semi casual business blouse and long grey skirt, nothing out of the ordinary for her regular dress for work. He watched as she removed her clothing, to put on some comfortable active wear and a t-shirt for the evening. He watched as she bent over to pull up her pants. He noticed her otherwise unassuming panties rode up the cheeks of her buttocks. I visualized her in that thong. He began to become aroused. He knew there was no chance to make love to her. She wouldn't have it, not in this current state of affairs. He turned and began to walk down the hallway, looking for his chilled beer glass in the freezer.

Molly watched him come into the living room, then turn to the kitchen. Once again, her loins burned with desire. Molly wanted him so very badly. She craved him. Raven craved him.

"Soon, Aaron. Soon." she thought. Moly considered her next step. She would have to plan her next move more carefully. She didn't know what had become of her panties, but she knew they would soon play a role. Molly exited from behind the shelf and quietly made her way out the back door. She slipped quickly into the night, with a plan forming in her mind. She knew that she had to make her presence known in Aaron's life. Molly was going to move in, whether he liked it or not.

Molly returned home and began to pace in her bedroom. She removed her blouse and hung it in the closet. She then turned and considered Aarons Harley shirt and the earrings that she had placed on the bed. Tomorrow, she would wear them. Tomorrow she would establish her place at Aarons side through the eyes of her coworkers. Molly sat down on the bed, thinking. She looked over at her nightstand, seeing a picture of herself from her younger days, as a teenager. She picked up the photo and plan flashed in her mind. She was moving in, literally ASAP. "Don't forget some photo's" She thought.

The next morning, Molly awoke with a renewed sense of purpose. She pulled on a loose-fitting pair of blue jeans since her belly was pooched and Aarons black Harley shirt. She put on Kelly's earrings. She spritzed a dash of perfume on her neck, grabbed her purse, stuffed a small photo album in it and then hurried down the stairs. Katy was up, eating breakfast. She looked at Molly and her attire. This was not molly's normal outfit for work.

"Where did you get that shirt? I didn't know you were a Harley fan. You've always been a sport bike girls, Yamahas, and shit." Katy spoke.

Molly turned to her sister. "It's Aarons. We have many common interests, that's what lovers do. He gave it to me the last time we made love."

Katy almost spilled her coffee. "The last time… What? When did you…" Kelly said, but Molly interrupted.

"We have a baby coming, and lately I've been super in the mood. Aaron has been taking care of that for me." Molly replied. Katy looked at her sister confused. Considering recent events, she could not wrap her head around the situation. Was Aarons still screwing her sister? Was he actually with her now? Molly waved at her sister as she stepped out the door and headed to work. She made one single stop before arriving, a local motorcycle shop. Inside, she began to browse. She found what she was looking for, a black chained leather riding wallet, just like Aarons. She purchased it, transferred her belongings into the card sleeves and put it on. When she got back in her car, she took a pair of black riding sunglasses over her face. She considered herself in the rearview mirror. Her plan, in her mind was flawless. They would see her walk in, wearing Aarons beloved shirt. They would question why she had it, and they would question why she had Kelly's beloved earrings. She would tell them that she had was moving in with him, that Kelly left him. Kelly thought about Aaron, and how she was going to get to him. He had no choice in her mind. They have a child on the way, and if he ever wants to see the child, he will come to her.

Molly walked into the office building like she owned the place. She approached Wayne, whom had a set of keys to Aaron's office. He looked her over a couple of times.

"Damn girl, you lookin' too fine in that…Aaron's shirt?" He glanced up at her earrings that sparkled in the bright florescent light. He could see only one reason for this. Aaron and Molly really were together.

"Can you unlock Aaron's office please? He asked me to pick up a few things for him, so he can get a few things done tonight after we have dinner."

"Uhh, yeah sure, Molly, I gotcha!" Wayne replied. He stepped over to Aaron's office door and unlocked it. "So uh, you and Aaron are really a thing now?" he asked.

Molly turned to him, looked into his eyes. "Isn't it wonderful? He and I are so happy together! With the baby on the way, we are starting a new life together, and I am going to become his loving bride." Molly replied. She turned to walk into Aaron's office. Wayne looked at her dumbfounded.

"So, curious, what happened to Kelly? Did she leave him?" Asked Wayne.

Molly stopped dead in her tracks, turned around and approached him. She looked at him with dark intent, almost furious. "That whiney little bitch is done for. Just you wait and see." she said, as she turned back and continued inside. Wayne looked at her as she walked away. "I guess it's all true!" he thought, as he walked away and pressed on collecting printer paper to restock the offices equipment.

Molly swung around Aaron's desk, swiping her hand slowly over his chair. She pulled it out and slowly sat down, feeling his energy, his power flowing through her. This was his office, and what's his, is also hers. She swung around and looked at a row of pictured on his cabinet. She selected a picture or Aaron and Kelly from their wedding day. She considered for a moment, then removed it from the frame. She tore off the half of the picture with Kelly in it. She inserted a picture of herself, adorned in a short black skirt dress and arranged it to appear as if it was Aaron and Molly together. She replaced it on the shelf. Her process had begun!

She proceeded to her own department and began her day. Everywhere there were looks, gazes. Roger approached her and handed her a handful of files for her to work on. He looked her over, deeply saddened by the turn of events. Aaron and Kelly, even though she herself didn't work there, were a staple in this place. How had things gone so wrong? They loved each other; everybody saw it. Now this? Molly?

How did she just swing on in and take Kelly's place? Roger looked at Molly in a new light now, no longer the bright young go getter he had met. She was a home wrecker. He knew it.

Molly turned to Roger. "Oh Roger, Aaron wants me working cut of his office and handling some of his duties while he's gone. I'll be taking my work in there now, thank you." She said as she grabbed the stack of files.

Roger looked at her in shock. Aaron's office was iconic! Everybody went there to see Aaron, not Molly. What had he done to make such a decision? What had she done? He nodded as a walked away. He was still her trainer and supervisor, but if Aaron made that call, so be it.

The rest of the day was spent doing her busy work, her feet up on Aaron's desk. She contemplated her next move. Tonight. Tonight, would be the night she made her move. She we leave work early, knowing Aaron's routine. Aaron wouldn't be home right now. Thursday is shopping day for Aaron and Kelly; they wouldn't be home for a while. She looked down into her purse, at the stack of photographs she has accumulated over the years. They will have a new home now.

Molly finished her day, and asked Wayne to lock up as she walked down the hallway to exit the building. AS she sat in her car, she pulled out a shiny silver key she had taken from a desk drawer in Aarons office. It was the key to Aaron's home, to her home as she saw it. She started the car and drove away, towards Aaron's neighborhood. She parked down the street where she had before. She went around the back yard, opened the door, and stepped inside. She carried with her a purse, and a small duffle bag with her some of her belongings. It contained socks, panties, a variety of sex toys, and toiletries. She made her way to the master bedroom. She looked at a pair of dressers arranged in the corner of the room and began opening drawers. She found a drawer that suited her, Kelly's own drawer of similar items. She emptied the contents onto the floor and began carefully arranging her own belongings inside. Item by item she carefully lines up her socks and panties. After another search she found another drawer, this one containing Kelly's own toys. Those too went to the floor. Molly neatly placed her own inside.

She proceeded to walk up and down the main hallway, considering the pictures on the wall. Anything that had Kelly in it was removed and replaced with a picture of her own. Molly's plan was in her mind perfect. Kelly would find the pictures, explore the drawers. Molly would write a note for Aaron and leave it on the table.

"Baby, I'm so glad you asked me to live with you. I've started decorating! You'll love it. I'll see you when you get home, I love you -Molly"

She used the restroom to relieve herself. After finishing, she washed her hands and looked in the mirror. Raven stared back at her.

"The child is the key, Molly. He won't abandon the child." Raven said.

Molly stared back. A smirk formed on her face. Aaron won't toss the mother of his child out in the streets she thought. Molly's vision was falling into place.

As Molly walked down the hallway and entered the living room, the lock on the front door turned. The door opened. In walked a young boy, maybe 13, carrying a backpack. His fluffy dark hair ruffled in the breeze as she stepped in. He looked up and saw Molly standing there on the other side of the couch. He was shocked and surprised at her presence. He recognized the woman. It was the woman from his father's office! He wondered what she was doing here.

"Uhm, hi!" Said the boy awkwardly.

"Well, hello there, Daniel! It's good to see you!" replied Molly with a smile.

"Uhm, you're the lady from Dads office! What are you doing here? Where's my mom and dad?" he asked.

"Oh, they will be along shortly. I suspect I'll be staying here for a while, Danny." Molly replied.

"Staying here? Why?" asked the boy.

Molly approached him, placed a hand on his head and ruffled his hair. The other hand went down over her belly, rubbing it gently. "Well, you see, you're going to have a little brother or sister soon. I'm going to be mommy to both of you!"

"But I already have a mom. What's going on here?" he asked.

"Well, Danny… your dad and I…" Molly was interrupted. The door opened again; Aaron stepped in followed by Kelly. Both were carrying bags of groceries. They both dropped them to the floor when they saw Molly standing there. They stood there in shock and silence, staring at each other.

"WHAT THE FUCK ARE YOU DOING HERE? HOW THE HELL DID YOU GET IN?" Aaron demanded.

"YOU FUCKING WHORE! I CAN'T BELIEVE THIS! GET YOUR HANDS OFF MY SON AND GET THE FUCK OUT! Screamed Kelly.

"I think not!" replied Molly calmly. "It's time to face the truth, Kelly. I'm the better deal here. You know that, and now Aaron and I have to plan for our future together, and you have to go."

"I ASKED YOU HOW YOU GOT IN HERE!" Aaron demanded again.

Molly produced the small silver key from her pocket and held it up. "You gave me a key Aaron when you asked me to move in."

"What the hell did you say? You lying little BITCH!" replied Aaron.

"Baby we've had this discussion before, that's no way to talk to your child's mother." Molly said, smiling.

"Danny, go to your room. NOW!" demanded Kelly. Danny ran down the hall and locked his door.

"I'm calling the police!" Kelly said. "You are done this time. GET OUT!" Kelly turned an ice-cold glare towards

Aaron. She pulled out her phone and dialed 911. She began describing the situation to the operator. "Police are on the way, ma'am." They replied.

Aaron turned and looked back at Molly, about to rip her a new ass. In that moment, he saw them. Cold dead black eyes had replaced her blue ones. An evil, sinister grin spread across her face. She began to laugh. Aaron stood frozen, in shock, unable to speak. Kelly saw it to, and she could feel the hateful energy germinating from within. The room went cold, Kelly began to shiver. She was not dealing with Molly now. Molly was gone, she had been for some time. Raven was here now. She strode over the Aaron and ran a finger down his chest. She chuckled. It felt like time had stood still. Neither Aaron or Kelly could speak or move. It was as if the energy was being sucked out of them.

The doorbell wrang, and the door opened. A pair of police officers entered. "APD, were responding to a report of a break in? What's the situation here. Molly's blue eyes had returned to normal. Kelly felt her energy return. She pointed an accusing finger at Molly.

"This woman broke into our house; she's become a stalker! She's not welcome here! The police moved to guide Molly out the door. They began to question her. Molly didn't speak as she was led to the police car.

Several hours had passed. A detective did a sweep and investigation of the home. He searched through rooms, checked drawers, looked in cabinets. Aaron, Kelly, and Danny were all interviewed. After they concluded the investigation, determining nothing was missing, they wrapped things up.

"We will be in contact with you Ma'am. Ms. Jenson is being questioned downtown. We will get in touch with you as soon as we have more information. They left.

Kelly paced up the hallway, Aaron did the same. Then, something caught his eye. The pictures! There were at least half a dozen pictures placed in some of the frames on the wall. Molly! She was unafraid and bold indeed. Kelly went to the bedroom and found her clothes on the floor. She had been too distracted to notice that earlier. Why were they there? She opened the drawer and her jaw dropped. Rows of well-lined thong panties lined the drawer. Neatly folded socks were on the other side. In another drawer, a complete set of ridiculously complex sex toys. Aaron screamed out in a rage cussing and screaming. He took all the pictures, one by one and ripped them to shreds. He threw them out of his hand, letting the pieces fall where they may.

Kelly pulled out the panties and chucked them against the wall. She grabbed a trash bag from the kitchen and tossed the foul sex toys inside it. She stood and glared at Aaron. Part of her felt absolute burning rage for him, but she couldn't grasp the challenge he was facing. This was not just some horny little office tart after him, this was something far more. Pure, unfiltered evil! She knew she wanted to lash out at him, but how to direct the rage in such a way considering the situation eluded her.

Aaron began to panic! He had gotten himself into this, but he had never seen anything like what he had.

"What the hell was happening around here?" He thought to himself. Kelly approached him, pointing her finger at him. "I can't take any more of this Aaron; I'm reaching my breaking point with that… thing! All of this because you had to go to a fucking bar with her, screwing around!"

Aaron thought back to what he had found yesterday, Aaron's temper began to rise. He too was at a breaking point.

"You're a goddamn fucking idiot, Aaron! You're too old to have made such a stupid decision!" Kelly remarked. Aaron became agitated.

"And how about you? You're a little old to be screwing around yourself! Aaron replied angrily.

"Excuse me? EXCUSE ME? SCREWING AROUND? YOU'RE THE ONE DOING THAT SHIT! DON'T YOU TURN THAT SHIT ON ME ASSHOLE!" she said.

Aaron walked over to the laundry basket, reached in, and

retrieved the panties he had found. "Do these look familiar? What are you doing, going out for revenge sex?" Aaron barked.

Kelly stood, confused. She didn't recognize those panties; they weren't her style. They were black, this, almost see thru, lacy…Stained. She reached out and took them from his hand, inspected them.

"What the hell? Aaron, these aren't mine! Where did you find them?" She asked, now calmly.

"They had fallen off the bed when I was taking my nap. I didn't recognize them as anything you had. I started getting the wrong idea." He said. A complete scenario began forming in both of their minds at the same time. Molly! She must have left them there! She must have come in before!

"Aaron, she was here before!" exclaimed Kelly.

Aaron thought out loud. "She must have been here while I was sleeping! She must have been standing right her doing God knows what to herself. She's trying to sew doubt between us!"

"That fucking little runt!" Kelly muttered.

Several days had passed, and a detective knocked on the door. Kelly answered and let him inside.

"Did you lock her up and throw away the key?" asked Kelly, anxiously.

"Ma'am, Ms. Jenson has been released. There is no evidence to suggest she broke in, and nothing to suggest she didn't belong here." He replied.

"EXCUSE ME?" Kelly begged. "What the hell do you mean." She asked.

"Look here's the deal. She had pictures on the wall when we looked around. She had clothing in a drawer, personal property. She had her own key that she said your husband had given her. We interviewed several of her coworkers, they all suggested that she and Aaron were in a relationship. There was a picture of her on his desk. We know that she is pregnant with his child, and we also know about the altercation in the lab between you and her, with several eyewitnesses giving statements."

The detective adjusted his tie. "Look, here's what I see. A desperate young woman who is pregnant is having an affair with your husband. Maybe they have some little arrangement between them behind your back. He gave her a key, she obviously has spent time here before, maybe while you're out and about. You just happened to catch her this time. This stuff happens all the time, but we don't have evidence to charge her with a crime here."

Kelly was in complete rage and disgust. If only the detective knew what she knew, they would understand. How do you tell a cop the woman is possessed by something malevolent. How did that deceitful little tramp set this all up? She had to have had a plan from the start.

The detective stood up, handed her some contact information, and excused himself as he walked out the door. Kelly fell to the couch, sobbing. She needed help. She needed Haley.

19 HALEY

Haley Higgins was a short, petite girl. Long strands of golden blonde hair lay over her shoulder as she lifted a small box of digital recorders into the black cargo van as she and her team were loading for their upcoming investigation. They had been contacted a few days before about an old, abandoned farm just outside out Prescott, Arizona that for some reason seemed to have unusual activity at night. Passersby reported seeing shadows, human like figures behind the broken weathered windows. Noises and screams had been heard. Police had been called to investigate, but nothing was found. Hayley's team, Palo Santo Paranormal, was contacted shortly after their recent investigation of an old, abandoned hospital just north of the Mexican border. They didn't pick up much that time. Just some scratchy voices on their EVP, couple of temperature drop here and there. Basic stuff, nothing that got Haley's blood flowing. She's been doing this for 20 years now. The work was exciting, but she had some scary run ins, in her day. This game wasn't one for the kiddies. She had to make sure her and her team were protected from everything that could be seen, and from what couldn't. Sage, prayers, holy water. It was all there. What couldn't be seen, was very much there and these things can provoke the unseen or clear them out, which is the primary purpose.

"Haley, I got two more boxes of microphones, some EMF's and other tools to get from the supply room. Then I'll grab the voice boxes." Said Mike, one of her younger tech guys.

"Cool. We'll head out in an hour. I want to get some lunch in me first. I'm ravished!"

"Alright." Said Mike, with his long dark hair swaying in the breeze. Haley had a bit of a crush on him, with his dark Hispanic skin and bright brown eyes. She would never bring herself to do anything about it. Mike was only twenty-three, Haley had just turned forty-one, although she didn't look it. She still enjoyed sneaking a peak from time to time as he walked by. Haley had just placed several more boxes in the van when her smart phone went off. She reached into her pocket and pulled it out.

Haley recognized the number on it, though she was surprised to see who it was. She hadn't really spoken to Kelly in years, not since they were dorm mates in college. She had missed her old friend, but life had gotten in the way, and they had fallen out of touch. She answered.

"Kelly, oh my god! How are you? I haven't heard from you since our college days, and how's Aaron, that sexy hunk of man you got?" Asked Haley, chuckling.

"Hi Haley, oh god, it's been so long. I wish I were calling under more pleasant circumstances, but I have a crisis here. I've been watching your shows and I thought maybe you could help me out with something." Said Kelly.

Haley tilted her head sat down on the edge of the cargo bay door of the van. "Sure, what's up? We've certainly been busy with this paranormal stuff. Everybody starts watching these shows and without warning I think there's ghosts in their silverware drawers." Haley laughed.

"This one…" Kelly stammered. "This one's real, Haley. Somethings happened, it's a long story, but I think Aaron may be in trouble. There's a woman… She uh, well she did something to my husband."

"Did what?" asked Haley.

"Look there is so much to this, you would need days to hear everything that's happened. This woman…" Kelly hesitated.

"This woman is pregnant by Aaron, but it's not his fault. She did something to him." Kelly continued. "I think… God I can't believe I'm saying this. I think she is possessed by an evil energy that has control of her. It's too strong to still be an attachment I sense." Kelly blurted. She still couldn't believe she said that.

Haley tilted her head to the side. "Kelly, this sounds more like something for a cheesy afternoon talk show, the one that usually ends in you ARE the father, and since when is Aaron the type to screw around on you?"

"I get that, this is actually different. I'm serious Haley, I confronted her, this woman. I argued with her. Something overcame her. I saw this something. I saw it in her eyes. I saw it in the refection of a mirror. The entity is dangerous, Haley, and as much contempt as I have for her, I can't shake the sense that the child involved needs protecting. I sense that evil wants the baby, somehow. I don't know why." Kelly said with surprise.

Haley considered her words for a moment. An actual possession? She had heard of such things before, she's even had teammates that suffered trauma in the past. She needed more details. She was intrigued. The last several years had been a string of haunted houses, rusty warehouses, dilapidated schools, and hospitals. Same old stuff. She hadn't been offered a case of possession in a long time, and the last one turned out to be just a case of mental illness, and yet, somehow deep down, she knew this one was one to pay attention to. This was an opportunity to film a real live possession. She didn't know how she felt it so strong, but she knew to take this case. "Kelly, I'll need some details first. What did you see? And are you still empathic? Clairsentient? I remember how your where in college, I told you I felt that in you." Asked Haley, curious.

"Yeah, I'm still all those things. It's only gotten stronger these days. I am sensing its increasing intensity. I've sensed something sinister. Haley, I felt that woman. From the moment I first met her, I picked up on her intent. I felt an energy I could not explain. This thing is out for vengeance, it wanted revenge, it was very angry. It hit me hard in the chest like getting punched with a wooden mallet. It takes hours for it to calm down. It hurts me physically and taxes me mentally. Aaron… he has his ability to. I can't believe he didn't sense it in her. I can't believe he didn't see her game from the get-go." Kelly began to break down. She wept over the phone as Haley listened in. She felt her pain, as if she were right next to her.

"Kelly, listen. We just loaded our van with our equipment for a local investigation. But this….this is more important. I'm going to pack some extra things and head out to you, a soon as possible. I always told you I would be there for you. That hasn't changed. I should be there tonight if we leave within the hour. That would put us into town at around eight, maybe nine tonight. Sit tight, we'll be on the way." Haley spoke softly.

"Thank you so much, this means so much to me." Kelly

replied.

"I'll talk to you tonight, make sure you have a bottle or two of Sangria ready for me." Haley said, giggling.

"Believe me, I'll have more than just that when you get here." Kelly replied. The phone call ended. Haley turned to her team, who were loading up the final boxes at that moment. She whistled at them. "Come on boys, we got a live one this time. Where headed to Albuquerque. Seven-hour drive ahead of us, so empty your bladders. We're not stopping for pee breaks this time, so you'll be stuck with empty Gatorade bottles. That's disgusting, so please for heavens sakes take a piss now and watch your fluids on the way over." Haley announced while trying to look serious. She knew that part was a lie, but hey whatever motivated them.

"What's the scoop, boss lady?" asked Lily, the short freckle faced redhead that worked as Haley's camera woman and background researcher.

"Possible possession. Maybe fierce attachment. Not sure if a malevolent spirit or a demon. It's for an old friend of mine from college." Haley said.

"Whoa, are we equipped to deal with a demon? That's the church's area of expertise." Remarked Mike.

Haley stood there for a moment. She pondered his remark. He was right. Demons are the Catholic churches department. She had worked alongside them before. She had a few connections she could reach out to. Father Riley had worked with her in the past. He was a good man, young and handsome. To handsome. Haley had a bit of a wandering eye around him, she remembered.

The road trip was long. Hot desert winds rocked the tall van from side to side as the crossed the Arizona desert. Haley's mind raced as she considered the potential of what they would face next. "Who was this woman?" Haley thought to herself. Haley remembered Aaron from her school days. Kelly had landed her quite the guy, he was kind, gentle, sweet… and always loyal to Kelly. Loyal. Aaron was loyal to her. How in the hell had Aaron managed to knock up another woman? What was going on? If there had been problems, Kelly surely would have confided in her about it. There was nothing. All of this seemed out of place.

Lily had been spending her time in the back of the van, researching information on spiritual possession during the drive. She pulled up several articles and books on her laptop, combing through what she could find. She scratched her head as the read and thought out several scenarios.

"I don't know boss lady; this possession seems more spiritual than demonic based on the info you've given me. It's seeming too thought out, too much intent. Methodical even. I suggest the possessed has some weakness that the spirit wants to exploit, some weakness that makes the spirit attracted to her. You said she's pregnant?" asked Lily.

"Yeah, why?" replied Haley.

"This is only a theory but is it possible this woman isn't the spirits intended target. I think she's only a temporary vessel. A means to an end." Said Lily

Mike interjected. "You're suggesting the child is her true goal? Can spirits do that?"

Paul, one of the other techs and researchers replied. "Anything's possible. Just because we haven't seen it before, doesn't mean it can't happen. I mean come on, if it can inhabit some old rag doll in a museum, or some other random trinket, I'm sure a human child can have it too. Something about this child could be the key to why this is happening in the first place." The drive went on for the next several hours. More questions and general chats about the case went on as research continued. Haley considered the prospect over and over again. The one thing that went thru Haley's mind was whether spirits haunt objects, or really possess them.

They pulled the van up in front of Kelly and Aarons house, after a grueling eight-hour drive. The door opened as they exited the van and Kelly stepped out, throwing her arms around Haley after these many years of not seeing each other. The woman cried together. After short introductions to the rest of her teams, they all stepped inside. Paul called a local hotel to begin setting up reservations for the team. The rest sat down and made themselves comfortable, as Kelly pulled out two bottles of wine and several glasses for them all. Lily wasted no time in opening one and began picking Kelly's brain on the details of the upcoming investigation.

"Can you tell me who the woman of concern is, Ma'am? Name, age, where she's from? Any details of which you can think."

"Whoa, slow down, Lily, she's been through a lot." Replied Haley.

"It's ok, Haley. I have a lot to get off my chest." Kelly turned to Lily at that point.

"Her name is Molly, she's a new research assistant at my husband's pharmaceutical company. She's from Michigan. She's the younger sister of woman named Katy, a friend of Aarons, who works for the same company. In fact, she helped Molly get the position there. She's here to train and gain experience for a similar position that they have at their other branch, up in Grand Rapids, Michigan. That's where she and Katy are from. I think she around twenty-six, maybe twenty-seven. She came here and immediately developed a crush on my husband. But I never thought she would go as far as to do what she did to him. She doesn't seem like the type. I mean the real her." Kelly spoke.

Lily asked curiously. "And what did she actually do ma'am."

Kelly looked to the floor, a tear running down her face. "I don't know with what, but she roofied him with something. I believe she stuck a drug in his beer at a local bar. She basically raped him at a nearby hotel. She hurt him, and now, she's pregnant with his child." Kelly cried.

The team fell silent, as Haley gently rubbed Kelly's back, with concern in her eyes. They looked around at each other, wondering how this leads to possession.

"When I confronted her, she began to change, physically." Kelly continued. "Her eyes, those pitch-black eyes, staring at me. Like black pits into Hell itself. Her voice was snarly and growly like. That wasn't her normal voice. It sounded like nothing I've heard. It wasn't exactly audible it was guttural. "

Haley looked around at her team. "Demon? Spirit? What do we think, team?"

Lily combed through her notes. "How did Molly behave before the confrontation?" she asked.

"She seemed calm for the most part. I didn't see anything that would indicate anything was wrong with her. Aside for the nature of our fight, I didn't feel like she had a demon in her. That is something else too. Raven. Molly calls this entity Raven." Kelly said.

Lily continued with her notes. "Hmmm, Raven. Definitely not a demonic name. Demon's don't like being called by their names so it's definitely pointing to a human spirit. Hmmm... Does your husband keep any crucifixes or religious items in his office?" asked Lily. "He has a crucifix on his desk. He also has a bottle of Holy water. He's not a very religious man, he's spiritual. He has little habits he keeps from his childhood. Why you ask?" Kelly said. Lily responded "Demons tend to shy away or attack when in the presence of religious items. It's usually referred to as religious provocation when crosses are present, biblical passages are said, or rituals are performed such as prayer and spreading of holy water. For the moment, I'm going to suggest it's a spirit since these things didn't seem to be detested by Molly is that correct?"

"Yeah. I didn't see any odd behaviors near these things." Kelly continued.

"What are we going to just walk up to this woman and sprinkle her with holy water? See if it stings her?" Paul chuckled.

"Not how this works, Paul." Haley replied. She turned to Kelly. "Is it possible to meet this woman tomorrow?" I think a personal interview is the best place to start."

"I don't want to see that wench in person right now, but I may be able to arrange something through her sister. I have her number." Kelly replied. "But I don't know how we are going to get her to go along with it."

Haley laughed. "Come on, look who you're asking. EVERYBODY wants to be on a TV show."

Aaron entered the room from the garage in the back yard. He had been hiding back there most of the evening, depressed, lonely, ashamed, and consumed with thoughts of failure. Just wanting some quiet time as he felt astronomically low. All this madness, this heart break, this uncertain future could have all been avoided if he only had used one simple two lettered word. "NO!" But he didn't, and now his life was in shambles, and now there was a group of strangers sitting around his living room. They turned to look at him, Aaron focused on the blonde in the middle as she looked familiar.

"Haley? Haley Higgins?" Aaron asked. He knew Kelly had intended to contact her, but he had no idea she would be right here, right now in this very moment. "What are you doing here? I haven't seen you in years! Aren't you running some paranormal team on TV now?"

"Hi Aaron, yeah that's us." Haley gestured around the room. "This is Lily, camera operator and background researcher. That's Paul over there, fellow expert and equipment tech, and this one is Mike, he's my go to guy on pretty much anything we do. Mike stepped forward and offered his hand. Aaron reached out and shook it.

"Haley, I thought you had moved to Arizona? How did you get here so quickly?" asked Aaron.

"Kelly called; she told us what's going on." Haley replied.

Aaron felt a sense of complete embarrassment surge through him. His face felt hot and turned a slight pink. He looked at Kelly. The sorrow in his mind was more than he could bare. His heart had just hit a new low. Did he even have a heart anymore? He had never felt so bad in his life. Aaron had been strong, resilient, rock steady his entire life. He always felt he could accomplish anything, lead others to do the same. He always wanted the best for his peers and pushed them to that that end. Now, Aaron felt like an empty, lifeless soul. He knew the next time he walked into work; his fellow associates would look down on him. Aaron, for the first time since his mother had passed away years before, wanted to break down and cry. But not here and not now. Aaron pulled himself together for the sake of the moment.

Haley stood up and approached Aaron. "Look, let's talk, privately." Aaron nodded his head, then they stepped into the kitchen. Aaron looked at Kelly, she nodded in uneasy approval. Haley and Aaron sat down at the kitchen table, out of ear shot of the rest of the group.

Haley spoke first, sensing the torment in Aaron's heart. "Look Aaron, I've known you and Kelly for a long time. This isn't you. You need to do something about this! I don't have all the details here, far from it. But how did you get so far sucked into this that now a woman is pregnant? What the fuck happened? You and Kelly…"

"Can't have any more kids. Kelly's started menopause. She hasn't had a period in I don't know how long. We had been trying for so long to have more. Somehow, that little fucking shit figured that out, and she used me, she fucking used it against me." Aaron replied. His body began to quiver. He started to cry. His pain was unbearable. He gave in to Molly's ploy and now a baby was involved. Fear echoed through him. "I FUCKED UP!" Aaron yelled, as tears ran down his face. "I should have seen her game. I should have known. I FUCKING should have known! GODDAMN IT! I just wanted to mentor and now this?!" Aaron yelled. Aaron slammed his fist in the table as he begin to bawl. Haley reached out a caring hand to him, as Kelly entered the kitchen. The alcohol had begun to flow through her veins. Her inhibition was lowering. The rage was finally beginning to rear its ugly head. The rage she was feeling, that had been pent up inside her, was about to emerge!

"You're fucking right you should have known, Aaron. I'm so fucking pissed off that you didn't read the signs. How could you have been so FUCKING stupid? How could you not open your eyes and see we what the fuck she was doing to you? And you let her convince you to go out for a few drinks after work? Kelly kicked a chair out from under the table. IT WAS FUCKING OBVIOUS SHE WANTED TO FUCK YOU! IT WAS OBVIOUS SHE DIDN'T FUCKING CARE ABOUT US, OR HERSELF, HER HUSBAND, OR YOU, OR ME, OR ANYONE! SHE DOENST FUCKING CARE ABOUT THE THIRTY FUCKING YEARS WE SPENT BUILDING THIS MARRIAGE! SHE DOESN'T FUCKING CARE ABOUT THE PLEASURE AND THE PAIN AND THE HARD WORK, THE LAUGHTER, THE TEARS, THE UPS, AND THE DOWNS. WE HAVE SPENT YEARS BUILDING WHAT WE HAVE TODAY. MOLLY ONLY CARES ABOUT ONE FUCKING THING! ONLY HER FUCKING PUSSY MATTERS TO HER!" Kelly took another drink from her wine glass. Sweat dripped from her brow. Hatred filled her heart. "FUCK YOU, MOLLY! FUCK YOU, MOLLY! FUCK YOU, MOLLY!" Kelly screamed. Kelly turned back to Aaron. "YOU FUCKED UP, AARON. You chose to go out, you chose to have an evening with her. Your decision led to this. Now PAY FOR IT!" Kelly broke down into absolute despair. She sobbed with tears falling like a waterfall. She took a few steps forward and stood in Aaron's face. She leaned in, inches away from his own. Kelly lowered her voice. "And now you are going to pay for that mistake, ! And if you think for one moment that I'm going to help you raise that child, FUCK YOU!" The alcohol flowed through her veins. She had become weakened. Aaron wanted to die in that moment. She was right. He was older, smarter, more experienced. He should have read her like a book. He didn't.

Haley stood up and stood before Kelly. "Hold on sister, there's something more sinister here. I feel it. You know why I got into this game to begin with. You know how I am, clairvoyant." Kelly, who had finally let the reality of the situation set in, paced back and forth in her kitchen. She was full of rage, hate, anger, and… her own resentment. She emptied her glass of wine, filled another, and swigged that one down too. The rage inside of her had finally hit a tipping point. She took the wine glass in her hand and threw it into the wall, over the sink. It shattered into shards and pieces. She stepped toward Aaron, looked into his eyes. She raised her hand and slapped it hard across his face. She had never done that before. Never once had she felt such rage toward him. She didn't care about some fucking so called ghost, inhabiting Molly. This was his fault. He let this happen. He went out for drinks. He gave her the opportunity to do this. Kelly screamed out in pain. In the next room over, the team heard the commotion. They huddled together as they considered what they were getting into.

"Man, this shit is hard core, and we investigate fucking haunted buildings, not domestic disputes. Should we even be here?" asked Paul?

Mike circled the living room. "I trust Haley on this one. Something drew us here. We need to be here. You see, entities can affect the living and it's possible this is what's going on and that's what I feel is going to be the pinnacle of this investigation, to find out if this is that case."

Lily rubbed her chin as she contemplated the situation. She stood up from the lazy boy she was sitting in. She looked at her partners. "I'm with Mike on this. We stay. Haley knows how to help them. Isn't that what we do? We're here to help people, guys, and these two NEED help." Lily spoke. "Plus, imagine the ratings!"

Mike and Paul reconsidered. This could be one for the ages. They started thinking "Emmy!" This one could put their show on her whole new playing field. This kind of drama was going to rake in a whole new level of viewers.

20 THE TIME HAS COME

Molly stood before window of her bedroom, gazing out into the rainy blackness of the night. It was monsoon season in Albuquerque. These storms seemed to pop up whenever they pleased. She stood, with her arms crossed behind her back, in quiet contemplation. James was out of her life now. That was fine in her mind. "He was pathetic anyway." Molly spoke under her breath. Soon her belongings will be sent to her. She will find a new home, away from her equally pathetic sister. "Treat me like a child why don't you, Katy." She muttered. Molly thought about the next day that loomed before her. Aaron. She will see her Aaron again, and she will take her place at his side, where she belonged. Molly gazed at her dull reflection in the window. Raven gazed back at her, with a sinister grin on her face. She spoke.

"The time has come, Molly."

"The time for what? What's next for me? What's my next course of action?" Molly asked.

Raven gazed at her. "Kelly must go, if he is to come to you."

"But how? How do I make her go away?" Molly questioned.

Raven tilted her head to the side. "You have everything that you need." Spoke Raven. Then, she was gone. Only Molly's reflection looked back at her now.

Molly questioned what Raven meant. She turned around, removed her clothing, and stripped down to her black bra and thong panties, and got into bed. She fluffed her pillow and went to thing, dreaming up a plan do deal with her nemesis. She slept.

The next morning, she got up and took a bath, got dressed in her tightest yoga pants and a classy blue blouse. She ate a grapefruit for breakfast, as she planned out her day. She applied her lip stick, sprayed perfume on her neck, making sure she would look ravishing for her man. She began to walk toward the front door when she heard a voice. Molly turned to face her sister.

"You're actually going to work today? I would let things simmer down over there first. There will be questions. Lots of them, and Aaron…" Katy was interrupted.

"And what about Aaron?" Katy asked, "What about him?!" Molly snapped. "He and I have a life together we need to plan out. He's going to be a father to a beautiful child. OUR child."

"You truly are delusional, Molly!" Katy said. She took a few steps close to her sister. "I don't care what happened between you two. What you've done is unthinkable! IT'S ILLEGAL." Katy blurted. "Do you honestly think Aaron isn't going to press charges against you? Have you fired? You could be facing a long time behind bars, Molly. This will end badly for you!"

"Leave Aaron to me, sis. If Aaron knows what's best for him, if he wants to be a part of our baby's life, Aaron will watch his steps around me. Aaron will soon realize that I am the best chance he's got at a happy life." Molly retorted.

"There's something else. I got a call this morning, while you were still in bed." Katy sighed. "You have a visitor coming in a few minutes. There are some people who want to meet with you.”

Molly looked at her sister witch shock and confusion. “What? Who?” demanded Molly.

“I don’t know, some investigators, I think. It might have something to do with the fight at work. I’m not sure the details, only that they are on their way.” Katy said.

Molly was irritated. Why now? Who were they? She had already been interviewed by the police, smoothed things over. Molly did not want to be delayed going to her man. The sound of a vehicle pulling up in front of the house startled her. Doors slammed shut. Footsteps, several of them could be heard. The doorbell rang. Katy went over and opened it. She was greeted by a short, attractive blonde woman, a curly haired redhead with glasses, and two dark haired Hispanic men carrying assorted equipment. Molly looked on confused. These weren’t cops at all.

“Good morning, I’m Haley with Pala Alto Paranormal. We’re out of Arizona, and we’re here to help out with a case. We spoke this morning.” Haley said.

“Yeah, I’m Katy. I know why you’re here. I spoke with Kelly just before you called. Come on in.”

The team stepped inside. Molly looked on, annoyed, as if random strangers had just invaded her private space. She looked back and forth between the group, wondering what the hell they wanted.

“This is my sister, Molly. The one we spoke about.” Katy said.

Haley considered her for a moment, then reached out a hand to greet her. “Hi, Haley Higgens. Palo Alto Paranormal. This is my crew, Lily, Paul, and Mike. We’d like to ask you a few questions. We’re here to help.”

Molly looked her over. Not wanting to be rude, she shook her hand, but said nothing. In that instant, Haley could feel the rush of a powerful energy flowing through her body. She could see now what Kelly was talking about. It came loaded with powerful emotion. In all her years as a Psychic medium, she have never before felt such a surge.

She knew she was in the right place. She shivered.

"Molly Jenson." Was her only reply.

Haley looked around at her crew, glaring at them. They knew what that glare meant. The had worked for Haley for years. It could mean only one thing. This… was the real deal. They knew what to do next. They set their cases down, extracted several various instruments, and prepared to take readings.

"So why are you here, anyway." Asked Molly, contemptuously.

"Molly, we do a variety of paranormal investigations for a show called "Palo Alto Adventures" And were here because we have reason to believe you may be subject to… an infestation of the mind and body." Haley replied. Molly was repulsed by this idea. "Who the hell do they think they are to come up in here and say that" Molly thought to herself. She felt agitated.

"Molly, you have people who care about you. It seems that some pretty rough stuff has been going on. We can help you with that." Said Lily, coolly.

In an instant, Molly felt a pressure release from inside her chest. It was as if some weight had been lifted. Raven was for the moment, away from her body. She hadn't left for good. Raven was in the house. She wasn't going humor these people into thinking she was actually there. Molly felt, for a moment, normal again. Haley sensed it too.

"Molly, I like to see myself as a psychic medium. I can sense things, feel things. I've only been here a few minutes and already felt that you have a presence in you. Normally I wouldn't come to such a quick conclusion without doing some research, but my goodness, I feel this one strong. It's hiding right now. It's trying to lay low. Can you tell me when you first encountered this spirit?" Asked Haley

Molly felt uneasy, not sure if or where to begin. Katy stepped over and sat down. "Alright, I'll start." All eyes were on Katy now. "Molly went out one night with a handful of friends who swiped alcohol and a Ouija board. They went to a cemetery and started doing rituals and taking drinks out the bottle. Well since Molly had participated in the séance she's never been the same. She started having memories that weren't hers. She had night terrors of an entity wanting to control her. Molly got into random violent rages. We didn't know what was setting her off so easily. Well, I had gone to the head stone where they did the séance with a sledgehammer I picked up out of my dad's old truck. The headstone was desecrated. It looked like a satanic ritual happened by the looks of the inverted pentagram that was on the headstone itself. I smashed it hoping it would help. Well for a while it did. Then things got worse. I noticed it coming back when I would see a reflection that wasn't Molly. It looked like someone else" Katy explained.

"Lily interjected as she jotted down notes. "Sometimes spirits can become tied to physical objects, perhaps this spirit was tied to the headstone. Ouija boards are not fun and games. There are away for portals to open for sprits or demons tc latch on to you. There's usually a weakness that attracts this spirit attach to you, Molly. Can you tell us a little about yourself?"

Molly became agitated again. She was restless. Who the hell were they to pry into her life? Molly jumped up and grabbed her purse. "I'm not going to sit here and take this shit! You can all go to hell!"

Molly stormed out the door, slammed her car door shut and drove off.

"Wow, such a sweet girl!" Mike joked.

"Such a hotty though. Did you see that ass?" Paul whispered over to Mike.

"Knock it off you two. Be professional." Demanded Haley. "Sorry about them, they can be obnoxious." Haley told Katy.

"No prob. Sorry about her." Katy replied, embarrassed by her sisters' actions.

"Don't sweat it, we see this all the time." Replied Haley.

"Victims of possession are under the influence of the spirit. I sense in Molly's case, it feels threatened. It's latched on to her. Remember, this isn't your sister acting out, it's the entity. This one feels powerful. We made the right choice in coming here. Team, thoughts?"

Lily sifted through some notes from her binder. "We need to determine the source of the entity's energy. We need to determine what the source, the vessel, that the spirit is inhabiting."

"Duh, it's inhabiting her!" Paul replied.

"Not necessarily. The spirit could also be inhabiting an object. Maybe something that Molly own's?" Lily replied.

Haley opened her case and produced several small religious objects, a crucifix, pentacle, candles, and sage. "I'm going to have to sift through my bag of tricks on this one. Katy, I need to see Molly's room. That's where I need to start my investigation. I need to feel the energy of the place, and her things. I also need to sage the whole house, and we need to set up some equipment." Haley turned to Mike and Paul. "Boys, get the EVP recorders, EMF detectors and cameras. Lily, get on your research and dig up anything you can. Katy where did you say you grew up when she used the Ouija board?" asked Haley.

"Michigan, small ranch just outside of Manistee, nor far from Grand Rapids." Katy replied.

"And you said this thing had a name?" Asked Haley.

"Yeah, it calls itself Raven." Katy replied.

"Lily, that energy I felt, it wasn't demonic. This is a very angry spirit. It was tortured, tormented, suffering and angry. I'll also say vengeful. Start with that."

"On it, boss lady." Lily replied. She sat down her laptop and began typing furiously.

Haley turned to Katy. "You may want to call in today, Katy. We need your help with this one."

"No problem here, I got too much use or loose leave anyway." Katy answered.

Aaron walked into his office to collect a few personal belongings. He'd decided he and Kelly needed time together to reconcile. He had decided to put in a few weeks of leave to work things out with her. The building was quiet. He went early to avoid any uncomfortable encounters. Katy wasn't there. Aaron was being quick about it, hopefully he could get what he needed before… Aaron turned around, startled.

"Molly!!!" Aaron jumped.

Molly didn't speak. She smiled at Aaron slyly, approaching him placed her hands on his chest and backed him into the wall behind him. She grabbed at his chest, almost purring at him. Passion burned in her eyes. Aaron became angry. He grabbed her wrists and threw her back with enough force to almost knock her over. Molly growled with excitement.

"Come on baby, you know I like it rough. You know it get me hot when you toss me around like a horny little rag doll." Her smile sharpened. She approached and reached out for him. Aaron grabbed her by the wrists and shook her.

"YOU STOP THIS RIGHT GODDAMN NOW. MY NEXT STOP IS THE HR DEPARTMENT, WHERE I'LL MAKE SURE YOUR SORRY ASS IS FIRED AND OUT THE DOOR." Aaron pushed her back again. Molly still smiled.

"Now Daddy, you know that's not going to happen. They are not going to fire a sweet little thing like me that you just physically assaulted in your office." Molly laughed.

"You insane little BITCH!" Aaron yelled. "How fucking dare, you…"

"Now, now ,now, babe. That's no way to talk to the mother of your child." Molly replied, rubbing her belly. She encircled him. "Things are different between us now. We have a bond to share, an energy between us. Can you feel it, honey?"

"We need to start making plans for our future together. You and me, as a team, as a loving couple raising their beautiful baby together. Would you have me and our baby out in the streets. I thought not. The best thing for us now is to face our new reality, our new future. Do you think I'm going to let you get away with paying child support for next eighteen years? No Aaron, we're a package deal, you, and I. I've wanted this for a long time Aaron." Molly leaned in closer to Aaron, whispered in his ear. "I always get what I want, baby. Always."

Molly pulled back and smiled at him. She turned to walk out the door and looked back at him one more time. She lifted her leg and wrapped it around the frame of the door, slowly humping it. She blew him a kiss as she walked away back to her desk in the lab.

"FUCK!" Aaron yelled, as he grabbed his brief case and stormed out of the building.

Back at Katy's house, Haley walked around Molly's room, looking at pictures and trinkets on her desk. She rummaged through her closet, looking over her clothes. She opened her nightstand drawer, observing her vast array of expensive looking jewelry and perfume. She opened another drawer in the chest near her bed. Rows and rows of neatly stacked lacey thong panties were there. Next to them, a vast variety of adult toys of various types lay neatly arranged by size.

There was something elusive here. An energy, but she couldn't place it. Was it a residual energy from Molly? Perhaps, yet it could be something else. She circled the room looking for anything that put out a tangible energy. Something caught her eye. Over the dresser across the room, stood a tall ornate mirror. It looked antique. She examined it. It was antique, maybe 100 years old. It seemed to call to her. What was it with this mirror?

Haley went downstairs looking for Katy. She found her in the kitchen, preparing lunch for them all.

"Katy, can I ask you something? You said you saw a reflection of Raven in a window once. What can you tell me about the antique mirror in Molly's room."

"It's old, I think it went as far back as my grandmother's in the early 50s'. Molly loves it, won't give it up now that she's here. Why?" asked Katy.

"Hold that thought. I just had an idea." Went to the living room and approached lily, who was typing away searching for information on Raven. "Lily, add something to your pile of work. I need you to look up info on antique mirrors and old superstations about them. Something familiar is on my mind that I read once, but I forgot some details."

"I'm all over it, boss lady." Said Lily.

Haley knew deep down that something more drastic than sage and prayers was going to be needed for this one. Somehow, the mirror was key. She felt it but didn't know what it was. She turned to Mike and Paul.

"I need you to go to Molly's room and take EMF readings in there, particularly the mirror. I think I may be on to something. Get a base reading and then check for spikes."

"Got it." Paul replied. They went upstairs. 20 minutes later, after consulting with Lily some more, Haley joined them. "What Cha got?" she asked.

Mike turned to her, with concern on his face. "Readings in the rest of the room run normal, but when I approach the mirror, the reading spikes right, but my batteries for the cameras are completely drained. I'm telling you they were fully charged! It's like this thing is sucking in energy from any source." Haley knew then immediately why she felt strangely about the mirror. It was drawing in her own energy; it was a negative space. Haley continued to wonder about the mirror. What was its history? What was its connection to Molly and Raven?

Lily entered the room. "Got something, old newspaper article out of Manistee. Says here that a young girl, Raven DeBardot, seventeen, had been found sexually assaulted and murdered behind a shed not far out of town. There were seven more murders of similar form over the next 15 years. Their bodies were found in the Huron national forest, but no killer was found until many years later when a victim managed to escape and provide a sketch of the suspect and location of where he lived. Here's another little fun fact. Looks like the killer came back to taunt his victims, carved satanic images in their graves. Wow this is gruesome stuff."

Katy entered the room, announcing lunch. "Katy…" asked Haley. "Does the name DeBardot mean anything? Do you remember what was on the grave." Katy struggled to remember, then it came to her. "It was kind of washed out, but yeah, a D, an O and a T were still visible, I think. Why do you ask?"

Haley considered it for a moment. Rape and murder? That could place a lot of anger on a soul. She turned and considered the mirror for a moment. A theory formed in her mind. Then she turned back to Katy. "Do you know where your grandmother got this? She asked.

Katy thought for a moment. "Let me ask." Katy pulled out her phone as the rest of the crew hungrily went to the kitchen to chow down on the chili dogs Katy had made for them. She swiped through her contacts and found her mom's number. She called through facetime. A few moments later, her mother answered. Her face appeared on the screen.

"Hey baby girl, how you are doing?" asked her mother.
"Mom, I'll explain the whole thing later. But for now, you know that old antique mirror of grandmas?"
"God yes, I do. Hated that thing. It was always ugly as hell. I can't believe you still have it. Looks like it came out of a French whore house." She chuckled.
"Where did grandma get it, do you remember?" asked Katy.
"Oh, good lord, you remember how your granny was!

Always at yard sales, estate sale, shit like that. Everyone else's junk was her treasure." Katy's' mom replied.

Katy thought for a moment, looked over to Haley for direction in questions to ask. "Ask her if it may have come from Manistee, or anywhere near that." Haley requested. Katy asked that question.

"Look honey, it could have come from anywhere. Your granny was a packrat. But yeah, she did most of her shopping in Manistee back in the day. I may be mistaken because she always liked to brag about the treasures she would find. I think that mirror came from some estate sale. An older couple was leaving the state for some reason. But who knows, it's been so long. Why are you asking about the mirror anyway? Sure, it's an antique, you trying to sell it. I doubt its worth a dime."

"Look mom, things got complicated down here. I'll call you back later with the details, I've got a few things to work out." Katy said.

"Well honey, if something is wrong, and something does sound wrong, tell me!" her mother replied.

"Mom, it's Molly." Katy replied. "Raven!"

Her mother's face went flat, her voice silent. She stared at her daughter through the screen and sighed.

"Katy, now you listen. Molly knew that stopping her medication was a bad idea. If her illness is back, that's on her. She's an adult. She's out there with you, and you work at that fancy drug company. Maybe they make something better that will work better for her? Don't you all have decent health insurance?"

Katy sighed. "Look mom, I'll call you back. I have to deal with some stuff. I love you, talk to you later." Katy replied.

Her mother leaned into the screen. "You watch over your sister over there, young lady. You remember what hell we went through when she stabbed that boy with the pencil. I love you, too." Her mother said. Katy ended the call.

Haley had overheard every word of the conversation.

Concern began to build inside. "Stabbed a boy with a pencil?" asked Haley out loud.

"Yeah, it's when she started acting out after that séance, you know the violent outbursts I told you about? That was one of them." Katy said as her heart began to sink.

Haley considered this. "Was she like this before the cemetery thing?"

"No, she was perfectly fine before that. Despite the fact she always was a little boy crazy. She was back to her annoying self after a smashed that headstone." Katy answered. " By the way, why all the interest in the mirror?"

Haley thought for a moment, then answered. "Katy, mirrors, particularly of this material, have been said to act as portals. They have physical properties that aid in this. There's old legends of people covering them with blankets during certain time of the day and night, so spirits can't see or enter our realm."

"You mean like any mirror is a portal?" asked Katy. "Like some ghost is always watching me naked in the shower?"

"No, not modern mirrors. Antique mirrors were made differently. They were coated with silver, gold, or chrome." Haley turned and approached the mirror, gesturing for Katy to follow. "This one, this one is coated with gold. Look there, you can see the patina." Katy looked closer. Yes, it was kind of yellowish, but she didn't think much about it. It just looked like cigarette smoke stain.

"What's so special about that?" Asked Katy.

"Gold is an excellent conductor of electricity. Normally it builds a charge of positive electrons, forms an electrical field from radio frequency waves, which is just barely detectable on a RF meter." Said Haley. She paused. "This mirror is different. It draws in energy from around its environment, as if its sucking it in. As if it's sending it somewhere else." Haley spoke.

Katy was dumb founded. She didn't know this kind of science. "What does this have to do with Molly? I mean she's only peering into this thing twenty time a day!" remarked Katy

"I have a theory, Katy. I think this mirror has a connection with Raven. I think it feeds her."

Molly was confused by the technical mumbo-jumbo. She was hungry, decided to join the rest of the crew for her famous chili dogs. She excused herself and left Molly's room. Haley turned back and refocused her attention on the mirror. She didn't realize a few hours had passed by while her crew was performing investigations and research downstairs.

As she gazed into the mirror, she began to feel a new energy. It was overwhelming. She lowered her head to collect her thoughts. She was getting lightheaded. She wiped sweat from her brow as a sense of nausea began to irritate her. She closed her eyes to focus. A moment later, she looked up at her reflection. She jumped back, startled! There, standing behind her right shoulder, in the reflection, was a young woman. Her hair looked black, wet, unkept. Her skin was wet with sweat. Hear eyes… those eyes… blacker than the blackest she had ever seen. Panic flowed through her veins. She turned around to see what was causing this image. "Molly!" Haley screeched.

Molly had entered the room without her noticing. She had come home from work now. She stood behind Haley, staring down at her with fury in her eyes. Molly stepped forward and stood inches from her face. Haley could feel her heated breath over her skin, as Molly looked down at her with a hateful stare. Molly raised her hand and pointed to the door. She inched ever closer to Haley, her nose almost touching her face. She propped her head to the side.

"GET THE FUCK OUT!" Molly yelled, threateningly! "GET… THE FUCK… AWAY… FROM MY MIRROR! MY FUCKING MIRROR!" Molly stepped closer to Haley, with her right fisted balled up. "GET THE FUCK OUT OF MY ROOM, BITCH!"

Haley stepped back, pulled herself away from Molly. She

inched her way towards the door. The hatred, the anger, the fury, flowed through this room. Haley knew who was in control right now. Raven.

Haley backed away. "Look, I'm only here to help you! That's what I do! I help people!" Haley backed into the hallway; her hands raised in a non-threatening gesture. Molly grabbed the door handle. She slammed it shut.

Haley hurriedly went downstairs. "Team, we need to get out of here. Pack your shit. I know what needs to be done here. Katy, avoid your sister! It's not Molly right now." Arturo walked in the door in his Air Force uniform. "What the hell is going on here?" Arturo asked.

"Sir, Molly is upstairs, but it's not Molly. Watch yourself around her!" Haley exclaimed. Withing minutes the team had their gear packed and loaded in the van outside. Katy dashed out of the house. "

What the hell do I do?" Haley turned to her. "Get a hotel for the night, this is going to get complicated. I know what needs to be done, but I need some outside help to do it. I'll call you in the morning with details. Keep yourself safe whatever you decide to do. But stay away from your sister!"

Arturo followed up behind Katy, having just overheard what Haley had to say.

"Fuck this shit, I'll pack some bags. We will stay at my mom's house tonight. That bitch is crazy!" Arturo exclaimed. "I thought you told her to fucking pack and leave?"

Katy turned to her husband, tears rolling down her eyes. "I told Molly to pack and leave. That's not Molly anymore." Katy began to cry.

Haley looked up at the second-floor window as she entered the driver's seat of the black van. Molly looked down on them, ominously. Haley could feel rage. Deep down inside, she also felt sorrow, pain. She felt the real Molly, the woman held hostage by this hateful spirit. Haley vowed to stick to her guns. She would find a way to save this young woman.

21 FATHER RILEY

Father John Riley was a humble man. He was still young, by most church goers' ideas, only in his mid-forties. His dark, faded hair and well-trimmed beard made him look distinguished to his flock. He was soft spoken, yet stern. His small group of believers, in the dusty down of Winslow, Arizona, Was loyal to him. His church, St. Bernadette's, was a small yet tidy and clean place. It was a place for his congregation to go for prayer and reflection. Yet, they did not know what kind of a man Father Riley was. They did not know the church housed an experienced exorcist. His knowledge was vast, as he was one of the few that had access to the Vatican's sacred archives, a place only a select few were given access to. There, he learned vast knowledge of demons, angels, and the arcane. He had chosen a life of simplicity, here in Winslow. The archdiocese of Arizona had hand picked him to lead this small church. They knew that his previous experiences as an exorcist had broken him down. It still made him a strong leader. For him, this was almost a retirement job.

Riley had just competed performing daily mass services. He retired to his office, removed his gown, and adjusted his frock on his black uniform. He considered the days sermon. Lust. One of the seven deadly sins. He had spoken of the weakness of man, and the many forms of lust. Lust leaded to infidelity which is a leading cause of marriage failure. He reflected on that. He himself had faced the lack of intimacy since he had given up that part of his life to be a priest. He paid a price for it once he was discovered but was able to keep on doing what he loved the most, leading people to the lord. This was his passion.

He settled down and dismissed his deacons as he rested his feet on a pedestal under his desk. The phone rang. Looking at the caller ID, he was shocked. It was her, the very subject that had been in the back of his mind during his sermon. Haley! The woman he wanted to share love and intimacy with in which he was accused of being lustful toward. Father Riley had been called to assist on a very important investigation, a possession, of a young boy that had fallen victim to a demonic tragedy. The demon that possessed this teenager was cunning. It then began to play on Father Riley's own weakness during the battle. Haley was beautiful. He desired her and deep inside he loved her. The demon saw this as a weakness since he was a priest and preyed on it.

Riley Shook himself out of his self-reflection, hesitated for a moment, then answered the call.

"Hello, this is Father Riley." He spoke.

"Uhm, Father Riley? John, it's me, Haley." She replied.

"Haley, what a pleasant surprise! How are you doing?"

"Well, myself I'm quite fine. There is something I needed to talk to you about. Do you have a minute?" She asked, with a hint of panic in her voice.

"Of course, we just finished mass. I've been taking a moment to meditate. How may I help you?" he asked.

In the back of his mind, a strange feeling came over him. Something told him this conversation was going to be complicated. Something in Haley's voice didn't sound right. Memories returned to him, the last time they worked together, things got complicated. He remembered… the looks they shared. He remembered the feeling he began to feel. He remembered the temptation.

"Listen, Father, I have a new case. This situation… it's the strongest I've ever felt. It's a possession, but I don't think it's demonic. You see, there's this young woman. Her name is Molly, here in Albuquerque. I sense something dark in her, but it's nothing I've ever felt before. It's like it's almost alive in her! I don't know how to describe it. I think an exorcism is the right path, but it feels more complicated." Haleys voice trembled, she was nervous after her confrontation with molly, after what she saw in the mirror.

Father Riley considered her comment for a moment. An exorcism? That's not something you just call some hotline to request. An exorcism must be sanctioned by the church. Formal requests, investigations of validity, this kind of request goes straight to the Pope himself. It could take weeks, if not month's for this to go through. What kind of desperate situation is Haley in that she would so directly inquire about this?

"Haley, slow down. Give me some background details. What's going on? I haven't heard from you in years, and now you inquire about an exorcism unexpected? Tell me, child I know you. You never panic like this. Is this young woman of the faith?"

"I don't know, I investigated her home, well, her sisters' home. I didn't see any religious artifacts. No crucifixes, holy water, anything of the sort. Why?" Haley asked.

"Haley. Exorcisms are a complicated subject. You know that we've been down this road before. One doesn't simply call up the local church and request one. You know the process. How serious do you sense this to be? It's not like you to be so direct in something like this. You're smart, resilient, confident.

I've never heard your voice tremble like this before." Riley spoke.

"Father, I saw something. I saw the spirit. I saw it in an old mirror, it's reflection. I turned. Molly was behind me, threatening me. I saw the evil in her eyes. I felt the fury, but it didn't belong to the girl. Father, this thing is something I've never encountered. I sense its growing power. The girl need's help! Soon! Of the faith or not, I know an exorcism is her only hope!" Haley exclaimed.

Father Riley considers this for a moment. He let her words sink in as memories of exorcisms past rushed through his mind. He had seen things. He had been threatened, tempted by demons. Horrible things! Yet a mirror… a mirror. This triggered a memory. Years ago, at the Vatican, He remembered reading an old text, a document that the church kept locked away in the archives that he studied. Mirrors. Mirrors were powerful portals, but not just any mirrors. Not modern mirrors. He began to recall several lessons he had taken from his readings. He needed more information."

"Haley, tell me about the mirror. What kind is it? What material is it made from" he asked.

Haley thought about it. "Hold on Father, let me ask." Haley turned to Lily, who was sitting on the edge of the bed in their hotel suite, researching. "Lily, what can you tell me about the mirror." She asked, as she turned up the volume of the speaker phone.

"Well, I can tell you it's no less the one hundred years old. But based on the style I'm thinking later 1800's. French, possibly. It wasn't made here for sure. The mirror is glass, chrome backing with a gold outer coat. They certainly don't make them like that anymore. That thing could be worth a fortune!" Lily replied.

Father Riley overheard Lily's comment. His mind began

to process what he had heard. Mirrors like that, he knew, where special. Their construction in those days made them special. With metallic coatings, they had certain potential abilities. Or so he had read. It was pure speculation at this point. They were said to be able to harness, store energies, acting like capacitors. With two metallic coatings, and a sheet of glass as an insulator, it was basically like an anode and a cathode. The theory was they could channel energy, opening a portal to the other side. This was forbidden knowledge by the church. Why the Vatican kept this arcane knowledge in the archives was a mystery to him. In his studies as an exorcist in his youth, he had been exposed to vast amounts of forbidden knowledge. Something inside him told him he was needed in this situation, but he knew the church would never sanction this. He knew, because he had once learned an ancient rite that exists, one that the church absolutely had forbidden to be performed for the last eighty years. Riley thought deep. The mirror. He would have to see it for himself, and he also knew what he owed Haley. She had risked her neck for him ten years earlier, during the last exorcism he performed. He sat back in his chair, weighed his options. If he got involved, this would be out of the church's domain.

"Haley, I need to tell you something. A traditional exorcism won't work here." Riley said "But..." Riley hesitated. There is another way. It's complicated."

"What? What is it?" Haley asked.

"Haley, I can't tell you over the phone. But... I can be there soon. It'll be a few hours' drive. I can be there this afternoon. But I need some info first, I need to know the physical condition of the possessed. What must be done, if I'm correct about what I sense is going on, will be quite taxing on her."

"She seemed to be in good health, as far as I could tell. She looks very fit. I know the physical challenges that these things bring on, I remember..." Haley was interrupted.

"Hey, don't forget, Katy said she's pregnant!" Lily spoke

out load.

Riley sat back in his chair again. Pregnant! The situation was worse than he thought. This added a new spin to the situation. Now he was certain. He had to help. He stood up and circled around his chair. "Haley, I'll be there in 3 hours, four tops. This is more urgent you can possibly imagine. If what you say is accurate, there is more at stake here than just the woman."

Haley looked confused. Father Riley sensed a greater danger than she did. What could it be? She was eager for him to get here. He knows something.

"Alright, I'll text you the address where we are staying. It's not far off of I-40." Haley replied.

"I'll head out in a moment; I need to make some preparations. I need to collect… my kit. Remember Haley, what we are about to do is outside of the church's knowledge and control. This is us, on our own again. Not unlike last time." Father Riley hung up the phone. He collected his thoughts. He turned towards a large, locked cabinet in his office. His kit was inside, aged, and dusty. It had been some time since he used it. This time, if he were right about what he sensed, would be a great challenge.

The drive had been challenging. Thunderstorms has struck off and on throughout his drive. High desert winds rocked his vehicle as he passed through miles and miles of hilly desert terrain. At last, success. He arrived in Albuquerque in the late afternoon. He pulled up to the hotel address that Haley had sent him. He parked, stepped out of his pickup truck, and went inside, looking for suite 145. He found it and knocked on the door. It opened. There she was, just as young and attractive as she had been ten years ago. She was a sight to see. Riley blanked his mind, such thoughts were forbidden.

"Haley, so wonderful to see you!" He remarked.

"Father Riley, thank God you're here!" she replied. The rest of the team stood up from various points of the room to greet him. They approached and shook his hand. He had already known who they were, as he had been a secret admirer of the show. He entered the room and sat a briefcase on the desk near the door.

"Folks, it's a pleasure to meet you all. I would love to spend time exchanging pleasantries, but I sense time is short. I need more information on this Molly woman, what did you witness, how did she behave, any strange mannerisms? I have reasons I need such details if I'm to confirm what I suspect." He spoke.

Haley turned to him. "Well, for one thing, her personality seemed to shift from normal, to angry, uneasy, even verbally hostile."

Paul added in. "Are you kidding, she a complete ass! With a nice ass!"

Lily scowled at him, then turned to Riley. "She displayed typical behaviors of possession, anger, irritability, discomfort. But there were also moments of relative calm, as if the spirit were being elusive."

"Haley, what was it that you saw in the mirror?" Father Riley asked.

"A girl, black hair, pitch black eyes, clammy grey skin. She had a look over pure evil on her face." Haley replied. Riley considered this for a moment. "Definitely not a demon, so this confirms my belief that we need to take a different approach."

Father Riley walked over to a chair and sat down. He looked up at the group. "There is old rite of exorcism that the church stopped using decades ago. It's complicated and dangerous, but it's the only way to truly rid this entity." He continued. "A traditional exorcism banishes a demon from its host, sending it back to Hell. That won't work here. Banishing this spirit simply frees it from her, releasing it to roam freely to attach itself to another person, or even Molly herself again." Said Riley.

"What more can we find out about this Raven? If she was murdered, I'm sure there are police records than can be researched. Lily, hop on that. I suspect we need to know as much as possible about who we're dealing with. Mike, get ahold of Kate and see how much more we can dig up on this mirror. Go there and physically examine it if you have to. There has got to be some kind of clue we can draw from it. Make sure it's when Molly isn't there though, I sense Raven is getting more powerful, more control over Molly." Haley ordered.

Mike called up Katy and set up a time to go over and inspect the mirror. They settled of 3 in the afternoon. Mike arrived and Katy let him in and led him to Molly's room. He looked around and found the mirror sitting on top of the dark wood dresser in front of Molly's bed. He approached and began to examine it. It certainly was old, Louis XVI style; he could tell by its patina that it had definably been around awhile. He moved it forward, it was heavy. The frame was made of a heavy wood, coated in fading gold paint. He looked at the frame, the glass, the light gold coating over it. He studied the back of it. There, on the lower frame, just to the left, was a faded stamp by the manufacturer. "1820, Paris, France" identified its age and where it was made. He looked further. He found a set of initials carved into the side frame. "R Debardot" It read. The discovery shocked him! Could this mirror have belonged to Raven? Had Molly's grandmother purchased this from her family's' estate? Did Raven once gaze into this mirror as Molly does now?

Mike pulled out his phone and called up Haley. "You, I think this thing once belonged to Raven, and now that Molly has it, it could be the vessel that Ravens spirit had inhabited after the gravestone was destroyed."

"Then the mirror is key. I've seen this before." Haley said. She turned to Father Riley, who had joined her for coffee in the hotel lobby. "Father, that mirror… it may have been Ravens. I think that's where it energy came from." Riley considered this for a moment. He sipped his coffee.

"Then we know what we need to do. Raven must be

exiled back into the mirror. The mirror must be destroyed.

Haley spoke into the phone. "Mike you and Katy to prepare for the exorcism. We need to surprise her when she gets home. We need to trap her in her room and subdue her while Father Riley performs the exorcism.

"Got it!" Replied Mike.

"Father, what's the plan?" asked Haley.

"We need to be there before she gets home. Prepare the room, make sure a crucifix is placed on the wall behind her bed, one on each wall beside the bed, and one on the ceiling. When Ravens leaves her body, she will avoid the crosses. She will be drawn to the mirror, her only place of refuge. Once its back inside, we need to act quickly. Have a sledgehammer ready, we need to smash it to bits." He sipped more coffee. "We need to act quickly though, once the portal is opened up, it becomes a two-way door. Raven can go back in it, but something else may be attracted to it on the other side and attempt to pass back through." He considered a few passages in the book he had in his hand, the "Rituale Romanum."

He knew he would need another tactic. He produced a second book, the "Atharva Veda." From his briefcase beside him. He referenced a certain section that suggested that a sacrifice, or offering, must be made. Something needed to further attract Raven back into the mirror. There must be blood. They would have to draw Molly's blood and apply it to the face of the mirror. They would have to cut her palm as a symbol of sacrifice.

Father Riley would have to recite the prayer against Satan and the Rebellious Angels. This would aggravate the spirit, forcing it to leave her body. It would be a tough fight, and a long night. He laid out his plan to Haley.

Lily entered the hotel lobby where Haley and Father Riley sat. "I dug up some information on this chick! So, looks like she was at some rave back in the 70, partying it up and getting drunk with friends. Apparently, some serial killer named Jason slipper her some roofies, and took her to his home where he bound her, raped her several times, then bet her to death with a geode. A freaking! Geode of all things! That's totally fucked up!" Lily said. "Later on, the defiled her graves stone with a pentagram etched into the face of it. Apparently, he did that to other victims as well."

Father Riley considered this. He began tapping his fingers on the table in front of him. "What time does she get home?" he asked.

"Katy said she's usually home by 6" replied Haley.

Lily spoke up. "I just talked to Katy a moment ago. Guess what! She got arrested and taken into for questioning downtown by the cops. Word is though she was released and because they couldn't find any evidence of wrongdoing."

"Arrested for what?" asked Haley

"Sounds like she had snuck into some guys house, I think her lover or something, not sure why. That's some weird shit." replied Lily.

Father Riley looked at his watch. It was 3:33. In his mind, this was a sign that now was the time to act.

"Let's go, it's time to begin preparations. Raven is almost in full control of her now." He said.

He stood up and gathered his kit and briefcase. The rest of the team assembled and headed to the van. They began the drive to Katy's house, where the ritual would begin.

22 THE EXORCISM OF MOLLY JENSON

The van pulled up and Haley instructed the team to empty out the equipment, then park the van down the street, out of sight. They complied with her instructions as Father Riley entered the house, went to Molly's room, and began setting up the Crucifix's, laid out holy water, laid out a bible on the nightstand. Next to it he placed a small statue of Michael the Archangel, one of Mary, and another of Jesus. He began to pray the "Our Father" and pleaded to God for strength in the coming battle.

Downstairs, the team hashed out a plan. They would have to subdue Molly and force her into her room, kicking and screaming if necessary. Their presence would anger her, so they had to be sneaky about it. Paul had a pair of arm and leg restraints that he would secure to her.

"Ha, this is going to be the fun part!" Paul joked.

"You're always such a pervert, Paul. Take this seriously,

it's not a game." Replied Lily

Paul shrugged as he made his way to Molly's room and attached the restraints to the bedposts at the corner of the mattress. Father Riley was busy springling the bed with holy water, and recited prayers as he did so. Haley, Mike, and Lily set up a variety of cameras and sensors in the room. EVP recorders where placed on a dresser at the side of the room. Lily turned on one of the cameras and began filming Haley as she began the intro to their next episode.

"This will be one of the strangest shows we have ever filmed! A real-life exorcism is about to take place and you the viewers get to watch along as we go through this incredible journey!" Haley spoke into the camera.

Father Riley had his misgivings about this being filmed. The Rite he was about to perform was no longer sanctioned by the church. He spoke with Haley about choosing angles that would keep his face concealed as best they could. Normally he would not permit this, but he knew they had a show to do, so he allowed it. He proceeded with his prayers and preparations.

"Alright team, here's what we have to do." Haley said, as Katy entered the room. "Molly won't want to be in here once she sees how its set up. We'll hide in the room on the other side of the hallway. When she opens her door, we sneak up and grab her. Paul, Mike, you grab her arms and try to lift her off her feet. Get her on the bed. Lily, you strap her down and make sure she can't move."

"Hey, I wanted that job!" Paul replied

"Shut up, perv." Said Lily.

Father Riley interjected with his own thoughts. "She'll fight you tooth and nail on this. Be strong, I don't expect the nicest language out of her. She'll say thing that will challenge your faith, which will make you question yourself. Don't listen. This isn't a demon so I don't know what she will tell you, but it's going to be foul. Katy, I suggest you not be in here for this. This is going to be very personal, and you know her best. She would target you the most."

"Got it." Replied Katy, who's nerves had her trembling.

"As soon as she's secure I'll begin with holy water and a prayer. She won't like that. This may take some time, so use the restroom now. Once she secured, I need to cut her palm. I'll apply blood to the mirror. This will draw Raven to it further."

"How will we know Raven is in the mirror?" Asked Mike.

"Prepare yourself, but I've done this before. You'll see her. She will be angry. Mike, you're the strongest of the bunch. Take that sledgehammer and smash the glass, do it quickly. Remember, it's a two-way door." Father Riley said.

"Got it." Mike replied.

The team broke up and prepared themselves. They ate, they used the restroom. They waited. Then the time came. Molly's car pulled into the driveway. A door slammed shut. The front door opened, then closed. Molly had come home.

The crew positioned themselves, ready to pounce. Molly looked darkly upon her sister as she entered the house. They didn't speak. Molly was angry and frustrated from her ordeal with the police. She turned and went up the stairs. Katy listened nervously for what she knew was coming next. Molly opened her door to her bedroom. She saw what it had become.

"WHAT THE ACTUAL FUCK IS THIS SHIT, KATY!" Molly screamed at the top of her longs.

, the team leaped into action! Mike and Paul grabbed Molly by the arms, the squeezed as they began to lift her off the floor. Molly began to kick at them furiously. Molly was strong! This was no longer Molly. Her eyes turned black as endless pits, her face went pale, her skin became cold and clammy. Her voice became something unbearable to hear, like that of a monster, cold and guttural. It seemed to resonate from somewhere beyond this world. Raven was in full control now. Molly was gone.

"WHAT THE FUCK ARE YOU GODDAMN ASSHOLES DOING, YOU FUCKTARDS! GET THE

FUCK OFF ME! LET ME FUCKING GO YOU BITCHES!"

Despite the Kicking, screaming, and spitting, they wrestled her to the bed. Lily swept in and quickly, though not easily secured her arms and legs to the straps. Father Riley slipped a rosery around her neck. Raven screamed in pain! Hatred of that thing made her wretch!

"WHY YOU FUCKING LITTLE BITCH! YOU LITTLE CUNT, UNTIE ME SO I CAN BEAT YOUR SCRAWNY LITTLE ASS!" Raven yelled. She turned to the priest. 'AND WHO THE FUCK ARE YOU SUPPOSED TO BE, . GET THE FUCK OUT OF MY ROOM!"

Father Riley produced a small knife, approached her, and made a small incision on her left pam. Blood began to ooze from the wound.

"OWWWW YOU FUCKING BASTARD! WHAT THE FUCK WAS THAT FOR? FUCK OFF!" Raven yelled.

Father Riley wiped up the blood with a small cloth and proceeded to outline the edges of the glass of the mirror. , the mirror began to vibrate and shift as if it had become alive.

It had been relatively warm earlier, but the temperature dropped as if the energy of the room had been sucked out of it. The crew could see their breath escape as they breathed.

"RELEASE ME YOU FUCKING CUNT!" Raven said as she looked towards Haley.

"Lily looked towards Haley and whispered. "I think we're going to have to bleep a few things out." Haley nodded as she looks on in terror. She had never seen such a manifestation. "Molly, if you can hear me, you need to fight her. You need to Fight!" Haley said.

"AND YOU NEED TO PULL THAT STICK OUT OF YOUR FILTHY TWAT, SKANK!" Raven replied.

Father Riley opened his Bible and proceeded to offer his blessing. "In the name of the Father, The son, and the Holy spirit! Raven, I command you to leave the body of this child of God. I command you to free her and return to your realm!"

"AND I COMMAND YOU TO FUCK OFF, OLD MAN" Raven replied. Her head twisted to the side in an unnatural way. She leaned closer to the priest. "I THINK YOU HAVE SOME ALTER BOYS TO PLAY WITH."

Father Riley continued. "Oh, heavenly Father, Jesus Crist, give Molly the strength to fight this beast." He leaned in towards Raven and placed his palm on her head. He began to pray. "Michael the Archangel, battle now this foul tormented spirit. Send it back to the other side!"

"NOOOOOOO…" screamed Raven in a demonic tone. Lily felt a shiver of fear run down her spine as the sounds reverberated through to room. Mike's blood ran cold as he gazed into the pitch-black eyes. Haley shivered as she moved to adjust the camera angle to re-image the scene. Paul struggled to manipulate the controls of the EVP but realized the batteries had completely drained.

Father Riley continued to press Ravens head down as he repeated his prayers repeatedly. For hours, sweat dripped from his brow as Raven twisted and turned. She growled and spit upon him. She uttered horrific insults. Her body shook as she wet the bed, and then for a moment, she settled down. Raven looked over to Paul as he replaced battery after battery.

In a calm voice, Raven addressed him. "I saw the way you were looking at me the other day, Paul. What do you say you and I have a little fun? Wanna fuck me? I'll let you fuck me hard!." Paul couldn't speak, rather he shivered in place. Raven turned to Lily.

"How about you, girly? I'll bet your pussy is tight!" Raven enticed her. Lily kept her cool and continued filming. "Fuck yeah my pussy is tight, but you'll never get it, ." Lily thought in her mind.

Meanwhile, Katy paced around the kitchen. The yelling,

screaming and obscenities she was hearing from upstairs was making her heart race. She thought of something! She needed to call Kelly and let her know what was going on. How could she have forgotten? She pulled out her phone and dialed up Kelly's number; the phone rang, Kelly answered.

"Hello? Katy is that you?" Kelly asked in a weepy voice.

"Yeah, it's me. Kelly, I need to tell you what's going on, this is huge!" Katy said.

"What is it, this sounds bad?" Kelly asked.

Kelly, already in tears from all the stress she has endured, sat down on the floor in her kitchen. Even though her anger at Aaron was flowing through her, she still decided to find the energy to make dinner for her family. She still provided for her family's needs.

"There's a priest here, with Haley and her team. He is performing an exorcism on her. It's hell up there. Molly is suffering! I don't know what to do. I'm scared!" Katy said as she broke down and began to cry. Kelly could hear the demonic screaming, cursing, yelling coming through the phone. It sent shivers down her spine. She walked over to Aaron's study, where he was sitting and contemplating what had happened when Molly had infiltrated his home. Kelly put the phone on speaker.

"Aaron, listen, Molly is getting an exorcism. Katy is on the line right now." Kelly told him. Aaron looked up, shocked. A burst of foul language in a horrific voice could be heard through the phone. Aaron stood up and approached his wife as she held out the phone. He looked at Kelly in fear.

"Are you fucking serious? Is Haley there right now? An exorcism is serious shit! How did that happen?" asked Aaron. Aaron knew about exorcisms, how taxing they can be on the mind and body. He knew this could last for many hours, even days, over several sessions. He feared for the wellbeing of the baby, he feared for Molly.

"Katy, is there anything we can do to help? We can be right over!" Aaron told Katy.

"I feel so anxious and alone right now. My anxiety is through the roof. Aaron I can't take this!" Katy replied.

Aaron looked over to Kelly. For the moment, their own personal troubles were sidelined. Aaron grabbed the keys from his desk. Without speaking he looked at his wife, they nodded in agreement that they needed to be there for Katy.

"Look, I don't know, there is so much going on right now. I can't even think straight. Molly is suffering.." Katy replied. Tears began to run down her face. She began to sob. She felt her sister's pain, it flowed through her. Kelly could hear more screams and yelling in the background. Her perspective on what had happened, what he had been through, and what was to come was making the situation come to a new light. Kelly felt a new pain in him. This one was of sorrow, dread, regret, and fear.

As they collected their things, Kelly called Susan, the mother of Danny's best friend, Jacob. "Susan, do you mind if Danny stays over for e few days? Things are going down over here, I'll explain later."

"Sure, no problem! Are you all ok?" asked Susan.

"You have no idea the chaos, but I'll tell you over coffee someday." Kelly replied hurriedly.

"Send him over, I'll set up the guest room." Susan replied.

They hung up and Kelly prepped Danny a bag for a few days. She blessed him and sent him down the street to Jacob's house. Aaron and Kelly locked the doors and hopped in his truck. They started it and sped off.

As they pulled up, Katy opened the door. They approached her and threw their arms around her. Kelly began to sob as she felt the emotions flowing throughout the house. Aaron entered the house. The yelling and screaming he heard from upstairs rattled his bones. He considered going up there but was hesitant. Kelly put her hand on his shoulder, cautioning him. He looked at her, and she could feel the fear in him. Kelly thought for a moment. There had to be some way to distract the trio from the stress. She decided to head to the kitchen, began rummaging through Katy's fridge. She decided cooking was a good stress relief. She pulled out some pork sirloin steaks and potatoes. Aaron began dicing the potatoes. Katy started brewing up some red chili. Kelly started a pot of beans. The smell permeated the kitchen. It was indeed the distraction they needed.

Arturo pulled into the driveway. As he exited his car, he could hear the evil foul language coming from his home. He rushed inside to find Katy, Aaron, and Kelly in the kitchen, preparing a meal. He was confused as to what was going on.

"Katy, baby, what the hell is this? What's going on?" he asked.

Katy pulled him to the side as more foul language could be heard. "Molly is getting an exorcism, Art. There is a priest and a paranormal team up there. They have been there for hours!" Katy replied. Art looked at her in shock. His eyes widened.

"You mean like in the freaking movie? He asked.

Katy laid out all the details of what had been happening. Art dropped onto the couch; his mind was racing. He never imagined things would come to this. Thirty minutes later, the group sat at the table, each picking at their plates of carne steaks that Kelly had prepared. They listened on in silence at the horrific commotion continued upstairs.

Several hours had passed, there seemed to be no progress. They had taken several breaks in the procedure. Each time, they discussed new ideas. They conversed with Katy, Aaron, Kelly, and Arturo. They determined Molly herself was unreachable. They had to appeal directly to Raven. Father Riley considered trying a new tactic. He thought to appeal to the spirit itself, to Ravens own pain and suffering. He reaffirmed himself, and the team went back to work. They re-entered the room.

"Raven, I know the pain you have endured. I know your suffering. Release it. Your killer is long dead. He has paid for the price for what he did to you. I command you to release Molly. She is innocent! She is a child of the Lord!"

Raven turned to the priest. "Innocent my ass. You should feel the thoughts that run through her mind. The desire, the lust, the sex; Molly is a whore."

"Raven, this body does not belong to you. Free her and move on! Jesus Christ compels you!" the priest demanded.

"You wanna fucking take me on? Do you think you can command me? You men can't be trusted." Raven spat at him. "All they think about is fucking PUSSY! You punk ass pedophile bitch, you're no fucking good. Your SO-CALLED GOD IS NO FUCKING GOOD! HE DIDN'T HELP ME! HE DIDN'T SAVE ME! HE ABANDONED ME! HE WILL ABANDON YOU!" Raven calmed her voice for a moment. She looked around the room. "Just like that fucker that took my life, I'll take Molly's. I'll get even, just you wait. As for Molly, she belongs to ME now, you worthless FUCK!" Raven growled. She began to chuckle to herself. Raven looked around the room at each of the team members. "Aaron… BELONGS TO ME NOW!" She paused for a moment. "Kelly… I WILL end her… one way or another."

Over the next several hours, running long into the night, Father Riley continued to bargain with Raven. It wasn't getting anywhere, Raven was too stubborn, too angry. , Lily angled her camera and bumped the mirror, almost knocking it over. Mike reached out and grabbed it before it fell.

"GET AWAY FROM MY FUCKING MIRROR, YOU LITTLE PUSSY LICKING WHORE! THAT'S MY FUCKING MIRROR! DON'T YOU FUCKING TOUCH IT!" yelled Raven to Lily. She spat at her but missed the mark.

Mike and the priest seemed to in that moment have a simultaneous epiphany. The mirror! The mirror was key! If only there was a way to get Raven full attention on it. Father

Riley looked to Mike, then gestured to the sledgehammer. Mike nodded. Raven saw what was going on. She became agitated. Her body began to shake violently as Mike picked up the hammer and held it threateningly towards the mirror.

"GET AWAY FROM MY FUCKING MIRROR, YOU DUMB PIECE OF SHIT! GET...THE FUCK… AWAY!' Raven screamed.

Mike swung the hammer back ready to strike. Ravens body arched violently, almost lifting off the bed! Over and over, it lurched. Her intent was to break free from the straps that bound her. Mike prepared to strike.

"NOOOOOOOOOOOOO……. STAY THE FUCK AWAY!" Raven demanded. Her voice came off as it came from the pits of hell.

a black cloud of energy seemingly ripped out of Molly's body and was drawn to the mirror, entering it. Father Riley continued his incantations as he turned to the mirror. There, a cold grey skinned young woman with black hair and evil dark eyes stood staring at him. "NOW, MIKE! DO IT!" demanded the priest. Mike swung the hammer with a furious swift swing, striking the mirror. Raven screamed! The mirror shattered into hundreds of shards of glass and broken wood. The room went silent. The temperature rose. It was warm again.

Molly had fallen silent. Her body lies motionless. Her breathing was weak. Sweat dripped from her body. Fortunately, her skin tone had returned to normal. Katy entered the room with wet towels to clean her up. She peeled back her eye lids to check and see of the blackness had left them. Molly's blue eyes had returned. Katy turned to Haley, who had been looking on over her shoulder.

"Haley, run down and get Kelly. We need her." Katy instructed.

Haley asked no questions. She hurried down the stairs and called out to Kelly to join them. Together, they rushed back up and entered Molly's room. Kelly looked down at the young woman, still bound to her bed. Katy looked over at her.

"Is it gone? Kelly I know you can feel…"

Kelly rushed over. She sat on the bed at Molly's side and placed one hand over her heart and the other over her forehead. Kelly closed her eyes and allowed Molly's energy inside her. She felt only Molly there. Raven was gone.

"Untie her, she needs to get to the hospital. She's hurt, and we need to find out about the baby. Somebody call 9-1-1." Kelly demanded. Lily rushed over and undid the bindings. Haley pulled out her phone and dialed emergency services. Aaron and Father Riley entered the room. Aaron looked around, then down at Kelly and Molly. His heart skipped a beat. The room had looked like a war zone, with smashed bits of mirror on the floor, bed sheets strewn about, a jewelry box that had been knocked to the floor. He approached his wife. What he saw had surprised him. His wife, whom had utterly despised Molly, was now cleaning her up and comforting her.

For a brief moment, Molly tried to open her eyes. She struggled to turn and look at the group around her. Her vision was blurry, her head pounded. For a moment she could see the group around her. Katy was there holding her hand. Kelly was wiping sweat from her brow. A priest stood at the foot of her bed, saying a prayer. Two strange men, and two unfamiliar women were wrapping up strange equipment in the background. She could see Aaron. She could not speak. She did not understand why she was in this condition. She could not keep her eyes open any longer. She blacked out once again.

An ambulance arrived within minutes of being called. EMTs arrived and began running an IV, while also checking Molly's vitals. Katy handed Molly's identification to their supervisor, a young woman named Amber, who looked to be the same age as Molly. She began filling in her information, name, age, height, weight… then stopped in sudden recognition. "Molly Jenson?" she remarked. "Molly from Manistee?" Katy looked at her confused.

"What? Do you know her or something?" asked Katy. Amber looked over at Molly and took a few steps toward her. "Molly?" she asked out loud. She turned back towards Katy. "I'm Amber White. I grew up in Rapid City, Michigan. That's where I went to EMT school. I had several classes with Molly! My husband is in the Air Force and got transferred here two years ago." she replied. She looked down at Molly with shock. Molly had been a friend of hers back then. She looked down at her friend, laid out and unconscious.

"What happened here?" Amber looked around the room, noticed the debris of the broken mirror. She looked across the room where a police officer was interviewing Father Riley. She examined the rest of the room, noticed the damage that had been done to various objects. She turned back to Katy. A memory flashed in her mind, a memory of a strange conversation she had once had with Molly a few years earlier.

Molly, Amber, and another young woman, Sarah, had been sitting at an outdoor patio at a local brew pub not far from their college campus. The three had ordered a round of beers as they unwound from their day. They gossiped about guys, laughed, giggled, and had a good time. Several beers in, Molly was getting a little loose lipped.

"So, Molly, how many guys did you hook up with in high school? What's your body count?" giggled Amber. "I had three football players myself. They ALL scored a touchdown with me!" She said, laughing.

Sarah chimed in. "Four here, two of them at the same time!" Amber punched her lightly in the arm, giggling.

Molly hadn't replied. She kept her mouth shut. She took a long swig of beer, deep in thought.

"None." She replied quietly.

"None? A pretty girl like you just had one?" laughed Amber. Sarah Chuckled along with her.

The memory of that night in the cemetery flooded Molly's mind. She decided to tell her story now that she was getting a little inebriated. "Do you girls believe in ghosts?" Molly asked.

"Ghosts? Sure, I guess." Replied Sarah.

"I don't know, I neither do nor don't I guess." Said Amber.

Molly took another swig of her beer. She leaned in. "Then let me tell you a little story about ghosts." Molly said. Molly told them about sneaking out with her friends, the drinking, the Ouija board. She told them about Raven, the possession, the headstone, all of it. The other girls listen on quietly. Sarah thought of it all as a drunken story to scare them. It was getting close to Halloween anyway. Amber on the other hand, she had an uneasy feeling about this. Something deep inside told her Molly wasn't making this up.

"So, your free of this… Raven… Now?" asked amber.

"Yup, that bitch is long gone." Molly replied. She finished off her pint and ordered another one.

Amber snapped back to the present. Molly was being wheeled out of the room by now. She compiled all she remembered in her mind and sized up the situation. Molly hadn't been free from Raven after all.

"Raven! Raven did this!" she uttered.

Katy looked at her confused. "You know about Raven?" she asked.

"Yeah, she told me about it years ago. I didn't know what to make of it then. Part of me thought it might be just a scary story, but another part… What really happened here?"

"Katy took a breath. "What you see here is the aftermath of an exorcism. Raven had come back. She had taken over Molly again. They've been at it all night long since this afternoon."

"An exorcism? Oh my God! Poor Molly. I mean a real-life exorcism! I thought that kind of stuff was just in the movies." Amber replied, deep in thought. "Listen, I got to get going with here. She's in bad shape. We're taking her to St. Mary's stat."

"I'll be right behind you; I'll go get my keys."' Katy said. She turned over to Aaron and Kelly, who had been standing in the front yard nearby. "You all, I'm following her down there. Art, I'll call you when I know anything.

Amber refocused on her job, finished her notes, and entered the ambulance. She looked back through the crew passage from the cab, back at her old friend. This was all so much for her.

23 UPSHOT

Molly woke up several days later from her ordeal in the hospital. The room had a window this time. She turned and watched as the sun began to rise over the Sandia mountains. A nurse entered the room, just as her previous visit here. Like before, she looked at charts and checked vitals. She verified that her IV bag had enough fluid to last. She approached Molly and looked caringly down on her.

"Good, you're finally awake. You've been through a lot of trauma, but your vitals are mostly good. Your blood pressure is a little on the low side, but it's been steadily rising. We've been getting you vitamin supplements, as your bloodwork showed you a little low across the board. The doctor will be in shortly to explain his findings, you've had a CT scan and MRI. The doctor will discuss the results."

Just as the nurse had finished that sentence, the door knocked and opened. An older Hispanic woman in a lab coat stepped in and sat at a chair near a desk by Molly's bed.

"Good morning, Molly, I'm Doctor Griego. I've been overseeing your care for the last few days, you've been through quite a bit, but the circumstances of how you got here aren't quite clear. If you're up to it, can you tell me a little about what happened?"

Molly thought for a moment. She couldn't recall anything. She had no idea how she got here. In fact, she could not remember much at all. The last thing she recalled was standing in front of the mirror in her room. Then she seemed to have blacked out after that.

"I… I don't remember anything. I was just coming my hair in my room, and then everything seemed to go black. Now, I'm here!" Molly said, trembling.

"Well, we've done some tests and run some scans. Your bloodwork showed low levels of sodium, very low. Your blood pressure when you got here was 90 over 50, so it's possible you passed out due to dehydration. Other key minerals in your system were also quite low. How's your diet? Do you eat healthy?"

"Uhm, yeah, I don't eat anything odd or unhealthy. What about the scans." Molly asked.

"The MRI shows no blood vessel damage, so we have ruled out a stroke or aneurism. The CT scan shows a little minor swelling, but nothing serious. I expect you have a bit of a headache. Do you recall feeling overheated at the time? Had you been in the sun that day?" the doctor asked.

"No, not more than usual. I actually remember feeling pretty good at the time." Molly replied.

"I do have some deeper questions for you, Molly. Your current living conditions, do you feel safe at home?" she asked.

"Of course, why do you ask." Said Molly

The doctor adjusted her wire frame glasses and lifted the sheet from over her legs. There, around each ankle, were perfectly circular, but fading bruises. The doctor also pointed out similar bruises around her wrists. Molly looked down, completely confused.

"I assure you there is doctor patient confidentiality. Anything you want to tell me is between us. Do you feel like you were held against your will? Perhaps and sexual fetishes that could have resulted in these?

Molly rubbed her head. Sure, she had been into a little light spank play in the past, but nothing like this had happened. Where did these come from?

"No, nothing that extreme, and I've never been held against my will." Molly murmured.

"Well, they do concern me. But if you feel safe, I'll let you be on that." Dr. Griego replied. "For the time being, I'm satisfied with you blood work, although I want you getting more fluids and sodium. Your sister is here in the lobby. We'll get you released so you can go home." The doctor spoke. Molly simply nodded.

Over an hour later, another nurse was pushing molly in a wheelchair out to Katy's waiting car. Together, Katy and the nurse helped her inside. Katy closed the door and began to drive away. Both women where quiet at first. Then, Molly lazily turned her head to her sister, whom had a distracted look on her face. "Katy? What happened? Molly asked.

Katy sighed, paused for a moment. "She had full control over you, sis. Something had to be done. Kelly called an old friend from Arizona. She, and a priest knew a few tricks. They freed you from her."

Molly, still drowsy, continued to stare at her sister with droopy eyes. "Who had me, Katy?

Katy turned and considered her sister. "How far back can you remember, sis?"

"I don't really know. My memory is kind a blotchy, bits and pieces, I guess. I was combing my hair in the mirror, then blackness." Molly said lowly.

"What about Aaron? What do you remember of Aaron? Asked Katy.

"Aaron, your boss? He's seeming like a nice guy. I've only meet him a couple time, though." Molly said.

Katy suppressed a chuckle. She gave Molly a little suggestive side eye. They continued into their neighborhood and pulled into the driveway. Arturo was already there with the front door opened. He stepped over to the driveway and helped Molly out and pulled her up. He and Katy each took a side and helped her walk in. They sat her down and Katy went to fetch her some iced tea. Art laid a blanket over Molly's legs and went to meet his wife in the kitchen.

"How is she?' Art asked.

"She doesn't remember anything, not since she first got here. She only barely remembers meeting Aaron. She doesn't know she's pregnant with his child." Katy replied.

Arturo looked at her wide eyed. "We better be careful on this one, honey. She's already in a delicate state in many ways. This could be too much for her right now."

"I agree. But she is still pregnant and needs to find out eventually. She'll eventually start to show and ask questions if we don't." Katy replied.

Katy looked into the living room from the kitchen. Her sister was laying down on the couch, dozing off. Katy worried that her ordeal had caused more mental damage than they had discovered at the hospital. She couldn't remember all that had happened, all that she had done. Katy wondered if she would ever remember. She thought back to their teenage years, searching for clues. Had Molly behaved this way before? Did she lose her memory then too? she realized something! She hadn't lost her memory! She thought deeper. Katy realized that while Raven had control of Molly back then, she hadn't taken such a deep level of control. Katy had smashed the headstone well before Raven could take such a grasp. She considered the mirror. It had been in Molly's bedroom back in those days in Michigan. Why didn't Raven re-acquire Molly then? It was because Raven had been weakened, yet still somehow attached to her sister.

Katy needed to be assured that Raven was truly gone, but who would be able to tell? KELLY! Katy grabbed her phone and pulled up Kelly's contact info, she hit the call button. Kelly answered after a couple of rings.

"Hello, hi Katy. How are things?" asked Kelly.

"She's home now. This mess has Molly really messed up. She can't remember anything. It's like a whole block of several month's is missing in her mind. She doesn't know she's pregnant. I'm worried about that, and I don't know if Raven is truly gone. I was wondering… I was wondering if you could…"

Kelly knew what Katy was going to ask. She was hesitant, but also curious. "You need me to read her I take it?" she asked Katy."

"Yeah, it's the only way to be sure. I, we, need to know Raven is truly gone." Katy said.

Kelly thought for a moment. She was right, considering the state of affairs, they did in fact need to know if Raven was truly gone. "I'll be right over, we just finished breakfast."

Kelly finished putting the dishes away and grabbed her keys. Aaron walked into the kitchen as she made her way to the door. "Where are you going?" he asked. Kelly looked over at Aaron. Still shaken by the last several weeks of events, she couldn't quite look at Aaron as she used to. She still very much loved him, but things were still to fresh, to raw for her.

"I'm going over to check on your little girlfriend, Aaron." She told him, sarcastically.

The jab hurt Aaron right down to the bone. He was still fearful and embarrassed of the situation. His heart sank to the floor when she called her that. He had never seen her that way himself. Yet, in a way, it wasn't far off the mark. He pondered however, considering Molly's pregnancy, if he should go.

"Katy said she doesn't remember anything. She worried that some trace of Raven may still be there. Grab your coat, lover boy. You need to be there too." Kelly said.

Reluctantly, Aaron did what he was told. He grabbed his

denim jacket from the coat rack by the front door. They locked up and headed toward the truck, started it, and drove away. A few minutes later, they pulled up in front of Katy's house. Aaron looked at it in dread, remembering the events from a few days prior. His memories, his thoughts haunted him. He knew what awaited him inside. They exited the truck and knocked on the door. Arturo let them inside. There, lying on the couch, dazed, was Molly. Molly looked up as they entered.

Kelly walked over to her, not saying a word. Molly, still drowsy, looked up at her slowly. She didn't recognize the red-haired woman who stood before her. Kelly bent down and lifted Molly's chin up to her. She gazed into Molly's eyes. There was an emptiness there, absolutely no sign of recognition in her. Kelly placed her other hand on Molly's face, positioning her thumb over her forehead. Kelly closed her eyes. Molly looked up at her, not understanding what was going on, yet not resisting. Kelly let molly's energy flow through her. She could feel her. She could feel the child within. She could not feel a trace of Raven inside her. Nothing remained.

Aaron looked on as his wife read Molly. His sense of astonishment overwhelmed him as the image of his wife, whom had otherwise despised Molly, now gently handled her and felt her energy flow through her. A few moments passed as Aaron, Katy and Arturo looked on. There was absolute silence. , Kelly opened her eyes and slowly pulled away. Molly slowly lowered her head back down.

Kelly gestured to the group to meet in the kitchen. They followed her as she took a stance at the far end of the kitchen table. She turned and faced the group. She lowered her head for a moment and took a breath. She looked back up and quickly glanced at her husband, who stood to her left, arms crossed. Arturo and Katy stood in anxious anticipation, hands in their pockets.

"Alright, here's the deal." Kelly began. "Raven is gone. I don't feel her presence anymore. Only Molly and the baby remain now. But there's a catch. Much of Molly is gone too, or at least suppressed. She's catatonic. What we see out there is almost like a shell of her former self. If there's anything left of her, it's buried deep down inside. We need to keep an eye on her at all times. She's been under Raven's influence for so long, she has forgotten her true self. I sense that she doesn't know who she is anymore."

The group looked around at each other. "What about the baby?" Aaron asked. Kelly looked over to him, concerned. For the moment she set aside her personal feelings and focused on what's important.

"The baby is healthy. I can feel it. I don't think Raven wanted the child harmed, so she left her alone. In fact, even before, when Molly was at our house, I felt like Raven wanted to protect it."

"I wonder what Raven's purpose for the baby was?" asked Arturo.

"Isn't it obvious?" asked Katy. "She probably thought she could be reborn through the child, if that's even a thing."

"A sort of reincarnation you mean." Said Aaron.

"Yeah, you see her life was taken by that serial killer. She may just want to have her life back, like as a way to live the rest of the life she had that was stolen from her. Sprits want to inhabit people who are weak or people who have gotten stuck in Astro projection, where the soul is in a different dimension and the body is soul free, because they crave life. They want to live again but they can't. So, in order for them to do that they have to have an empty shell if you will so that they can have a host to join the living. This is also true for demons. In fact, which is the main reason dolls were invented. So that the dead can inhabit them and have a place to live, hypothetically speaking." Kelly said.

"Is Raven truly gone? Destroyed? Or simply banished?" Asked Katy.

"I remember something Haley had told me years ago. There are two realms, the physical and the spiritual. Raven used the mirror as a portal between the two. By sending her back and smashing the portal, Raven is trapped in the spiritual realm. She can't return unless she's somehow invoked."

"Could she use another mirror?" Asked Arturo.

"Not a modern one, an antique. Haley had told me that antique mirrors were made differently. They had an energy all their own." Kelly replied. "Haley also said that the mirror may have belonged to Raven in the past, she may have had a special connection to it."

"Well, for now let's not go buying up any antiques." Katy replied.

Aaron considered Molly from the doorway of the kitchen. He considered his options. She looked broken. She looked pathetic. She no longer looked like the perky, chatty, flirtatious young woman he had come to know. "There has got to be something in there left of her." Aaron muttered to himself.

Kelly eyed him from behind. She knew what he was about to do. "Be careful what you say to her Aaron. She fragile. She can't take any more drama right now. She's been through enough." Aaron turned back at her and nodded. He stroked his silver goatee, stepped into the living room, and rounded the couch. He sat on the edge of the wooden coffee table in front of it, interlaced his hands and leaned in towards her.

"Molly. Molly, do you remember me?" Aaron asked. Molly slowly lifted her head and looked into his eyes. Something inside of her stirred. She knew she had met him a couple of times before, but somehow, she knew this man had something more to do with her.

"Mr. Aaron, uhm, Hi. How are you?" Molly asked.

Aaron sighed. It was worse than he thought. She really didn't remember him. She didn't remember the flirting, the favors, the advances. She didn't remember the sex. She didn't know about what's growing inside her.

"Molly, I need you to get as much rest as you can. You've

been through a lot." Aaron said softly. He knew Kelly wouldn't much care for this next part, but he reached out and cupped her hands in his own. "You have recovering to do now, Molly. You need all the rest you can get now."

"Do…" Molly struggled. "Do you know what happened to me?" she sobbed.

"I do, Molly. I know all too well what happened. But for now, we are all here to help you recover." Aaron spoke.

"But I have to get back to work! I just started working with Roger on that new project." Molly continued.

"That doesn't matter right now, Molly. What matters is you. Molly needs to help Molly now." Aaron replied.

Kelly looked on at the pair from the kitchen. It seemed strange to see her husband sitting there, comforting a woman that she had previously thought that she had so despised. Kelly, however, had a deeper recognition. It wasn't Molly that Kelly hated. Molly was just a young, misguided girl who happened to have a crush on her husband. So What? She was certain that Molly wasn't the only one. There were lots of pretty girls at Aaron's office who gave Aaron the eye. Kelly at times even thought it was cute. In Kelly's mind she knew it was time to look ahead to the future, one where Kelly and Aaron stayed together, even if Molly had to be weaved into the fabric that was their life now.

"I'm very tired Mr. Aaron. I need to get upstairs to my bed. Can you help me up the stairs?" Molly asked.

"Yeah, sure. It's just Aaron by the way, Molly." Said Aaron. "Katy, her room? Good to go?"

Katy nodded. "Yeah, we cleared it out, cleaned it up and replaced a lot of stuff, including the bed."

Aaron helped Molly off the couch. He slowly guided her up the stairs to her bedroom door, opened it, and helped her to the bed. She laid down, fluffed her pillow, and almost instantly fell asleep. Aaron threw a blanket over her, then looked around the room. Yes, several of the furnishings had been replaced. The mirror was long gone. It felt almost peaceful in here again. He exited the room and closed the door. Walking down the stairs, he thought to himself the irony of the situation. Him, here, with Molly and Kelly at the same time after all that had happened.

Kelly was helping Katy with dishes when Aaron walked back into the kitchen. She glanced over at Aaron as he sat down at the kitchen table, next to Arturo. "Well, looks like you got her into bed a second time, Aaron." She said in a sarcastic tone. Aaron was annoyed. He knew what he had done but was tired of the jabs.

"Kelly, enough." Aaron snapped. "I've already got enough on my mind."

Kelly sighed. He was right, but she still had the right to be upset. Maybe she would cut him a little slack. Maybe.

"So where do we go from here? Raven is gone. Molly's still pregnant. Lord knows what her mental state is now and what it will become." Remarked Aaron.

Katy considered the question as she wiped dishes and put them in the cabinet. She turned to Arturo. They didn't speak, but their gaze said volumes. Molly had to stay. Katy wouldn't kick her out, not in this state. Aaron was right. Raven was gone. Molly was pregnant. It would be a wonder if she could even hold down a job at this point. Arturo turned to Aaron with a smile on his face and slapping a hand on the table.

"Well come on buddy, looks like you and I are building a bassinette!" Arturo said.

Arturo had set up a pretty handy wood working shop in his garage. He loved the idea of a new project. This was just the thing for him, and to have Aaron over helping out was the right idea.

"There's a lot more to figure out before, pal." Aaron replied.

"I get it, I get it!" Arturo chuckled. He seemed to be the only one around making light of the situation.

Kelly finished helping Katy and they all sat down at the table. The time for "The talk" had come. Kelly seemed to take the ring- leader position in the conversation.

"Alright, here's my deal. I have a lot of personal issues with Molly that I need to work out, but I'm not setting a timeline on that. It'll happen when it happens. Aaron, we know what YOU need to start thinking about." She rubbed her fingers together, signaling money. "And the baby… Does it go back and forth between Molly and Aaron? Shared custody?"

Katy sat in contemplation. She looked up in the general direction of her sister's bedroom, considered her current mental state. "There's another idea." She spoke. "I know she just got out of the hospital, and she's tired, but I have a feeling what happened did more damage to her than we can see. If she can't pull herself together, I can't see her as able to raise a child in any capacity. Aaron, you could technically take full custody."

Aaron looked at her in surprise. How would Molly ever consent to that? That's her child too! Who would give up their child? This was too much to fathom for Aaron.

Molly woke up just after noon. She sat up, feeling more refreshed, but still lacked any memory of what happened. She looked around her room. It seemed unfamiliar to her. Something was off, here. She could feel it. She slowly stood up and walked to the dresser across from her. Something was missing. She usually combed her hair here. Her mirror! Where was her antique mirror? She opened her drawers. Several items of clothing seemed out of place. Where were her things? Not everything was missing, but many things were out of place. Molly liked order and coordination. This was off! She began recall her most recent memories. The mirror…the comb in her hair… , a fragment of a memory flashed in her mind. A girl, one that at that moment she didn't recognize. Who had that been?

Molly was hungry, she hadn't had a solid meal in days. Although still a little woozy, she made her way down the stairs. She could hear conversation coming from the kitchen. As she rounded the corner, she could see Katy, Arturo, Aaron from the office, and the unfamiliar woman from this morning. The woman looked at her rather cold as she spoke. Molly kept out of sight as she listened in on the conversation.

"Look, you think I'm going to sit here and be all happy-go-lucky about raising that woman's baby? Aaron, if you get fully custody…"

Aaron understood where she was coming from. The tension was building in him. He was ready to scream and yell, but he wouldn't do that in Katy's home.

"Look, I know what the implications here are. I know you could never look at the child the same as our son, considering who the mother is. That puts me in a hard place, Kelly." Aaron said.

"Oh, quite playing victim here, Aaron." Said Kelly, sharply.

"Alright lets calm down here!" Katy interjected. "There's time to figure this out. We need to find the right time to tell her she's pregnant first."

"Pregnant? Who are they talking about that's pregnant?" Molly thought. Her stomach growled. She rounded the corner and walked into the kitchen.

"Who's pregnant? Anybody I know?" asked Molly.

The group silenced. They all turned to look at her. How long had she been standing there? What else did she hear? The woman, Kelly, apparently looked like she was going to shoot lasers out of her eyes at her.

"Cat's out of the bag now!" remarked Arturo.

"Molly, sit down, we need to tell you something." Said Katy.

Molly, confused, did as she was told. She pulled out a chair and lowered herself in it. She looked around her. Everyone was staring at her. She felt very nervous. She wondered what was going on. Katy thought of the best way to tell her. She decided to test her memory.

"Molly, I need you to think back to our teenage years.

Raven. Do you remember?" asked Katy.

Molly thought back. Her memory was still fuzzy, but… YES. She began to remember. She remembered those dark days. She nodded. The group looked amongst each other, then back to Molly.

"Hey, by the way Katy, where's my mirror? I need to comb my hair." Molly asked.

"Molly, the mirror is gone. Destroyed. Raven came back Molly. Thru the mirror." Katy told her. "Raven possessed you again, only stronger this time. That's why you don't remember."

Kelly interjected. "Let's cut the crap and get back to basics." She turned to Molly. "Molly, you little shit… you, while under Ravens control drugged and fucked my husband." She slammed her hands down on the table. Molly jumped, startled. "And now, Molly, your pregnant." Kelly said, with contempt. Molly looked on in shock! She slowly turned her head over to Aaron, her mouth wide open.

"What? I did what?" Molly asked. "Raven came back for me. But how? Katy you smashed the headstone."

"The headstone was just part of it Molly. The mirror! The mirror was at the true vessel." Katy replied.

Molly looked at Aaron. "I'm pregnant? With your baby? Why… why can't I remember?

Aaron took a sip of iced tea. "You invited me to join you one night for drinks after work, and like a idiot I decided a couple cold ones couldn't hurt. I went. You slipped something in my beer. I drank it, and I fell under the effects of whatever you used on me. You took me across the street to the hotel. The rest speaks for itself. Now, we have a situation on our hands."

Molly's hands began to tremble. Raven! She had come back for her! How? Why hadn't she felt her before? "How long had Raven been with me? In me?"

It was Kelly's turn to speak. "Here's my theory, Molly." Kelly said coldly. "When Katy smashed the headstone, it weakened it. It found its refuge in a new vessel, her old mirror."

"That mirror? It belonged to Raven?" Molly asked. Katy added her piece. "When you moved out for collage, you left the mirror behind. When Art and I married and moved here, we brought it with us. We used it to decorate the spare bedroom, your bedroom."

Kelly spoke up again. "When you moved here molly, Raven attached herself to you through the mirror. It was weak. It couldn't take you over. Then that stupid little trip to Pennhurst made it stronger, more powerful. It was finally able to enter you, slowly taking you over. Eventually, it found a way to manipulate you. Your lust, for my husband, made it stronger. It took you over completely."

"Then it's not my fault! I didn't drug Aaron, Raven did! I'm innocent in all this." Molly remarked.

"No, bitch! Raven was influencing you but didn't have full control yet. She only enticed you to act on your desires. The actions you took were still your own!" Kelly stood up and slammed a first down. "NOW OWN IT!"

"Kelly, ease up on her, please." Katy begged. "How do you know Raven wasn't in full control?"

"Haley explained it all to me before they went back to Arizona. You see spirits don't attach themselves to just anybody, they look for someone with a desirable weakness. They attach themselves to them and work to exploit it. The more Molly gave in to her lust, the more powerful it became."

Molly began to cry. She sobbed for a solid five minutes. When she stopped, she asked. "Where is Raven now? How did she leave me?"

Kelly answered. "You've had an exorcism. It was long, and intense. It took a lot out of you, out of all of us. They were successful, banishing Raven back into the mirror, the portal that it had become. They smashed it and destroyed it. The portal is no more. Raven can't come back. At least not easily."

Molly slumped into her chair, lowering her head. It was

beginning to make sense. She was slowly beginning to remember now. It was piece by piece coming back to her. The Bar, the beer, the sex. It was all coming back to her. She considered Kelly's comments. Molly realized something. She remembered what she was thinking when she was combing her hair before she blacked out. She had been fantasizing about Aaron. She had been planning to get into bed and pleasure herself to him. That was the final straw Raven needed. That is when she had full control. How foolish could Molly have been?

"What do I do now? I'm not ready to raise a child. I can't do this!" Molly cried. The group remained silent.

"Alright, I'm going to lay out some options." Katy replied. "I'm not going to sugar coat this. Option one. You have the baby; you share joint custody with Aaron. You raise it together, but separate. Option two. An abortion. I know Aaron has his reservations about that, I don't know how you feel. Option three, surrender custody to Aaron, I know Kelly has her own reservations about that. But that's the deal as it sits. You can stay here during your pregnancy. We need to see where you are mentally and physically, after all that happened."

Molly sniffled and wiped her tears away. She looked to Aaron. "What do you think, Aaron?"

Aaron contemplated his response. "I'm obviously willing to raise and support this child. I won't walk away from this. But I won't make a move without Kelly's support. I need her in this, whatever we do. I love my wife. I always have. I always will. That will never change."

"But Aaron, I didn't do this out of lust. It was love! I love you Aaron!" Molly cried. Kelly's draw dropped.

Aaron, furious at her stubbornness, jumped out of the char and slammed his hands down on the table. Molly jumped again. "Now listen here you goddamn stubborn little entitled shit! You fucking princess bullshit ends now! YOU HAVE NO IDEA WHAT THIS WOMAN AND I HAVE ENDURED OVER THE YEARS. YOU HAVE

NO IDEA THE HARD WORK AND TEARS WE HAVE SHARED! YOU HAVE NO IDEA WHAT THIS WOMAN HAS DONE FOR ME, WHAT SHE'S BEEN THROUGH! YOU DON'T JUST WALK INTO A RELATIONSHIP AND THINK YOU CAN TAKE WHAT YOU WANT! YOU EARN IT, MOLLY! KELLY HAS EARNED MY LOVE AND MY RESPECT IN MORE WAYS THAN YOU CAN COUNT! I LOVE THIS WOMAN, NOT YOU! I LOVE MY WIFE! I LOVE KELLY!"

Aaron slowed his breathing and sat back down, glaring at Molly. "You do NOT wreck lives, and now we both must pay for your mistake. What part of that don't you seem to understand. Love. What the hell do you know about love? Jack shit is what you know."

Aaron looked over to Kelly, who face was so red its almost matched her blood red hair. She stood up and began pacing. Aaron knew something big was coming, something nasty. She always paced when she was red in the face and had something to get off her chest. She stopped and glanced at Aaron, then Molly. She crossed her arms and spoke.

"You two have taken the most intimate part of myself and trampled all over it. You have no idea what it feels like to have two people disregard you in such a way that you decide to go out and have a child I desperately want. I have limitations in which God himself gave me. It's not my cup of tea, I did not ask for it, and I feel that it is the cross I bare every single day. I consider myself less fortunate. I am not always the person you take home to mom because I am a strong opinionated and very defensive kind of person. So, when I get an opportunity to have something in my life, I don't take it for granted. For ANYONE to go down to the depths of my soul and just shit all over me because they don't have enough of what they want from me. That is the lowest form of torture you could ever inflict on me. Congrats you've managed to be about as cruel as you can be to a human being. For either of you to expect me to just take this laying down and expect me be understanding? Your sadly mistaken. So as far as your little rendezvous is concerned you can take it, and all the consequences that come with it, and shove it right up your ass. I have zero fucks about how that makes you fucking feel. If it hurts your soul, good. Maybe you'll have some God damned empathy for a fucking change, especially MOLLY. You can learn a thing or two about how actions have consequences. That being said. There is a child here that did not ask for the position they are in right now. If you even dare to treat that child in anyway form like you treated me, you'll have me to deal with. I'll be damned. You don't hold something a person has no control over against them" Kelly was heated.

Everyone was quiet and their eyes were dancing. "Children are not like dolls or trophies. They are human beings that need love, guidance, attention and above all trust from their loved ones. You don't play games with children and their lives. You don't put children in the middle of adult games like that! Pull your head out of your ass Molly and see the light of fucking day! Your selfish actions to crumble my life is just the most disgusting thing I've ever seen. What's worse? You targeted my HUSBAND! Why? Because princess lost her tiara and didn't get her dick-in for that bun in the oven she wanted from her hubby at home? I don't blame him for dumping your sorry ass."

Molly felt like the tiniest person in the room. She began to bawl. She jumped out of her chair and quickly headed to her room, slamming her door shut like a child who didn't get her binky, like a teenager who thinks her parents are unfair.

Katy and Arturo both looked white as a ghost. This had been building up for some time now. They looked at each other with a touch of fear in their eyes. Shit had indeed hit the fan now.

"Let's fucking go Aaron." Kelly demanded. She turned

to Katy and Arturo. "I'm sorry you had to see that, guys. This isn't your fault." Kelly said. Both nodded silently as they grabbed their coats and walked out the door.

24 DESTINY

Five months had passed since the exorcism. Although the pregnancy was progressing well, Molly's mental state had deteriorated. She struggled to eat, to walk, to think, or to talk. Katy had taken her to her latest ultrasound. The sex of the baby had been revealed. It was a girl. Katy had been throwing names at Molly for days. They had narrowed it down to three.

Katy, Molly, and her newly rediscovered friend, Amber, were driving down to a small local burrito joint. Katy and amber giggled as they played with names.

"Alright, we're down to Desiree, Destiny, and Dana." Katy reminded her sister.

Molly couldn't pick one. She had wanted something that started with a "D." Her mind, however, was still loopy after all this time. She struggled to focus. She could barely think.

Depression had set in long ago, since the day Kelly tore her and Aaron to pieces in her sister's kitchen. She was hopeless. Her old job was gone now. In her mental state, there was no way she could focus on her assignments and duties. She resigned on the following Monday after that wretched fight. She found work at a local insurance company office, filing paperwork and processing claims. It was boring work, but it paid the bills. She thought about finding a position as an EMT, but in her current situation that was completely off the menu. She had been reunited with an old friend, Amber, who was the supervisor of her own unit. She hadn't seen Amber in a few years, not since college. It was good to have at least one friend in her life. Amber had called her about a week after the big fight. They went to lunch, caught up and chatted. They shared stories of days gone by, current situations and sometimes just "How's the weather?"

Amber had recognized signs of depression in her. She made it a point to keep in contact with Molly, be her friend again. This was one of Molly's few escapes from reality. Amber was concerned for her friend. The problem was, how could she help her pull out of this rut? She knew that for some reason, she had to keep Molly going. She was growing fearful of Molly's mental health. Physically, Molly had been far more taxed than the average woman in her current trimester. Amber questioned whether she should be working at all! There was something unseen going on that Amber could not figure out.

"So, what is the decision, how are you going to do this? You chose against an abortion. I respect that. But what's next?" asked Amber to Molly.

"She will be the only part of Aaron I get to have now." Molly replied.

"You're still fucking obsessed with Aaron! You know what happened. You know what you did! Replied Katy. "That is why you're in the state you're in now! I thought you had learned something, Molly!"

"Have you heard from James, Molly? I know you're in the middle of a divorce. That can't possibly be doing anything good for you. How are you coping?" asked Amber.

Molly sat in quiet contemplation as she considered Amber's question. James. It had been so long since she had heard from him. She remembered back to a couple of weeks after the confrontation in Katy's kitchen. She had felt so alone, so desperate, that she called James and begged him to take her back. He wouldn't have it. He would didn't even want to hear her voice. He had her belongings shipped to her from Michigan shortly after the fight. He was if anything thorough. Everything was labelled and organized. The boxes were well packaged. Nothing of hers seemed to be missing. There was one final insult, however. All the pictures of her and James, when they were together, had been torn in two and placed back in the frame. Over her image in each picture, her had written the word "WHORE" over her face. When Molly read them, her heart sank. Aaron's rejection during the fight had in its own way torn her in two. When Kelly added her piece, it felt like being crushed with a sledgehammer. There was little left of Molly now. She had lost James; Aaron had rejected her. Her job, what little she could do with it, sucked. It had all come crashing down for Molly. She knew who was to blame, but she still struggled to accept it.

"Coping… how am I coping? I'm not. I'm in hell, amber. I'm in a hell of my own creation, and I have no way out." Molly replied, lazily.

"Well, that's why we got you in those counseling sessions, Molly. How are you going to be a mother to your daughter if you can't pull up your big girl pants and face the future?" asked Katy.

Molly thought on her question. She closed her eyes. A vision, a memory struck her. Raven, with her cold, black eyes, staring back at her through that cursed mirror continued to haunt her. She wished she hadn't regained her memories after the exorcism. Each time she remembered Raven; it sapped all the energy out of her. She would become unable to function for hours, sometimes even days. She could barely feed or cleanse herself. Sometimes even Katy would have to remind her how much she stank. The counseling wasn't helping. They couldn't possibly understand what she had been through. They couldn't possibly understand the power that Raven had over her. Her latest therapist had suggested she had become a delusional sociopath. How can she be a loving mother under those conditions?

"Destiny." Molly spoke

Katy looked at her, wide eyed. "So, you finally picked one! I love that name!"

Amber nodded in agreement. "Sweet feet! Finally, you're making some decisions!"

A tear rolled down Molly's cheek. She turned to her sister. "I don't know if I can do this, Katy/ I don't know if I can raise a child by myself." Katy turned to look at her sister. She felt pain and sorrow in her sister. She thought about how their youngest sister, Mac, was struggling with. Even with her husband at her side, times had been challenging for her too. Two am feedings, diaper changes, all the crying in the middle of the night… it had taken its toll on her. How was Molly going to make it through?

Aaron had been pacing around in his study at home. He was frustrated. It had been several months since the argument at Katy's between Kelly, Molly, and himself. The life of their marriage seemed to be draining away. Kelly had become distant. She barely spoke to him anymore. He couldn't remember the last time they had made love. He had no drive left in him anymore. Work had become just as bad. The relationship with his coworkers had changed. What once was a friendly and cordial environment, had now become tense and formal. People didn't look at him the same anymore. It had become a day in, day out routine for him. He lost the passion for his work.

Aaron was at a breaking point; he couldn't take this silence anymore. He felt like he needed to scream inside, but who would listen? Who would care? Kelly stepped in the room and dropped a pile of mail on his desk, then turned around and walked out. She didn't speak, she didn't even look at him. This irritated Aaron. It lit a fire inside of him that was about to burst. Rage built up inside him. When was this going to stop? Aaron stood up and stormed out of his study, trailing after Kelly who had sat down on the couch in the living room.

"When is this shit going to stop?" demanded Aaron.

Kelly looked up at him, shocked. Her husband had always been a quiet, laid-back kind of guy. This time, she sensed a furious rage building inside him. It was powerful, angry, it scarred her.

"Aaron, what's going on with you?" asked Kelly.

"What's going on with me? WHAT'S GOING ON WITH ME? Are you serious? What the HELL do you think is going on. I had some batshit crazy woman having my baby! I have a dead-end job that is leading nowhere. I have coworkers that keep looking at me with suspicious eyes, and what's worse?" Aaron steamed.

"What's worse? My own wife, the LOVE of my life, my rock, my SOULMATE, the woman who I endeavor to spend the rest of my life with, won't even talk to me! You won't even give me the time of day!" Aaron said.

He began to pace around the couch furiously. Sweat was dripping from his brow now.

"Every day! EVERY DAY you get your little jabs in at me! Your girlfriend this… your little tramp that. It never ends with you. Kelly I am YOUR HUSBAND! NOT YOUR WHIPPING POST! I KNOW I FUCKED UP! NOW I HAVE TO DEAL WITH THOSE REPERCUSSIONS. GIVE ME A GODDAMN BREAK!" Aaron yelled.

Kelly looked on at him in shock, speechless.

Aaron calmed his voice. "Kelly, after over 30 years my love for you has never faltered! It had never failed! I failed us. I failed you. I failed myself. I'm truly sorry for the pain I have caused you. I need you Kelly, I love you. I always have. I always will. Molly will never understand that I am loyal to you and you alone! This baby changes nothing of that. I love YOU Kelly. I fucking love you to death!" Aaron cried. Tears began to run down Aaron's face. He fell to his knees at his wife's feet.

A rush of emotion flowed through Kelly's veins. She could feel his pain, his torment. She could not stand to see him like this. She dropped to her knees and placed her hands on his shoulder. Tears began to fall from her eyes.

"Your right. We need to help each other, Aaron. I'm fighting battles right alongside you. What's gone is clearly telling me that we need to quit pointing fingers, dropping the ball and just flat out ignoring the problems we are facing. Understanding is a two-way street, Aaron. I'll work on my end, but I have to work too. It's not just my job, but you job too. That's the fucking problem. We are to invest in what we think our roles are instead of just supporting each other. I want you to have a voice. You need to start using it instead of idling by, honey." Kelly spoke, softly.

She moved in to wrap her arms around him.

"I can't help you with communication if you're not saying a peep. You can't help me if I'm not saying a peep. I have to remember that you are a victim here, you didn't do this of your own free will. Molly did this. Raven did this. I promise to set aside my own problems and be with you on this. I love you Aaron.

Aaron and Kelly cried together in warm embrace. They kissed, passionately. He ran his hands down her back. She felt good to him. She was soft and warm. They both were aroused now. He reached down and removed her shirt, as she removed his. He undid her bra and pressed himself against her. Her soft breasts pressed against him. Soon, the pair were wildly making love on the floor of their living room. They hadn't felt this kind of passion in a long time. It would be a long night for them.

Molly slowly paced in Katy and Arturo's kitchen. She was frustrated. She was tired. Katy looked dover to her sister, concerned. She stood up from the table and approached her sister, placing a hand on her shoulder.

"What is it, Molly?" Katy asked.

Molly turned to her. "I can't go on like this not talking to him. His child is growing inside of me every day. How can I keep this up, without at least having some sort of communication with him? I acted so horribly that day when Aaron and Kelly were here. I was wrong, I was a fool. I acted like a child. What was I thinking?"

"Molly, be careful the road you take in this. They probably never want to see you again." Replied Katy.

"I have to try. I have to fix this. Aaron is going to be a part of my life, despite what I've done." Said Molly.

"What are you going to do then?" asked Katy.

Molly continued pacing. She stopped and turned to Katy. "I'm going over there. I have to try to speak with him, with them both."

Katy looked at her with concern in her eyes. "Molly, you go over there and ruffle up feathers, I can't protect you from what happens. You remember what Kelly said, right?"

"I have to try." Replied Molly. She stepped into the living room and grabbed her car keys from the wall rack. She opened the front door and stepped out. Katy followed after her. "Molly, be careful. If you do this, you may find only more pain. Do you really need that in your life?" Molly stopped and turned around. "There's only one way to find out." Molly stepped into her car, started it, and drove away.

10 minutes later Molly pulled up in front of Aarons and Kelly's house. Molly was nervous, trembling. She gripped the steering wheel so hard her knuckles turned white. She turned off the car, gathered her courage and stepped out. It was getting dark as the sun was setting. She paused for a

moment, then walked up the walkway. She stepped on the patio and began to place her finger on the doorbell. , out of the corner of Molly's eye, through a crack in the curtains to her right, Molly could see them inside. They were naked as jay birds, their bodies wrapped in erotic embrace. Molly watched on as Aaron mounted his wife and pumped vigorously. She could see the sweat dripping from both of their bodies as Kelly moaned with passion. Molly could not turn away as the thought of her own experience rang in her mind. She remembered how good he had felt, how robust his penis was. She could feel him inside of her.

Molly put her hand down to her hip as she gazed at the entwined couple. Molly had a revelation. They had made up; they had forgiven each other. After all Molly had put them through, Kelly still loved him. Aaron still loved her. Molly knew in that moment that no action of hers would ever break that. Molly felt a sense of loss in that moment. The heartbreak she felt coursed through her veins. Her feelings for Aaron would never be allowed to surface again. She would have to shelve them from here on out.

She pulled out a notepad from her purse, along with a pen. She began to write. "Dear Aaron and Kelly. In these desperate times, I feel so alone. I know that no apology can ever fix the horrible things of done to you. I hope that one day you can find it in your heart to forgive me, but I know that like asking for the moon. Destiny will be here soon. She will be with you, always. -Molly"

She tore the note from the note pad and stuck it in the door. She looked down at her swollen belly and considered the future of her child, a future she will never be part of. She shivered at the sound of Kelly's orgasm inside the house. She turned and returned to her car. As she got inside, she let out a burst of tears. She bawled like a baby as she started the car and drove away.

"God, please forgive me! What have I done? I can't do this alone!" She screamed out as she drove home. When she arrived, she was all dried out. All that was left in her was pain, realization of what she had done.

The sun rose the next morning, and light entered Molly's bedroom window, illuminating her face. She sat up, slipped out of bed, and slipped into her pink bunny slippers. They weren't much, but they gave her at least a little joy. She opened her door and waddled downstairs. Katy and Arturo where already up. Katy was on the phone when she entered the kitchen. Katy returned to her sister as she continued her conversation.

"Yeah, Kelly. I'll let her know. She'll be there, I promise." Katy said into the phone.

Molly couldn't hear the other end of the conversation, but Katy soon hung up.

"Who was that? Kelly? What did she want?" asked Molly.

"Kelly said she found your note on the door, last night. She wants to meet with you for lunch, over at Brenda's Deli down on 4th street. She said she will be there at eleven."

Molly stood, shocked. She wasn't sure if she could handle another verbal beatdown from her. The last speech left her in shambles.

"Geez, I don't know. What if she attacks…" Molly said but was cut off.

"No Molly, Kelly wants to be candid with you. She wants to make amends." Katy interjected.

Molly stood in a state of shock. Kelly wanted to make amends. Molly sat at the kitchen table, trembling. This couldn't be happening! Molly wondered what the conversation would bring. Molly stood up and went to the fridge, grabbing herself a small container of oats and yogurt. She pondered how the day would pan out. She was nervous, but hopeful. She went upstairs, showered, and prepared for what was to come.

Kelly had arranged for her and Molly to meet at a delicatessen. Molly was sitting on a red vinyl seat booth. It was gently raining outside. The smell of fresh baked sourdough bread and chicken soup filled the air. It wasn't too busy. The lunch rush wouldn't be for another hour. She didn't understand why Kelly wanted to meet up. Molly's feet had swelled up, so she had on soft slippers. One of the many nuances of pregnancy she wasn't adoring. Kelly walked in the door and shook off her hoodie. She stopped and looked around hoping to spot Molly. She caught a glimpse of where she was sitting and approached the booth. She took her satchel from over her shoulder and sat it down while scooting herself toward the middle of the red vinyl cushion. "So, I'm guessing you want to know what is going on here?" Kelly started. "Yeah" Molly said softly. "Molly, we need to get on solid ground here. Your baby should have the most love and care without me, you and Aaron having spats left and right." Kelly took a deep breath. "Molly, when I was in my early twenties Aaron, and I broke up over a disagreement. He had a childhood friend, Oliver, which worked at a local retail store. Well one day I went up to him and we started talking. We had exchanged numbers and started seeing each other. I was under the impression that he had talked to Aaron and had he wasn't opposed to us seeing each other. Well, I was misled. He had seen us out in public, and he didn't know anything about what was going on between Oliver and me. Well, they ended up in a fist fight. It was ugly. Oliver had a broken nose and Aaron's left eye was swollen shut. They looked so pitiful!" Kelly chuckled. "Oh my god you're serious? They fought over you, really? That's so wild!" said Molly in amazement.

"Oh yeah, and they didn't talk to each other for years after that. Oliver found out he was terminally ill with cancer. He got a hold of Aaron, and they patched things up and were able to make amends. The point is Molly, nobody is perfect. We all get consumed by things we want and forget about what we have. We make choices thinking about ourselves and thinking nobody will really get that hurt. Especially when we want to make our own pain go away. Well, I did that, and I was wrong. Sometimes we need to slow down, look around, and embrace what gifts God has given us. We need to watch what we say and think about the consequences of losing what means the most to us. If we don't, we rip people apart for years. We cause pain to ourselves and to others for very little reason. I know you have disappointments. We all do. The point is that even though things aren't going in your favor, it doesn't mean you can't have a good life. There are so many good people out there. One of them is right for you and you deserve that, Molly." Molly grabbed a Kleenex and dabbed her eyes. "Kelly, I don't know what to say, I'm so embarrassed I just completely screwed up everything. I don't know how to fix all this"

"You don't need to say anything Molly. It's what you do next that counts. You start by picking up the pieces"

"How do I go from here? How do I get what I need from Aaron without all the tension?"

"That will be between you and Aaron. My best advice is to be respectful and be mature in the situation. Molly, I'm sorry for all the things that went south on you. I do feel you deserve better than the hand you were dealt that landed you in this predicament to begin with. Just know that you deserve grace in your life, and I want you to know that I am giving you as much as I know how to give. I know this is rather bizarre right? Doing the right thing isn't always the popular response, and I'm okay with that. I am okay with doing the right unpopular thing because my conscious lives with how things end up and not everyone else's. Causing more damage or pain isn't worth it in the long run. That type of satisfaction is temporary and its painful long term. It can even cost people more than it should. I want you to know that I forgive you Molly. I must let all of it go because your wellbeing and Destiny's wellbeing is more important than a shit flinging contest."

25 VISIONS

Aaron got home from work early, it had been a mentally exhausting day. He had been busy planning out an upcoming companywide training session. He had considered his circumstances and decided to build a positive outcome from all that had happened to him. Kelly wasn't home yet, so Aaron thought he would take a nap on the couch before she got home, and they got started on dinner. He kicked off his shoes and laid down, closing his eyes.

, Aaron began to feel a strange sensation. He felt a buzzing in his body, and a tightness in his chest. He knew what was coming. He had practiced lucid dreaming for the last several years, and this is always how it started. Aarons realized what he had unintentionally done. Afternoon naps where the most effective time for him to induce a lucid dream, but this felt different. In a flash, Aaron up and looked around, but something was off. The clock on the wall had no hands, and the digital readout from the kitchen displayed random numbers. His body buzzed, but it wasn't his body. He looked down, behind him. His physical body was still there on the couch. This was no lucid dream, Aaron realized. This was an out-of-body experience. He became excited, as these happened more rarely. He turned around and approached the front door. He opened it and walked through. He expected to see an ethereal version of his front yard, but instead he found himself in a wide-open meadow, dotted with trees and bushes. He proceeded to explore his new surroundings. He was fascinated. Aaron had Out of bodies before, and each time brought him something new to learn. There had always been something to take away from these things. When Aaron explored, objects that he was meant to focus on seemed livelier to him. Other spirits, fellow travelers appeared to him from time to time, their eyes always glowing blue.

He turned to a small patch of trees, where he saw what appeared to be a young dark-haired woman, standing in profile to him. He approached her, recognized her. Molly! What was she doing here? Aaron approached her but did not speak. White butterflies seemed to dance around her. Molly's gaze was focused on something. He followed her gaze and saw what she was looking at. Three groups of three people each were all having rapid conversation about something. Aaron could not focus on them well enough to understand what they were talking about, but he got the general feel of it. They were all talking about Molly, trying to make decisions for her. Molly seemed disinterested in those decisions. Something stuck out to Aarons. Something caught his eye. The middle group of people were doctors, and the one in the middle stood with his back toward Aaron. He was holding a clipboard, writing something down on it. Aaron approached and looked down on the paper. There were two words, underscored three times Pulmonary Concerns. Aaron wondered what that could mean. He turned back to Molly and approached her. She did not respond to his presence.

, the vision began to fade. Aaron was pulled back into his body. He woke up. He tried to sit up, but it took a few moments for his senses to return after these things happened. Kelly and Danny had come home, it was the sound of the front door closing that woke him. Kelly looked down at him. Her senses knew when Aarons was having an experience. She had once told him that she could see him asleep, breathing, but his energy was not there. Kelly reached down and ran her fingers through his hair.

"Did you have another vision, babe?' asked Kelly.

"Yeah, and this one was the strangest yet." Replied Aaron. He considered telling her about it, but since Kelly and Molly had a reconciliation recently, he felt at ease. He told Kelly everything he had seen in his vision. Kelly listened intently.

"That's strange. The number three seems to be a theme in that. Three groups of three people? Those words underscored three times. There's a lot of meaning in numbers you know." Kelly replied. She had long studied numerology. Haley, back in college had introduced her to the concept.

Aaron got up and began considering what he had seen. Was Molly in trouble or danger? With a baby at stake, he couldn't risk not finding out. He picked up his phone and called Katy.

Katy had been at home, scarfing down a sandwich. She was still chewing when she answered.

"Herroo?" she said, voice muffled.

"Katy, this is going to sound strange, but I need you to check on Molly. I had another one of my crazy visions and Molly was there. A think something is wrong." Aaron said.

"Molly, ah shucks, she's fine. She's upstairs taking a piss for the thirtieth time today." Katy said, annoyingly.

"Oohhh k, didn't really need to know that dork. keep an eye on her. This vision had a different feel to it." Aaron replied.

"Will do, old man." Katy said. They hung up. Aaron

proceeded to help Kelly with dinner. Kelly studied him as he diced potatoes. She could feel his energy, something was indeed off. This worried Kelly because Aaron had been right about certain things from his visions before. He once had a vision of a white van. Kelly eventually bought a white van. There were other things too. Little things, really. But they were right. Aaron let the thought pass as he refocused on tomorrow meeting.

The next day arrived, and Aaron woke up with a new sense of purpose. He arrived at work and entered his office. Gathering his notes and materials, he realized how messy his office was getting. He thought of the irony of the situation. He was about to perform a meeting that would lay out the events that led to his current situation, about Molly, and yet, if Molly were here, she would have had this place polished up and cleaned out hours ago. He couldn't help but chuckle.

Aaron went around the complex announcing a meeting to his coworkers. Several snacks were laid out on the break room counter along with paper plates, napkins, and red solo cups. Small sandwiches were arranged on a platter along with fresh fruit, vegetables, crisps, and two drink dispensers one with pink lemonade and one with water. As people gathered in, they helped themselves to the pleasantries and sat down at the tables.

Aaron walked in and gathered everyone's attention. "Okay everyone let's settle down. Now, I'm sure you're all wondering what is going on and why I have called this meeting. Several months ago, I met up with a colleague of ours, as I'm sure your aware of whom, for casual talk and a few beers. Turns out the beers were being laced with a party drug called Lotus, and I was sexually assaulted as a result of the effects of this drug. I was also drugged here on the job. It is true I have fathered an unborn child as a result of this. I am deeply embarrassed on how this situation has been handled. I let my guard down with very honest and different intentions.

"I have hurt myself, my wife, and my credibility. I prefer to keep my troubles and my life private. This is the first time I have faced a more public situation like this." The room gasped. Everyone felt a deep pit in their stomach. Eyes were dancing. Eyebrows were raised. "I've come to know all of you as good people and friends in which I am privileged to work with each day. I want to gain your respect back, and your trust. I know that it will take time. I want to use this experience to make some positive changes. I would like to propose that we implement training with qualified professionals to amend company policies. First proposal would be training on sexual harassment and sexual assault yearly. Second, I would like to propose random drug testing. It's come to my attention that some employees like to use street party drugs and pass them around on company property."

"This brings me to proposal three. To implement professionals who would investigate anything related to these things and to recommend proper courses of action. We are a pharmaceutical company that is helping to develop drugs to save lives and improve the quality of lives not promotion of using illegal ones. We need to uphold that standard. That said, proposal number four. I believe that we should offer alcohol and addiction resources to those of you who need it or know of someone who would benefit from it."

"Safety is our priority here at Oracle. If you are using drugs or have drinking habits that are causing issues at work, it can cost you. By proposing these resources, it would be giving people a chance to take care of themselves and not lose a life, credibility, or a job here. Proposal number five. I want to take the stigma out of mental health and replace it with awareness and treatment. If you or your loved ones need counseling or just an hour with a counselor, I want to make that available as well. To make these proposals a reality, I would like your support and ideas in persuading our upper management to help us implement these into our company. So here is a petition I have drafted. I have made enough copies for everyone to look at. If there are any suggestions or amendments you wish to discuss, I am more than willing to listen and take the time to make every one's voice heard. You matter to me. OUR voices must be heard. OUR voices matter."

The conference roared with various conversation between employees. Aaron was approached by many of whom had doubted him, offering their condolences and apologies. Aaron felt a sense of relief as many others shared their own stories. This was a success. He felt redemption. He felt reconciliation. Yet there was one more reconciliation he felt needed to happen next It needed to happen soon. If Kelly had found grounds to forgive molly, what was holding him back.

Aaron began driving home, feeling accomplished. His meeting had really hit the mark. Something, however, was nagging him. Deep down inside, he knew what he needed to do. Instead of turning down his road to his home, he continued onward to Katy's house. He pulled up and parked next to the sidewalk. Feeling energized from his day, he exited his truck and made it up the walkway. He rang the doorbell; Arturo answered.

"Aaron, buddy, come on in. Katy should be home in a few minutes. Let's grab a beer!"

"Thanks Art, I could really use one." Aaron said. Arturo led him to the kitchen, opened the fridge and handed him an IPA. "I'm not here to see Katy though, I just saw her at work. I need to see Molly."

A look of surprise flashed in Art eyes. "Is everything ok? Last time things didn't go over to well if you remember."

"That's why I'm here. It's time to bury the hatchet. It's time for Molly and me to move on and move forward." Aaron said.

Arturo nodded in agreement. He had known deep inside that this day would come, ever since Kelly had made peace with Molly herself. "Alright buddy, do what you got to do. She's upstairs. I'll get her for you. You can use my study, it's more private in there."

Aaron walked through the living room to Arts study. He wasn't ready to sit down just yet. A few moments later, a very pregnant Molly appeared sheepishly in the doorway.

"Aaron?" asked Molly, quietly.

"Hey, you." Aaron said in a low voice. "Listen Molly, with everything that's happened, things had spiraled out of control. Raven, our little night out, the baby, all the fallout that goes with it, has taken its toll on all of us. You're in your third trimester now. Destiny, in a way, awaits. You and I have work to do."

Aaron pulled out the chair from Art's desk, gestured for Molly to sit down. She sat down. She lowered herself carefully into it. Molly turned her full attention to Aaron.

"I'm willing to look beyond what happened, Molly. I needed time to fully embrace the bigger picture of what happed between us. Raven. Raven was in control. Raven fed on your lust, you temptation. But you're not the only one who feels lust and temptation. I've made my mistakes to, Molly. I'm not innocent of that. I need to accept my part of what played out between us. I felt that temptation too. That burden is mine to bare."

"Aaron, we both know what needs to happen now. I'm a walking wreck. I can barely function in daily life. Raven did a lot of damage to my mind. How can I dare say I'm fit to mother a child. Destiny belongs to you, Aaron, not me." Said Molly.

"I understand that Molly. If that is the decision you chose, I'll respect it. Destiny will have a good home with us, a loving home. But… if you and I work together on this, if we can set the record straight, you will always be a part of Destiny's life. You're still her mother. One day when she grows up, she's going to be curious about you. She will want to know where she came from. You will have to be there for her, to help guide her. I'll make you this promise, Molly. If you can make the effort to better yourself, get the help you need, and confront your demons, Kelly and I will be there for you."

"Aaron, I wasn't helping your situation either. I took advantage of your problems hoping to fix my own. I know you were trusting me to be a friend and I used that to my advantage, for my own gain. You didn't deserve that. I betrayed your trust. I hope you can forgive me." Said Molly. "I know we are both responsible for our own actions. I was wrong to do what I did. I sent you down a path you didn't deserve. Now I have my price to pay. I've lost my home, my husband, many friends. My actions come at a heavy price. I apologize to you for paying the price too."

"I forgive you Molly. Let's push on with this. I want you to keep an eye on your health. Your body has already been through so much. I mean, come on, a freaking exorcism? While pregnant?"

Molly let out a little smile. She felt a sense of relief now that she has so craved for so long. Katy burst into the room. She looked at Molly, then over to Aaron. She was confused as ever.

"What the hell's going on here?" Katy asked.

"Relax, Katy. Molly and I are just patching a few things up. We're moving on, putting this whole mess behind us, and looking to the future." Aaron said.

Katy breathed a sigh of relief. Aaron looked over to Molly. "This means keeping me in the loop, Molly. I'll be going with you to the rest of your prenatal appointments. It'll be awkward at first, but you'll get used to it." Aaron said, as he began to make his way out of the study.

"Wait, Aaron…" Molly said. Aaron turned around, while taking a final swig of his beer. "I promise I will never let my feelings interfere with your life ever again. I promise to address my issues." Molly said.

Aaron turned back to her and nodded. He made his way

to the front door when Katy stopped him.

"Aaron, Molly truly does have feelings for you, but I know she's genuine in her promise. I'll be keeping an eye on her. I've decided to let her live her permanently. She can't do it on her own anymore. From here on out I'm my sister's keeper." Katy spoke in a low tone.

"How bad is it, Katy. Truly, how bad." Aaron asked.

Katy looked around making sure Molly was out of earshot. "It took her years too deal with the things she had done as a teenager the first time Raven had taken her. The guilt was almost too much to bear for her. Stabbing that boy in the neck with a pencil? Once Raven was gone, she took that hard. It's a wonder she only got suspended for it and his parents didn't press charges. Then again, they were always too drunk to seem to care anyway. It took counseling then to deal with her trauma. But then, Raven didn't have as much of a hold on her as she did this time. I'm so fucking glad that Raven is destroyed."

Aaron made a serious face at Katy. "Katy, you're missing the point. Raven wasn't destroyed. Her portal into our world was. She was only banished to the spirit world. Raven still exists, and if were not careful, she could come back."

Katy considered that for a moment. "Even if that's the case, in Molly's broken condition, why would Raven still haunt her? Molly is a fractured shell of her formal self. My sister isn't who she used to be. It breaks my heart to see her as she is." A tear rolled down Katy's cheek.

Aaron threw and arm around his friend. "Then we all make efforts to protect her, from this realm and the next."

"Aaron, how is it that you can be so forgiving after what Molly did to you? All the sudden Kelly, then you, make amends with her? Things are just all the sudden all is forgiven. Everyone is best buddies?" asked Katy.

Aaron looked into her eyes, intensely. "Katy, what would you do? Live the rest of your life in anger? Despair? Hatred? I can't live my life like that. I can't live my life feeling that way, raising a daughter, and hating her mother.

At the end of the day, we all need forgiveness. Like I told Molly, I'm not exactly innocent in this myself. She deserves a chance. I'm going to give her that chance. I would ask the same if I was in her shoes."

Katy began to cry. She put her head into Aaron's shoulder and sobbed. "Thank you for this. Thank you for being good to my sister. She needs this. I need this."

"We all need this, Katy." Aaron said. He considered his next comment carefully. "In a way, were a kind of family now. You've been a dear friend to me for years. I've always seen you as a little sister, and now both our bloodlines will flow within Destiny."

Katy threw her arms around Aaron. She patted him on the shoulder when she let go.

"You better get going, big bro. I know Kelly makes Tacos for you on Tuesdays, and I hear your tummy grumbling." Katy replied. Aaron hugged her again, then walked out the door to his truck.

As Aaron made his way down the walkway, a vision entered his mind. Raven! He felt her energy. He felt her intent. Molly was never her true target. She was just a tool for her plan! It was Destiny! It was always Destiny!

A month had passed since Aaron and Molly had made amends. Aaron had felt refreshed. His coworkers were treating him with the old respect they once had. At home, Kelly had never felt so attracted to her husband as she did now. They made love every moment they had, in almost every room in the house, at almost any time of the day. Aaron, as promised, attended Molly's prenatal appointments with her. Molly had kept to her promise. She made no advances, no moves. Kelly had attended the appointments as well, from time to time. Molly was progressing well with the pregnancy. She continued to seek counseling, although progress there was slow. She still had memories and dreams of Raven. Even though she was free from the spirit, Raven still haunted her.

One afternoon, like usual, Aaron got home from work before Molly and Danny. It had been another one of those "meter after meeting" kind of days, and his brain was fried. He plopped onto their bed and kicked his shoes off. He thought about Kelly. It put a smile on his face as he thought of their next love making session tonight. He laid back on the pillow and closed his eyes. He was more tired than he thought as he began to drift off. Once again however, he found himself feeling a buzzing sensation in his body. His muscles tensed up. Just as he had before, he felt his astral body pull up and out of the bed. Once again, he looked back and saw his body lying as if in stasis. He looked around, performing what he a called a reality check. He looked at the clock on the entertainment center next to him. Just as he suspected, it displayed no numbers at all. He had entered another out-of-body experience. He began to walk to the door of the bedroom, and into what should have been the main hallway. This time, it wasn't a hallway, it was a kitchen. Specifically, it was Katy and Arturo's kitchen. Nobody seemed to be around. He looked for clues as he explored the place, something that was sticking out like a sore thumb. He found what he needed to see. There, on the stove top, was a shiny metal pot. Inside of it was either soup, or a stew slowly simmering. Next to it, two large soup spoons and a ladle were placed perfectly on the countertop next to the stove. Aaron approached it and studied it. He wasn't sure what the significance of this was. He wondered what soup could have to do with anything. In that moment, he heard shuffling behind him. He turned to see who it was. A very pregnant Molly had slowly made her way into the kitchen. She reached up to the cabinet, opened it, and pulled out a small stack of bowls. She placed them on the countertop in front of her and closed the doors. She turned and made her way to the pot on the stove. Molly took a spoon and stirred the soup. She tasted it and nodded approvingly. She placed the spoon back down on the countertop and made her way to the kitchen table. She slowly sat down and began scrolling through her cell phone. Aaron walked up behind, wondering what the significance of watching Molly do mundane tasks was.

He spoke out loud. "What is the significance of this?"

, Molly raised her head from the phone, as if startled. This in turn startled Aaron. She hadn't seen him standing there earlier, but could she have heard him? He approached her from the left and knelt next to her. He considered her for a moment. Then he spoke again.

"Molly, can you hear me?" Aaron asked.

Molly, looking concerned turned her head in Aarons general direction, but not directly at him. She HAD heard him! She had to have! In an instant, the vision began to fade. Once again, he was pulled back into his body. Aaron woke up to see Kelly standing at the foot of his bed, rubbing his feet.

"Hey there sleepy head, were you having another vision?" asked Kelly.

Aaron slowly sat up, rubbing his eyes. "Yeah. This one was strange."

"Aren't they all strange, babe? Let me guess, Molly again. I can feel her energy in you. By the way, what did you have for lunch? Something smells good in here." teased Kelly.

Aaron was relieved that any mention of Molly these days no longer produced sarcasm or outbursts, but it was a strange feeling to hear his wife bring up her name so casually.

"Lunch? Just an apple and a couple of fruit cups is all I had time for today. I don't smell anything myself." Aaron replied.

"Really? It smells like chicken soup in here, kind of yummy." She said.

Aaron looked at her, shocked. "Kelly, the vision I had… I was watching Molly stir and taste soup! And when I spoke, she acted like she heard me." Aaron said.

Kelly looked at him, confused. Among Kelly empathic talents, she also had another curious little ability. When spirits were present, from time to time, she could smell the scent of flowers. These were smelling that Aaron could never pick up on. When she was younger, she was always confused as to why she and only she could pick up on it.

Aaron opened the drawer in the nightstand next to him. Inside was a journal, a dream journal. Aaron had been using it for years to take down notes on his most significant dreams. He took the pen he kept inside it and added bullet points of the details of the vision. The journal was half full by now. It detailed dreams going back at least eight years. As he flipped through the pages, something caught his eye. He found a page that dated back over three years earlier. He looked down the list of details that he had written back then. There, written in black ink, was a detail of a young, dark haired woman with blue eyes. She had been standing in a field, surround by small white butterflies, fluttering around her. This triggered a memory in Aaron. He began flipping through his later entries. He had forgotten these! In all, there were three separate dreams that detailed a young brunette, surrounded by butterflies. He flipped back to the entry he had made after his last vision. Molly, standing in the grassy field, had white butterflies fluttering around her.

"White butterflies… What do they mean?" asked Aaron to himself. Kelly was listening.

"What's this about white butterflies, hon?" asked Kelly.

Aaron stood up and began pacing the room, thinking out loud. He began to have a realization. He had dreamed of Molly before he ever met her! Could those dreams have been a premonition? Could it have been a warning of things to come? Aaron hadn't remembered those previous dreams. They were too random to have been relevant to anything at the time, so he brushed them off. But now, they could have a meaning. He looked over at Kelly. She felt what he was thinking. Molly had some other significance that has existed for some time.

The next morning, Aaron sat in his office typing up daily

reports. Katy came in and entered her office across the hallway. She sat down yawned as she grabbed a pile of files that had been placed in her in box. Aaron looked over to her, thoughtfully. He got up, walked out of his office, and stood in her door frame.

"Morning, dorko!" teased Katy.

"Good morning, shrimp." Aaron teased in return. "I've got a question for you, Katy. What did you all have for dinner last night?"

Katy looked up at Aaron with a confused look in her face. "Molly made her famous chicken soup last night. It's a variation of our grandmas' old recipe. Why do you ask?" she said.

Aaron rubbed his chin, deep in thought. "Did Molly say anything weird last night, like hearing voices?"

Katy thought for a moment. Molly had mentioned just that morning that she had thought somebody had called her name, but nobody else was home. "She thought somebody called out to her, but me and Art were out. Molly just brushed it off. Why?'

Aaron stepped a little closer to her. "I had another one of my visions last night, Katy. I was in your kitchen, watching Molly stir soup and scroll on her cell phone. Tell me, do tiny white butterflies mean anything to you?"

"Kind of, I guess. I remember in the springtime back in Michigan we would get a lot of them out in our grandpas' field. Molly and Mac used to chase them around as kids." She replied.

This was the information Aaron needed. There had to be some connection to Molly even before they met, but what was it? Why had he dreamed of her before? Did this have anything to do with what happened? Aaron thought deeper.

"You look like your slapping clues together in your head, buddy. What's going on?" Asked Katy

Aaron looked back at her. "I've got a theory bouncing around in my head, but I'm not ready to share it just yet. I need more information. I'll get back with you on it."

Aaron walked out of Katy's office and returned to his own. He sat down at his desk and pulled out his phone. He decided to call up Kelly's friend, Haley Higgins. It had been months since the exorcism, and he was curious about how they were doing with their episode. He had a few questions for her as well. He dialed her number, it rang.

"Hello, who's this." Answered Haley.

"Haley, Its Aaron Eastman from Albuquerque." Aaron replied.

"Oh, hey Aaron, how are you since that little adventure?" she asked.

"It's complicated, but things are looking up. How's it going with your episode?" he said.

"Can't do it, we would have to bleep the whole thing out. But we got amazing research material, lots to work with." She replied.

"Hey, I was hoping to pick your brain on something. I have questions on dreams and out-of-body experiences." Aaron spoke.

"Oh, my favorite subject. Are you keeping a dream journal like I told you about in college?" she asked.

"Yes, very much so. Let me tell you what's going on. I think I had three dreams about Molly, three years before I met her. She was always in a field, surrounded by white butterflies. Then I had an out-of-body where again she was in a field, with the butterflies. She was watching three groups of three people each having discussions. One of those groups wrote on a note pad, pulmonary concerns, underscored three times. That one happened when molly started her third trimester. There were three soup spoons next to the pot of soup. Then yesterday I had a vision of being in Katy's kitchen watching her make chicken soup, which turned out to be true. I also think she may have heard me when I spoke to her. What could all this mean?"

"Whoa there, big fella, there's a lot to go on here. Let's start with the dreams. dreaming of someone whom you later meet means that you are meant to, for whatever reason, cross paths with that person. But the out of bodies, that a whole different ball game. So, you have had two consecutive visions of her? I would expect a third soon. It seems to me that you are meant to see something, maybe prevent something. Pay close attention to the details and be precise when you write them down. The tiniest details can mean the biggest things." She said.

"What about all these threes? What could that mean? I remember you were big into numerology back in the day." Replied Aaron.

"Still am. Here's the deal, three is a powerful number. It has a lot of meaning to it. Pay attention in your day-to-day life for more appearances of three. The number corresponds with creativity, communication, optimism, and curiosity. Think about which of those applies to your situation." She said.

"Hmm, creativity, not so much. Optimism, maybe. Curiosity, that could apply. Something, however, makes me think communication is key. But for what purpose?" Aaron asked.

"Like I said, look at the details. There is something more going on here. You have my interest peaked. You mentioned the dreams, you were meant to cross paths. That was before you met Molly. There were three of them, three years before you did. There's something about that, that has me thinking. If you feel strongly about the communication part, listen to your gut. You may be on to something. When you have your third vision, and trust me you will, focus your mind. Use your voice, ask questions, even if not directly to anyone. Sometimes just speaking out in these visions can reveal answers, so don't just look around." Said Haley.

"I never thought of that! I'll give that a shot." Aaron replied.

"Let me ask you a question, Aaron. Have you ever focused your mind on Kelly, really feel her energy? Try this exercise. Close your eyes in a quiet place. Focus on her, feel her, let her in no matter where she is. I sensed great power in you when last we met, harness it. I have a theory here. Call me back when you do and tell me what happens. If I'm right, I think you find a little surprise." Said Haley.

"Thanks Haley, I'll give it a shot." He said. The pair said their good buys, Aaron hung up

Aaron wasn't sure what Haley was getting at, but over the next several days he did as she asked. At first, he could feel her like normal, but then he had an epiphany. Aaron had been practicing lucid dreaming and out-of-bodies for some time now. He had an idea. He would put himself in a trance like state, shutting the world out and focusing on the tiny movements of his fingers. Eventually, all awareness of the world around him, and the sensations of his own body would vanish, he would enter the dream. He tried this procedure now. He laid down on his bed and shut the world out. He focused on Kelly, searched for her. All of the sudden, she was there! Even though she was miles away, it felt like she was right next to him! It felt amazing, he felt as if he could almost...

Something changed! All of the sudden, a second energy began flowing through him. This energy felt familiar, but he had never felt it like this before. The energy was neither negative, nor positive. Kelly's was very much positive. This one was neutral. Where was it coming from? Who could this...Molly! Aaron had a connection to Molly! But why? How? Was it because of the baby inside her? Did that create a bond between them?

Aaron snapped out of it, overwhelmed. He stood up and shook it off. He had a connection to Molly.

Aaron picked up his phone and typed out a text to Haley.

"Haley, I did it, I felt Kelly like she was right next to me. But there was something else, a second connection, Molly. Somehow I can feel her to!" Aaron typed.

Aaron paced in his study waiting for an answer. It came ten minutes later.

"Aaron, my theory is right then. You have some sort of

connection with her. Use the next vision to find out what it is. Remember, use your voice, and ask." Haley replied.

Aaron was confused. How could he have two connections? How long had he had it? He had so many questions, no answers.

Time passed by quickly. Molly's due date was fast approaching, it was a matter of a couple weeks now. Aaron walked into his house carrying a box of baby clothes and diapers that he added to the collection building up in the new nursery he and Kelly set up. There were bottles, formula, a newly fashioned bassinette that he and Arturo had built in his garage. Dressers were filled with baby clothes. So much had been done to prepare. Aaron thought about what Haley had said. There would be a third vision. Aaron was impatient, waiting. the thought occurred to him. He could induce it himself! Something in his gut encouraged him to do so. It was a Sunday afternoon. Kelly was having lunch with friends; Danny was out playing ball at the park. Now was the time.

He put down the box and made his way to the bedroom. He laid down. He closed his eyes. He began his ritual. He had gotten good at this, that the buzzing sensation soon overtook his body. Once again, his spiritual form lifted out of his physical one. He stood at the foot of the bed, did his reality check, and proceeded out the door. This time there was no hallway. This time, he found himself in a hospitals operating room. Before him was an operating table. A young dark-haired woman was laying down on it. Around her, three nurses tended to her. Aaron stepped forward. He could see that it was Molly. He looked across the room. There was a dry erase board on the opposite wall. On it were the words "Patients Name: Melissa"

"Melissa?" Aaron said. "Who is Melissa?"

In that moment, he heard footsteps approaching him. He turned to his right to see an older gentleman with white hair, and a silver and white gown. His eyes had a bluish glow to them. He stopped at Aarons side and turned to him.

"There is no need to be alarmed, my friend. Your mate and her child will be fine. There are however precautions that must be made." Said the old man.

"My mate? She's not my mate, doctor. That's Katy's sister. Her name is Molly, not Melissa." Aaron replied.

The old man smiled at him. "That may be true in the physical realm, Aaron. But in this realm, her spirit still remains bound to you. Melissa was your mate from another time, another life."

"Bound to me? I'm married to Kelly! She should be bound to me." Said Aaron.

"And she is! You are thinking through the laws of man, who would suggest one spirit may only be bound to one other. But the laws of the universe are such that one spirit may be bound to many, and many to the one. Now we must act fast, Aaron. Time is short in the physical realm. Molly will be going into labor within the next forty-eight hours. She desires a natural birth, at home. But this cannot be. There are complications arising. She must have a cesarian section, and it must be you who convinces her to do it. She will only listen to you."

Aaron looked at the man, wide eyed. "Why only me?"

"Because you possess an ability that others do not. Only you have the ability to come to this place." Replied the man. "Go now!"

The vision faded. Aaron woke up.

The Labor

Katy had been keeping an eye on Molly as she started contractions. They were getting closer together. The five-minute mark wasn't quite met so Molly had been breathing and taking it easy on couch as the contractions progressed. Once she hit the five-minute contraction mark the midwife monitored her as she dilated. Molly had started to push had had been for some time. She had slept a little on the couch and had shuffled trying to get comfortable. Her blood pressure was up, and the baby's heart rate was slowly decreasing, and it was causing concern with the midwife. The baby wasn't budging. A c-section was looking increasingly imminent. Aaron had a vision that something was again wrong and called Katy several times throughout the last few hours. Molly had been insisting on not going to the hospital thinking she could wait it out and have a natural birth at the house in the pool that had been setup. Katy had fought with her for an hour before Aaron and Kelly had shown up. It had been at least 36 hours of labor. Aaron went to Molly who was in the pool. "It's time to go to the hospital Molly, let's call an ambulance"

"No, I think I can stick it out for a little bit longer." Said Molly. She was feeling a huge sense of loss as she was about to hand over a child that she desired more than anything sometime soon. Aaron got frustrated. He had sensed that if Molly persisted, the child would suffer. Even without Raven in the picture, Molly surely had a stubborn pull.

"LISTEN, ! IT'S NOT ABOUT YOUR SENSE OF STUPID SELFISH PRIDE, IT'S ABOUT THE HEALTH AND WELLBIENG OF THE BABY NOW, SO WADDLE YOUR FAT ASS DOWN THE STAIRS AND GET READY TO GO!" Yelled Aaron

Molly looked at Aaron in shock but complied. The ambulance was called, and she was rushed to the hospital. The baby's heartbeat had dropped. They got Molly hooked up to IV's and gave her medication for the c-section. Aaron stood by Molly's side as the c-section procedure was performed and the baby was delivered. Destiny was taken for a quick clean up and check over. Molly was stable and doing well. She was in a state of deep depression with everything going on. She was able to eat, and Katy stood by her making sure she was taken care of. Aaron had traded places with Katy off and on. Kelly had waited in the visitor area. She had a lot of mixed emotions. She had been very quiet, though she was pleasant. She had excused herself to the bathroom to hide her tears in the stall on the potty so nobody would know she was crying. She was feeling broken.

She was hiding it as best she could to support Aaron and the new baby, Destiny. In a way she was hoping this would help her heal. It wasn't quite what she expected with the rush of things she wasn't expecting to experience. As she came back to the lobby Aaron was waiting. He knew by the vibes Kelly was giving off that she was trying very hard to keep it together. He hadn't seen her yet and he already knew. Kelly looked up and noticed Aaron. He came over and gave Kelly a warm embrace. "I know, honey, you're doing the best you can, I know, let's go see the baby, c'mon" Kelly and Aaron went to the room where Molly and Destiny was at the hospital. Kelly felt the lump in her throat and fought back tears as she laid eyes on Destiny. She didn't know if it was the best or the hardest day of her life. She just knew she wanted to let out everything, but she didn't feel right about it, so she held it all in. Aaron rubbed her back and looked at Kelly with knowing eyes. He knew this day was coming. He had visions of this very moment but kept it to himself. There they stood quietly admiring a sleeping little girl they never expected to enter their life. Kelly came to Molly and held her hand. "Hey how you feeling there?"

"Pretty tired and pretty yuck. The aftereffects of this are a little rough, Doc says no lifting for six weeks"

"Ahh okay. Did you eat?"

"Yeah, they gave me a weird piece of steak, some Jell-O, and some want to be potatoes. It's alright for hospital food"

"I bet, it's not exactly Vern's Steakhouse here is it?" Kelly chuckled

"Haha isn't that the truth!" Molly chuckled. "Kelly I never had the chance to say thank you for everything. I owe you and Aaron a debt of gratitude for everything you're doing for me. Thank you for being a friend to me when I needed it the most. Even when you could have not been."

Kelly gave Molly a gentle hug and a kiss on the forehead. "Molly you are cared about no matter what okay? You always have been, always will be" They sat, and it was quiet. Kelly held Destiny in her arms for the first time. She felt a sense of emptiness in Molly. Kelly's ability kicked in and she started to feel Molly's state and understood for the first time where Molly was coming from and how much she would be going through. She felt a sense of duty in a perspective that she wanted to be supportive and make the best of a very taxing situation. Kelly didn't take this opportunity for granted. She wanted to become the best mother figure and be able to be the best support for Destiny in the event the truth about Molly being her true mother would be revealed.

Molly held Destiny knowing she only had small time before she wouldn't see her for at least a very long time. Molly's mental condition as a result of the exorcism had left her with violent outburst and fits of rage. Molly was concerned for the safety of Destiny. She felt as if she had failed her before she was even born. She had been seeking care for herself since Raven was banished from her. It had not been easy to talk about since these sorts of events Molly went thru are subject to whether or not people choose to believe the existence of paranormal entities in a battle between God himself and Satan. Molly just wanted redemption but not at the cost of the wellbeing of her daughter. It was the most heartbreaking choice she ever had to make in her life. It meant giving up the one thing she wanted most, to be a parent. Molly was beginning to understand a pinch about what it must have felt like for Aaron and Kelly losing the ability to be a parent. She also learned what it was like to lose someone you loved more than you thought you did, and how that person chose to move in a different direction for their own happiness. Though Molly was gaining maturity she still had a long road ahead before her life would once again be whole.

Raven could see the events taking place. Her realm was a dark place, cold and lonely. Her opportunity was lost. She was so close to embodying the child that had grown inside Molly. She needed a new plan. Raven had sensed an energy in her, one that would grow and mature in time. This would be her path to the child. Raven could no longer breach into the world of the living, but Destiny would be able to cross into her own. Raven sensed the child's ability. She sensed her power.

Raven looked upon the child from her place of darkness. Only one thought ran through her mind.

"Destiny, you belong to ME now."

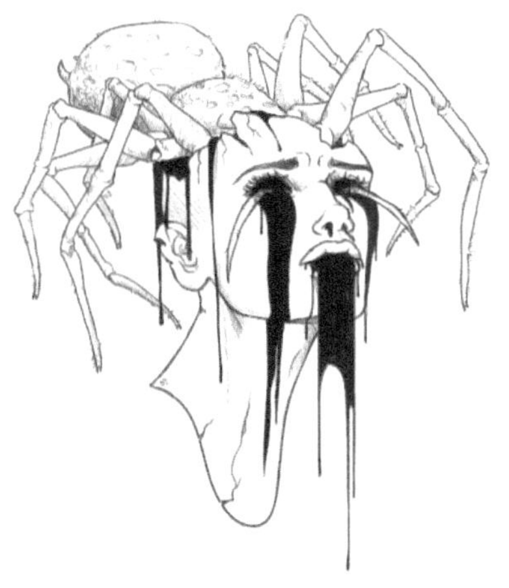

Epilogue: NIGHTMARES

Twelve-year-old Destiny Eastman walked down the street on the way home from school. Her long black hair was flung over her shoulder, almost blending in with the black Harley shirt she was wearing. She loved Harley shirts, just like her father. Tight blue jeans and grey sneakers completed her outfit. Piercing blue eyes darted around, looking for hidden dangers. She watched people going by, cars zooming past. She kept her eyes open for hidden corners. Her father had taught her from a young age to be street smart, to always be aware of her surroundings. He taught her to never trust anybody she didn't know, and even to be cautious around those that she does. He taught her that no matter how well you think you know a person, you will never know their true intentions.

Destiny often wondered why her father had been so adamant on the subject. Had something happened to him in the past that made him this way? Maybe one day he will tell her. Both her parents had been nervous about letting her walk to and from school. Destiny insisted, however. The school was literally only around the corner from the house, and she had her emergency cell phone always with her. Fortunately, her neighborhood never had any real crime, and everybody there all knew her and greeted her as she walked by. Destiny arrived at her home. A black jeep was parked in front of the house. Dads' friend, Katy, was there. Mom and dad were also already home. It was unusual, as her mom usually worked late on Fridays.

Destiny opened the door and stepped inside. She could hear the three of them in the kitchen, probably sitting at the table. She could hear that they were having a very serious conversation but trying to be quiet about it. Destiny sat her bag down on the couch. Curious, she listened in.

Aaron sat with his beer in hand. He listened as Katy rambled on about her predicament. Kelly paced back and forth as Katy spoke.

"Molly is deteriorating. She just can't let the guilt go. She can't let the hate go. She holds on to it like some twisted teddy bear. There are times when I walk up to her in her room, and she's just standing there, staring out of the window, sometimes for hours! Getting her to eat is like battling a moody teenager! It's like she's sixteen again. I'm just out of options! The counseling worked for some of her issues, the medication keeps her calm… most of the time. Her anger over… you know who… is all pent up inside. She wants to vent and rage at that…thing… so bad. But how does she do that? That thing is gone forever!"

Aaron sipped his beer. "Molly made her own choice, Katy. She thought she was a threat to her daughter. She feared that being around her in any capacity would put her a risk. She recognized that her violent outbursts could hurt her. She made a difficult choice to not be a part of her life. It was a wise choice, but one that bears a heavy price."

Kelly gave her own input. "Molly had the wherewithal to realize that she could not control her violent rage. She loves her daughter enough to keep her safe from herself. She admitted it herself that night in the hospital, when her daughter was born, that she would see her as a constant reminder of the mistake that she made, of the lives that she hurt. She feared that she would take it out on her. It was the most difficult decision a mother could make. It pains her horribly. She has no outlet to vent, and as for… you know who… she will never get a chance to unleash her fury and pain at the one that caused so much damage."

Aaron stood up and walked toward the kitchen window. He thought back to the night his daughter was born. Molly was dying. There were only moments left for the doctors to birth Destiny. He thought of Molly's words.

Molly was tired, sweating, and weak. "Aaron, if I don't make it, I want you to know this. You and Kelly redeemed me, you forgave me. I will always love both of you for that. Thank you for having a heart that I could never have. I'm far to selfish and insecure. The damage that bitch did to me has made me weak, and sour. The fury in my soul has made me dangerous. She is you and Kelly's daughter now. Not mine. If I survive, don't you dare bring her near me. I will always love her, but I'll always see her as the reminder of the pain, sorrow and suffering I caused. I want her in a safe and loving home. The two of you can provide what I cannot. I will always love you both."

Aaron came back around. He crossed his hands behind his back. He turned to Kelly and Katy, the sun highlighting his now fully chromed beard.

"We are not giving up on her. We are not going to let her rot in her own torment. She deserves better. She needs support. She needs love. She needs caring. If we want God to forgive us in the end, we must give the same to our fellow human beings, no matter what was done."

A tear rolled down Kelly's face. She moved in and threw her arms around her husband. He kissed her.

Destiny decided it was time to make her presence known. "Mom, dad, I'm home!"

Destiny walked into the kitchen. The three adults looked at her, wondering what she had heard. Katy looked at her niece, realizing she was growing up to be a perfect reflection of the younger sister she once knew. She quivered with the sense to cry, but she held back the tears. Destiny didn't know that Katy was her aunt. Molly made sure of that.

A few hours later, Aaron and Kelly were sitting on the couch, binge watching horror movies. Destiny walked into the living room, cussing like a sailor.

"Fuck this shit! How many fucking essays do I have to write in a week just for one stupid fucking English class?"

Aaron stood up and yelled. "Watch your fucking language, young lady! And yes, daddy gets to use it, you don't until you grow up and pay some bills around here."

Kelly slapped her palm to her head. "Were do you think she gets it from, ?"

Aaron looked over to Kelly and shrugged. He turned back to Destiny. "Brush your teeth and go to bed. Its late, and don't forget to give mommy and daddy a hug and kiss."

Destiny did as she was told. She showered, brushed her teeth, and put on her pajamas. She went to her mom and dad's room and gave them kisses and hugs. She walked down the hallway, into her room, and slipped into bed. She thought about the conversation she had overheard this afternoon.

"Molly? Who the hell is Molly?" she thought. She had heard the name before. Mom and dad had spoken of her many times. They always downplayed it when destiny asked who she was.

"She's an old friend of your father."' She remembered her mother saying.

"Someone I knew a long time ago." Her father had spoken.

Destiny gave up on the subject, as she closed her eyes. Destiny was tired. Stupid English class. She just wanted to sleep. It didn't take long. She was out like a light in a matter of moments. Then, the dream came.

Destiny found herself in a field of dead grass. It was dark. Broken, black clouds hovered in the air. An angry red moon stood high in the sky. Before her, there was a dark ominous forest. She stood up and looked around. She found a worn-out path in front of her, it led straight into the forest before her. She began to follow it. Soon she found herself surrounded by dead or dying trees. Their branches drooped down towards the ground, like arms ready to grab her. She walked on. Everything seemed grey. There was a creepy mist floating through the air. The howl of as wolf could be heard in the distance. The sounds of unseen animals running through the woods could be heard. Destiny felt like she was being watched. Further and further, she walked, stepping over dead limbs, hearing creatures surrounding her. Fear enveloped her. Everything was cold and dark. All the trees were dead or dying. Their limbs hung low to the ground, as if to grab her. There was a strange scent in the air. It smelled like sulfur. The mist blocked most of her view. Yet, in the distance something shined, sparkled in her direction. She walked on and approached it. The mist hovering over the ground obscured it. Soon, she was right in front of it.

It was a rectangular object, with ornate edges in a goldish color. It was a mirror! The mist obstructed the reflection. Destiny stepped closer. She looked deeply at it yet seeing nothing in the reflection. Moments later the mist cleared. In the mirror, a girl appeared. Her hair was jet black, just like her own. Her eyes were closed. Her hands were crossed behind her back. The sounds of crawling creatures echoed in the background. Destiny looked closer, realizing the reflection in the mirror was not her own. It did not reflect her own movements.

"Hello, hi there." Destiny spoke. The image did not respond. Destiny stepped closer.

"Uhm, who are you?" Destiny asked. The reflection did not respond.

She reached out to touch the mirror. An energy began to flow through her. Destiny was overwhelmed!

"Can you tell me your name?" asked Destiny. The image did not respond.

"If you tell me your name, maybe we can talk?" asked Destiny

The image did not open her eyes. She stood there wearing a black tee-shirt and a nose ring. Her hair was just as black as Destiny's. Her eyes remained closed.

Destiny began to pace in front of the mirror, a habit she had picked up from her father. She kept looking at the girl in the mirror. She considered her appearance. She looked out of time. Her skin looked cold and gray. Her hair was slightly mangled. There appeared to be a gash in her skin, just below her bangs. Destiny felt icy cold. A strong sense of despair began to flood her. Destiny wanted to flee, but she felt trapped where she was standing. She could not move.

"Please, tell me who you are! I can help you!" Destiny called out, frantically.

Moments passed. The girl in the mirror slowly opened her eyes. Destiny looked on in horror. The girls' eyes were pitch black, like looking into the blackness of space.

"Who the FUCK are you?" Destiny demanded. A small moment passed.

The girl in the mirror finally spoke, her voice guttural and demonic.

"Raven!"

ABOUT THE AUTHOR

Kerri West was born in 1979 one month and three days later than her husband. A native of Albuquerque New Mexico, Kerri loves the peace and serenity of the outdoors. Kerri is an avid chili aficionado and a foodie. The answer to the New Mexico question "Red or green?" is always followed by a "Yes!". She loves music of many genres. She will start with classical music, move to heavy metal, and then listen to country music all in the same thirty minutes. Kerri is passionate about finding personals emotional connections with many forms of creativity and story -telling. She believes that when there is a connection, then others will remember that shared creativity, and when that magic happens, people will respond and that work will be successful. Kerri has a unique sense of humor. Molly is the first novel written in collaboration with her husband Stephen.

Stephen West entered this world in July of 1979. He is a life-time inhabitant of New Mexico. He spent most of his life in Albuquerque but lived for two years in the village of Cedar Crest on the east side of the Sandia mountains. It was there where he received his first taste of the paranormal, having been exposed to a malevolent spirit as a young boy. This experience, paired with his own sense of clairvoyance is what drove his fascination with the supernatural and the sixth sense. He is a long-time reader of many great novels on the matter. His youth was filled with Books, comics, and horror movies of many genres. Together, with his beloved with and best friend, Kerri, they have put their heads together to create their first novel, inspired by real life events. Their journey together in the adventure is bound to continue.